Acclaim for the authors of
The Magic of Christmas

CAROLYN DAVIDSON

"For romance centering on the joys and sorrows of married life, readers can't do much better than Davidson."
—*Romantic Times BOOKreviews*

"Her novels go beyond romance to the depths of the ultimate healing power of love."
—*Romantic Times BOOKreviews*

VICTORIA BYLIN

"Ms. Bylin is a growing talent in historical fiction and her magic pen touches both your emotions and your soul with each turn of the page."
—*Romance Reviews Today*

"Bylin captures the aura of the Wild West as skillfully as she creates memorable characters. The fast pace is tempered by the gentle passion that shimmers through the pages, bringing readers a wonderful experience."
—*Romantic Times BOOKreviews* on *Midnight Marriage*

CHERYL ST.JOHN

"Ms. St.John knows what the readers want and keeps on giving it."
—*Rendezvous*

"*Prairie Wife* is a very special book, courageously executed by the author and her publisher. Her considerable skill brings the common theme of the romance novel— love conquers all—to the level of genuine catharsis."
—*Romantic Times BOOKreviews* [4 1/2 stars]

CAROLYN DAVIDSON

Reading, writing and research—Carolyn Davidson's life in three simple words. At least that area of her life having to do with her career as a historical romance author. The rest of her time is divided among husband, family and travel—her husband, of course, holding top priority in her busy schedule. Then there is their church, and the church choir in which they participate. Their sons and daughters, along with assorted spouses, are spread across the eastern half of America, together with numerous grandchildren. Carolyn welcomes mail at P.O. Box 2757, Goose Creek, SC 29445.

VICTORIA BYLIN

Victoria Bylin has a collection of refrigerator magnets that mark the changes in her life. The oldest ones are from California. A native of Los Angeles, she graduated from UC Berkeley with a degree in history and went to work in the advertising industry. She soon met a wonderful man who charmed her into taking a ride on his motorcycle. That ride led to a trip down the wedding aisle, two sons, various pets and a move that landed Victoria and her family in northern Virginia.

Magnets from thirty states commemorate that journey and her new life on the East Coast. Feel free to drop her an e-mail at VictoriaBylin@aol.com or visit her Web site at www.victoriabylin.com.

CHERYL ST.JOHN

Cheryl St.John says that knowing her stories bring hope and pleasure to readers is one of the best parts of being a writer. The other wonderful part is being able to set her own schedule and work around her family and church. Working in her jammies ain't half bad, either! Cheryl loves to hear from readers. Write to her at: P.O. Box 24732, Omaha, NE 68124, or e-mail CherylStJohn@aol.com. Visit her Web site, www.tlt.com/authors/cstjohn.htm.

CAROLYN DAVIDSON
VICTORIA BYLIN
CHERYL ST.JOHN

The Magic of Christmas

HARLEQUIN®

TORONTO • NEW YORK • LONDON
AMSTERDAM • PARIS • SYDNEY • HAMBURG
STOCKHOLM • ATHENS • TOKYO • MILAN • MADRID
PRAGUE • WARSAW • BUDAPEST • AUCKLAND

ISBN-13: 978-0-373-29515-9
ISBN-10:   0-373-29515-4

THE MAGIC OF CHRISTMAS
Copyright © 2008 by Harlequin Books S.A.

The publisher acknowledges the copyright holders of the individual works as follows:

A CHRISTMAS CHILD
Copyright © 2008 by Carolyn Davidson

THE CHRISTMAS DOVE
Copyright © 2008 by Vicki Scheibel

A BABY BLUE CHRISTMAS
Copyright © 2008 by Cheryl Ludwigs

www.eHarlequin.com

Printed in U.S.A.

CONTENTS

A CHRISTMAS CHILD

Carolyn Davidson

Dear Reader,

My memories of Christmas are many and varied, but within all the most precious are the continuing themes of love, of commitment to family, of faith and hope for the future. For without the true spirit of Christmas within our hearts, we have little faith in ourselves or those who surround us.

During this season of the year we find ourselves more willing to forgive, more considerate of others and able to give more freely of ourselves and our resources. Certainly that unselfishness is but one result of the blessedness of the birth we celebrate. Christmas is a time for family, both related by blood and unrelated except by compassion, for we can find ourselves just as caught up in love and caring with strangers as with our own.

May each of my readers seek out some way during this most holy of seasons to find ways of expressing your love for all mankind. May your holiday be happy and your heart be made joyful.

Carolyn

My story is dedicated with love to a babe born during the years of my youth, my niece, Marianne. She has grown to be a woman of perception, a concerned, caring mother and a dear friend.
To her I offer this story with all my love.

Prologue

The room held the fetid odor of death, and the babe who sounded his first wail in that hot, stale air waved thin arms and legs in a frantic motion, as though he sensed that his cries might be futile, that his future might be as dark as his past. For the woman who had given birth had already breathed her last. Her only contribution to the future lay in the doctor's hands, and already he was eager to leave this chamber of death for the clean, pure air he might find out of doors.

The sun was setting, the sky ablaze with color, and such beauty of nature seemed almost unholy compared to the pall of death that hung low over the small clearing. The small cabin and outbuildings represented the life's work and dreams of Joe and Charlotte Winters, both of whom lay abed in the cabin, their souls no longer of this world, their hearts no longer beating, only a small, scrawny infant boy child left to wail his sadness aloud.

The country doctor made haste to wrap the boy in a flannel rag, and carried him into the chill air of the December evening, rushing to the house that lay just over a small hill to the west, a place where the child might find warmth and nourishment, for he was small and weak and his chance of survival seemed slim.

The door of the farmhouse opened wide; a plump lady

peered out and greeted the doctor with an uplifted arm. "Come in. Come in. Bring that child inside where it's warm and let me find a blanket for him."

"It's best if I drop this flannel rag outside," the kindly doctor said sadly. "It's no doubt full of germs. Needs to be burned."

"It'll wait till morning," Mrs. Baker said quietly. "It's below freezing out there and the germs won't live long in the cold."

"Typhoid seems to be a hard thing to kill," the doctor told her. "But maybe we can get this little mite washed up and into clean clothes and keep him alive. His mama's last words were that he be cared for."

"Charlotte was a good woman," her neighbor said, tears running down her cheeks as she took the wide-eyed infant in her arms. "I've got hot water in the reservoir and lots of soap and washcloths. Reckon I haven't forgotten how to wash a newborn."

In but a few moments the tiny babe was covered with soap from head to toe, each particle of his body cleansed and rinsed in clear water. The woman who held him to her breast shed tears of sorrow as she worked, her mind on the future of the babe she held. It seemed that fate had decreed this child have a dark future, for he'd been left with but one remaining relative—a sister—barely able to care for herself, let alone an infant.

From the ladder that led to the sleeping loft, a voice called down, a cry of sadness that held but faint hope of good news. "Is Mama all right, Mrs. Baker? Did the doctor get here yet?"

"Come on down, Marianne," Mrs. Baker called out softly. "The doctor is here and he brought us a wee bit of a present tonight."

The girl, for she was not yet a woman, backed down the ladder, garbed in a white flannel gown, her long hair caught up in a braid that lay over one shoulder, and her feet touched the wooden floor of the cabin as Mrs. Baker turned to her with the child in her arms.

"Meet your brother, Marianne. Born just a bit ago, the last chore your poor mama managed to finish up before she died."

"Mama's gone?" As though it were a foregone conclusion, the girl spoke the words with gravity, her eyes dry, as though she'd already shed tears enough for the occasion, and now faced the future that awaited her. Her arms moved to take the babe and her head bowed over the tiny boy, eyes wide, mouth open, hands flailing the air. From the looks of things, he was primed to blow.

"I'll bet he's hungry," Mrs. Baker said softly. "I've got a bottle around here somewhere I had to use for Joey years back. Let me look a bit and find it."

She bustled across the kitchen floor, opening the cupboard doors that hid the shelves of dishes and dry goods. Poking around amid the plates and cups, behind the bowls and pitchers, Mrs. Baker came up with a round bottle, topped with a rubber nipple—used but still in working order.

"This oughta do it," she said with satisfaction, turning to the sink to rinse and clean the small vessel. "I've got fresh milk in the pantry and it won't take long to fix that baby up with his dinner."

Marianne watched the proceedings, ensconced in a wide rocking chair, holding her baby brother in arms that delivered warmth to the infant and love that would nourish his soul. She bent over the tiny head, her nostrils catching a whiff of the sweet baby scent he bore, and tears streamed down her cheeks as she thought of the woman who had borne him but minutes since.

Her heart's cry was for the woman she'd known as mother, the woman who had raised her and taught her the skills of a woman, who had been best friend and confidante to the young girl who had yet to find her own way in life. And whose path now seemed to contain a child, not of her own, but of her mother's flesh and blood. A brother to love and care for.

Mrs. Baker brought the bottle to her and Marianne settled down for the first time to the task of feeding her infant brother, acknowledging the swell of love that filled her as the tiny mouth sucked at the nipple with an eagerness that expressed his hunger. He seemed to be a survivor, she decided, and if there was any way she could help him to do that very thing, she would set her sights on his future and do all she could to make it one worthy of him.

Joshua. She'd call him Joshua, for her mother had decreed that it be so, just days ago before the fever took hold and laid her low in a sickbed from which she would never rise. Papa had died the day before, but Mama had lived to deliver the child they had so longed for, had prayed for and were to finally see. The baby boy they had yearned for for so many years, with small graves in the orchard attesting to the failure of Mama to bear live children.

Now they had a boy, Joshua, almost a Christmas baby, for it was but three weeks until that most wonderful of holidays. One that would mean little this year, with the outlying ranchers and farmers burying their dead in the wake of a typhoid epidemic. To think that such a tiny bundle would survive, when all about the countryside strong men had succumbed to the dreaded sickness.

Marianne rocked and whispered soft words of comfort and love to her small brother that night, then changed his make-shift diaper and wrapped him in a bit of flannel that Mrs. Baker found in her trunk. He'd need new clothing, for the things sewn for him by his mother must be burned in the cabin, lest the epidemic be spread by their use.

In the morning Marianne watched as the menfolk of the surrounding community burned her parents' cabin, knowing that such a dreadful thing must be done in order to contain the germs within. Only her visit with Mrs. Baker over the past days had kept her from the disease. Helping her neighbor had been a godsend in more ways than one, for she would surely have been a victim herself had she not volunteered her services to aid the neighbor after a bad cold had put her to bed with a fever and a case of the quinsy, leaving her house without a cook and someone to mind her three-year-old.

Mrs. Baker had a small son, but her other children were grown, most of them gone from home, and she had a wonderful husband who worked hard to support them. With spare rooms aplenty now that her young'uns were mostly grown, there was room for Marianne and the baby.

Yet Marianne knew that she must soon be on her own, that she must make provision to take care of herself and little Joshua as soon as she could. And to that end, she made her plans.

Chapter One

The horse she'd borrowed from her neighbor was less than perfect, but sometime in the past her mother had dutifully told her something about beggars not being choosy about what they got, and Marianne smiled at the memory. The old mare was swaybacked, had but one gait beyond walking, and that jolting trot was less than comfortable to the young woman's sore bottom. She'd been riding for long hours, appreciative of the loan of the horse, but weary to her soul as she considered the future lying before her.

Mrs. Baker had written out instructions to her sister's home in the small town of Walnut Grove, Missouri, and sent Marianne on her way, the baby, Joshua, wrapped tightly in flannel blankets and with a small supply of diapers and wrappers for the child. Enough to last until Marianne could find work and a place to live. Her sister was Sarah, a woman with four children, but surely with enough goodness of heart to help a young girl on her own, Mrs. Baker had said.

December seemed to be an unforgiving sort of month, with snow on the ground and more in the air, causing dark clouds to hang heavily over the land, hiding the sun. Marianne had ridden for a day and most of a night already, stopping only to rest in an empty barn in the middle of a field. The house was gone, only stones and burned upright boards remaining to mark where once a family had lived. The barn had been warm—at least warmer than the windswept fields—and, huddled in a stack of moldy hay, Marianne had kept herself and her baby brother warm.

The prospect of meeting Mrs. Baker's sister, perhaps even today, kept her going, even as she ate the last of the biscuits and bits of cheese Mrs. Baker had sent along. The baby had drunk from his bottle, the milk not warmed but nourishing, and yet even that was coming to an end, for the bottle now held the last of the supply she'd carried with her.

Ahead of her lay a small town, the main street lined with shops and buildings on both sides, houses lined up neatly as she approached, a sign beside the road designating it as Walnut Grove. Children ran to and fro, not caring that the snow threatened, calling out to each other, playing in the road. They all had homes to go to, Marianne suspected, warm coats to wear and mothers to tend to their needs.

For the first time in a week, her loss seemed overwhelming. The planning and working to accomplish this trek had taken her mind from the perils she would face—a woman alone, a newborn child to care for and but enough cash to buy a meal or two.

The map in her pocket was clear. If she would but turn her horse to a side street, down this alley and then turn right, she would arrive at the home of Sarah Nelson, Mrs. Baker's sister. A kindly lady, she'd been told. And yet as she rode the mare close to the front porch, she heard a thundering roar from a man who erupted from the front door, fast on the heels of a young boy. Snatching up the child, the man delivered several hard swats of his palm against the boy's backside and tossed him back into the house, then turned and looked at Marianne.

"You lookin' for somebody, lady? Or just enjoying the scenery?"

Marianne froze atop the mare and shivered. "I was told that

Sarah Nelson lives here," she said quietly, to which the man snorted, then opened the door and shouted words that echoed back from the hallway.

"Sarah. Somebody here wants to see you."

A small, skinny soul who bore but a slight resemblance to the sturdy form of Mrs. Baker came to the door, and a tentative smile lit her face. There was a resemblance after all, Marianne decided, there in that fleeting smile.

"I'm—or rather I was—a neighbor of your sister's, ma'am," Marianne began. "She told me I might find you here."

"I'm here, all right" was the harsh reply. "What do you want?"

"A place to get my little brother changed and warm and some milk to give him in his bottle."

The woman's face softened a bit and then she looked up at the man who towered over her. "Ain't got no room for anybody else in this house, girl. I'll give you a cup of milk for the baby, but that's the best I can do."

Marianne's heart sank. Mrs. Baker had been so sure…so certain that her sister would welcome the travelers. She watched as the skinny woman closed the door and waited until her return, just minutes later. Carrying a cup in her hand, she approached the horse, peering up at Marianne with a look of sorrow.

"Sorry I can't be more hospitable, but my man don't hold with givin' away the food he buys. I couldn't give you this, but I'm the one milks the cow and makes the butter and I told him it was mine to keep or give and I chose to give it to the babe."

"I thank you," Marianne said, well aware that there was no welcome here for her, hoping that Mrs. Baker would never find out how desperate her sister's situation was.

"Head on into town. You might be able to get some help at the general store."

Without awaiting a goodbye, the woman went back into the house, the door closing with a solid thud behind her. Marianne turned the mare and rode back down the drive and onto the road. The lights of several storefronts were still ablaze and she halted before the general store, sliding from the mare's back in a quick motion, holding her small brother to her breast.

The store was warm, redolent with the scents of leather and pickles and smoke from the potbellied stove that reigned in one corner. Behind the counter a woman watched her approach and bent a smile in her direction. "Hello there, young lady. You just arrive in town?"

"Yes," Marianne said quietly, shifting the burden of her brother to rest him against her shoulder.

"You got you a young'un there. Looks pretty much like a newborn, don't he?"

"He's three weeks old now. My brother, Joshua." Marianne pulled back the blanket and displayed the dark-haired child she held, his flawless skin pink and healthy looking.

"Sure is a good-lookin' young'un," the storekeeper said. "Where you heading, honey?"

"Nowhere, just looking for a place to stay for a bit. I had instructions to find a friend's sister, but she apparently doesn't have room for me, so I rode on."

"Who did you say you saw in town?"

"Sarah Nelson is the sister of my old neighbor. She sent me here, but Mr. Nelson didn't seem too hospitable."

"Hospitable! Hah, that's one word you couldn't apply to Henry Nelson. He's a mean one, gives poor Sarah a hard time of it. Treats those young'uns like slaves."

"Well, anyway, I won't be staying there, and I was wondering if you knew of anybody who needed help, maybe in the house or with their children. I'm a good hand with cooking and cleaning and such."

"Not around here, girl. Things are pretty tight in town, and with Christmas here, everybody's pretty well taken up with their own business. Them with kids is doing their best to make it a good holiday, baking and cooking and knitting up mittens and such. It's a poor town, sure enough, and barely enough to go around. I don't know of anybody who'd be needing help. At least, not help they'd be willing to pay for."

Marianne's heart sank. She'd expected no more, but her hope had been that she would find a place to rest her body and keep the baby warm. Even that seemed to be a dream, for there was no help to be found here.

"Tell you what, girl," the storekeeper said quickly. "I'll let you sleep in the storeroom for the night if you like. There's a kettle on the stove and tea in a tin out there and I can scrape up a loaf of bread and some milk for the baby if you like."

"I'd be ever so grateful," Marianne said, her heart beating rapidly as she recognized that she had a place for the night, and something warm to put into her stomach. "My name's Marianne. Can I do anything to pay for the room? Sweep your floors or something?"

"You just get yourself into that back room and lie down on the cot and we'll find some fresh milk for that baby, and you can sleep a bit." The woman was kindly, Marianne thought, bustling back and forth through the store, locking up the front door and leading the way to a warm, dusty room where a small potbellied stove held the cold at bay, and offered a warm place to sleep.

A kettle atop the stove indeed held hot water, and a cup appeared with tea in the bottom of it, the leaves floating on the hot water that splashed into its depths. The water turned color as Marianne watched, and the scent of tea arose to tempt her nostrils.

"I haven't had a cup of tea since my mama died," she said, fighting back the tears that begged to be shed.

"Well, this one oughta make you feel some better, then. There's milk and sugar to put in it if you like, and a piece of fresh bread and some cheese to eat with it. I'll just wash out that baby's bottle and fill it up with milk for him."

The woman hummed beneath her breath as she pumped

water and rinsed the bottle, then refilled it with milk and snapped the nipple in place. "That oughta be enough for him to last till morning."

"He doesn't drink a whole lot yet, about half a bottle at a time," Marianne said. "This is just fine. He'll have enough for his breakfast."

"I'll be back in the morning," the woman told her. "My name's Janet. Me and the mister live next door and we open up right early. Tomorrow's gonna be busy, being the day before Christmas, so I'll be back at dawn."

By the light of a candle and the glow from the stove, Marianne watched the woman leave from the back door, heard the click of the lock as she was safely left inside and settled down to feed Joshua and drink her tea. The bread was good—fresh and still soft. The cheese was nourishing and the milk seemed to agree with Joshua, for he drank his fill and then burped, loud and long, before he snuggled against Marianne's bosom and closed his eyes.

She lay down on the narrow cot, thankful for the warmth surrounding her. Her heart rose as she considered the generous spirit of the woman she'd just met, thankful she'd been given a bed to sleep in and food to eat. With no questions asked.

Joshua slept the whole night through and when the back door opened in the dim light of morning, Marianne sat up and rubbed her eyes, peering at the man who entered the back room of the store.

"You still here?" he asked roughly. "I told the missus you'd probably be off with everything you could carry before we opened up this morning, but she was sure you were a good girl. Guess she won this bet." He moved on through the room, leaving Marianne stunned as she sat up on the cot, watching his progress through the doorway into the store.

She rose and brushed her hair back, wrapping Joshua more securely in his blanket before she placed him on the cot and followed the man into his store.

"Sir, I want to thank you for a place to sleep last night. I appreciated the warm bed and the milk for Joshua."

"My wife's a soft touch," he said, turning to watch Marianne with narrowed eyes, his gaze covering her slim form quickly. "She said to tell you she'll let you stay here another night if you want to, but we can't do much more than that. She sent over some oatmeal she cooked for breakfast and a cup of milk for you and the baby. There's still tea in the tin for you to use if you want it."

The man's welcome was not warm, but Marianne was pleased at his offering of food, especially that of milk for Joshua's bottle. She rinsed out the dregs from the night before and filled it again, placing it beside the bed for when he would wake and be hungry. The bowl of oatmeal she held in her lap, sitting again on the cot and eating it quickly. Warm and nourishing, it filled her stomach and she was thankful.

She rinsed the bowl in the sink, washed her face and hands and brushed her hair back, dampening the sides to hold it in place.

From behind her, the gentleman spoke. "My Janet said to tell you to come on over to the house and tend the baby if you want to. She's got hot water and soap and such you can use."

"Thank you ever so much," Marianne said. "Just point me in the right direction and I'll be on my way."

In minutes she was rapping on the back door of a two-story house behind the general store. Janet opened the door for her. "Come on in, girl. I'll warrant that baby needs a good washing up and some clean clothes to wear, don't he?"

"I'd surely appreciate a washcloth and a bar of soap for him," Marianne said quietly. "He hasn't had a bath in two days. And my mama always said a baby should be washed up every morning."

"Your mama was right, and your little one there looks pretty healthy. You musta been taking good care of him."

"I've tried my best," Marianne said stoutly. "He's doing pretty well, putting on a little weight and sleeping pretty well."

"You're a good mama to him, girl. Just go on over there and use that basin and towel and clean him up a little."

Marianne washed Joshua and put a clean diaper on his bottom. Janet came up with a used but clean small kimono she said she had no use for.

"My Robbie is three years old, and he hasn't worn this for a year or better. You might as well have it for your young'un," she said kindly.

"I'll wash out Joshua's other two gowns and hang them up to dry if I can," Marianne said softly. "His diapers need to be washed, too."

"Use the bath water if you want to," Janet told her. "You can hang them behind the stove. They'll dry there real quick."

By noon, the small stash of laundry was dry, including Marianne's underclothes and her dress, and she folded the few diapers and gowns and placed them in her bag. Donning her own clothing, she determined that she would offer Janet cash for the food and care she'd received at her hand. The offer was turned down without hesitation, and Marianne was pleased to find such kindness in the woman.

"I can't thank you enough for your help," she said, her words sincere, even though her smile wobbled a bit. "I'm going to set off and look for a place to stay, a job of some sort that will allow me to keep the baby with me."

"Had you thought about letting some couple take him to raise?" Janet asked. "He might be better off with a father to care for him."

"Well, his is dead and gone," Marianne said, "and I've thought of giving him up to a family, but it seems that most everyone has enough of their own to take care of."

"The Thornley family, out east of town, might take him," Janet said. "They're good folks, with no little ones of their own. Maybe you could ride out and see them."

"I'll think about it," Marianne said slowly, not willing yet to give up her brother, remembering her mother's hopes for his future and unable to turn her back on her own flesh and blood while she could still tend to him herself.

"Ma'am, if I could help you some in the store or in your house today, I'd be pleased to earn out my bed for last night and maybe tonight. I don't like to take your food and impose on you any without paying back in some way."

Janet hesitated, then nodded. "I appreciate your honesty," she said, scrubbing at a skillet in the sink. "If you'd like to lend a hand, I've got to get our Christmas dinner ready for the morning. My man's folks will be coming in from out of town later on today to spend Christmas with our young'uns. They always come early so's we can go to church on Christmas Eve together."

"I'll do whatever you'd like for me to," Marianne answered with a smile. "Maybe by morning I'll come up with something else to do. Might be if I go to church for the service tonight, I'll see somebody who might need a hired hand or help around the house."

"Being a hired hand is no work for a woman," Janet said bluntly. "The places hereabouts are pretty well run already. Can't think offhand of anybody who'd need help. But it won't hurt to ask around if you go to the service tonight. It's Christmas Eve and folks are in a softer mood than usual this week. I'll ask around, too—maybe between us we can find something for you to do."

Marianne spent the day scrubbing and cleaning Janet's house, using a brush on the kitchen floor and a dust cloth on the furniture in the parlor. Late in the day Janet's husband, Tom, dragged in a tall spruce tree, freshly cut from the woods north of town. He quickly formed a stand for it with four small pieces of wood, and it stood in the corner of the parlor, almost touching the ceiling.

Janet's four youngsters gathered around as their father carried boxes of decorations from the attic and placed them on the floor. "Have at it, young'uns," he said jovially. And with glad cries and laughter, the four children hung glittering stars and angels on the tree, the ornaments showing signs of the years past, but shiny and bright nevertheless. Marianne watched with sad eyes, remembering the Christmases she'd spent with her family, her mother and father always making a fuss over the tree and the decorations they made from pinecones and bits of ribbon.

They'd had big plans for this holiday season, with a new baby due to arrive, her mother finally able to carry a babe full term after years of losing babies, one after another. And now there was little to celebrate, it seemed to Marianne, for her family was gone and she had no future that she could see. Only a darkness that threatened to overwhelm her.

Silently she wrapped her small brother in his warm blanket and set off from the house, unable to bear the joyous laughter of the children and the happiness in the house she left behind. It was growing dark, for winter brought long nights, and even though it was but suppertime, the sun was setting and the houses she passed on her slow trek were well lit from within.

The bright candlelight from a Christmas tree caught her eye as she passed a large white house, and from inside she could hear the voices that carried on the night air. Happiness seemed to surround her, but left her on the outside, looking in, and her heart ached with the pain of loss.

The small village church was dark, but it would soon be time for the late service to begin, probably within an hour or so, she thought, remembering that she'd told Janet she would attend with her family. She slowed as she passed the white building, a bell tower high overhead with a cross atop it catching her eye.

On the grass before the church was a Nativity scene, set up by loving hands apparently, for the figures were freshly painted, the robes of the Virgin mother and the kindly Joseph glistening in the final rays of the setting sun. A final beam of light cast its glow across the setting, and drew Marianne's eyes to the empty manger. Sheltered just within the framework of a makeshift shed, it was rough, unpainted and held straw, or perhaps hay, providing a bed for the child who would be born this night.

She'd heard the story for years, read from her father's Bible—a tradition in the family, that they hear the chapter in Luke that told the tale of shepherds and wise men who came to worship the babe in the manger.

From the house next door to the church, a door opened with a clatter and a man stepped onto the porch, shutting the door behind him, then stepping from the porch to walk toward the center of town, nodding at Marianne as he walked past her. Probably the minister, she thought, noting his young age. For her own pastor in days gone by had been an elderly man, with grown children. From the looks of the man she turned to watch as he strode toward the general store, he was but thirty or so, younger than most ministers in her experience.

Drawn by an urge she could not explain, she walked across the width of the churchyard, approaching the manger scene, and peered within the small, rough bed itself. And with no warning she heard a voice within her speaking.

If you leave Joshua in the manger, someone will want to keep him and give him a good home.

She looked behind her, seeking the owner of the voice she'd heard, for it had been distinct and the words seemed to vibrate in her mind. Without hesitation she bent, placing her brother in the wooden container, one meant for a holy babe on this, the most holy of nights. And if a baby was all the scene needed to make it complete, surely there was a reason for her being here in this place, a reason for her to do as she had. The thought of abandoning her brother was enough to break her heart, but perhaps this was the answer to her dilemma. And Joshua would be the better for it, if a man and woman without a child of their own should see him and claim him tonight.

She shivered, the warmth of her brother gone from her arms, and as she bent to him, she whispered words of farewell, unable to foresee the outcome of her actions, only desperate enough to hope that it would work out for Joshua's good.

Running quickly to the side of the church, she waited in the shadows, knowing that it would soon be time for the baby to eat, and he would arouse from his slumber soon, hungry and anxious for his bottle.

Chapter Two

David McDermott faced his first Christmas in his first church. A graduate of the seminary in St. Louis, he had been sent to Walnut Grove, Missouri, to serve as their pastor in the small community church there. With his wife, Laura, he'd made his home in Walnut Grove, making friends and working to spruce up the building he'd been given as a parsonage during his tenure there.

Bearing her first child was to have been a joyous event that first year of their marriage, but the birthing took its toll on Laura, and she succumbed to the loss of blood and horror of a childbirth gone wrong. The babe she bore lived but hours and breathed his last as his father named him and held him close, aching for the future he'd lost, in the death of those he loved best.

Buried in the church cemetery, Laura held her child in her arms within the wooden casket created by the town's carpenter. They lay beneath the ground with but a simple wooden cross with two names engraved upon it. "Laura McDermott, wife of David." And beneath those words was the name of his son, "Darren McDermott." Simple words that seemed barely enough to describe the youthful beauty and dignity of the woman he'd married, and the son she'd borne.

David had worked hard all summer long, painting the small church, cutting the weeds that threatened to overcome the grass before the parsonage, and in general keeping busy, day by day, his heart aching with the loss of his wife and child.

For nearly a year he'd lived alone and served his parish, loved by the people he served, and after a while he became a target for the young women, who saw him as a prime catch. He was tall and admittedly good-looking, for he saw his face in the mirror every morning and knew that his features were pleasing—dark hair that waved just above his collar, and blue eyes that held a remote sadness.

It had been a hard year, and by summer's end he'd felt a renewed interest in his work, found that the townsfolk had taken to him with a warmth he hadn't expected. Perhaps because of his loss, maybe because he'd made it his business to visit the sick, pray with those who needed his comfort, and in all things had done his best to serve the people of Walnut Grove.

He'd received several invitations for Christmas dinner from various members of his congregation and had accepted none of them, unable to find in his heart any joy in this season of the year. If only… His thoughts returned to the family he'd buried and he shook himself abruptly, knowing that self-pity was the last thing he needed to indulge in tonight. For the Christmas Eve service was scheduled to begin in two hours and he still hadn't purchased his groceries this week.

Donning his hat and a warm jacket, he made his way out the front door, determined to put the sorrow of the past behind him and concentrate instead on the joyous message he would bring to his congregation in just a short while.

The walk to the general store was short, and in less than ten minutes he'd gathered up the basic necessities needed for his kitchen. Not much of a cook at the best of times, he managed to make do with fried eggs for breakfast, bread and cheese and sometimes sausage or bacon for his dinner hour and often was the recipient of casserole dishes from the ladies nearby, who tended to drop off dishes for his supper.

Perhaps they knew that cooking was not a skill he'd mastered in his life or maybe they felt he needed the nourishment of hot meals on occasion. Whatever the reason for the generosity shown him, he appreciated the chicken casseroles and hot vegetable dishes left at his front door several times a week.

Tomorrow was a day that loomed long before him, a day of happiness for the children in town, a day of feasting in most of the homes of his congregation, several of which would welcome him with open arms.

He lingered in the store for but a few minutes, speaking to Janet and her husband, knowing they were anxious to close the door and return to their family in the small house next to the store, where their four children were no doubt enjoying the lights of a Christmas tree in the parlor.

Waving goodbye and reminding them of the service that would begin in an hour or so, he walked the short distance back to his home, his arms full of bundles—the coffee, bacon and sack of eggs he'd purchased. A tin of lard hung from his index finger and he shifted the wrapped parcels to free his hand to open the front door.

The Nativity scene caught his eye and he admired the fresh paint he'd applied to the figures just last week. The shepherds were tall and stalwart, the sheep and donkey suitably humble and the young parents knelt beside the manger. All was ready, awaiting the addition of the small statue of a babe he would add to the scene after midnight, when the service at church was finished and his parishioners were once more in their homes.

He'd heaped the manger with hay, deeming straw to be harsh for a babe's fragile skin, even though the small statue was but an imitation reminder of the Christ Child and neither hay nor straw would damage its hard surface. The sun had set and the moon was making an appearance in the sky, sending down beams upon the scene he'd created for his church and its people.

The manger seemed to glow with the light of the moon upon it, the simple brown cradle awaiting the final touch that would— David halted suddenly, his breathing loud upon the silence of the evening. For there, waving in the moonlight, was a small hand, a tiny arm. And the sound that reached his ears was that of a babe, a whimpering cry, escalating into a wail of distress.

Placing his packages on the frozen ground, he reached the manger in half a dozen long strides, reaching into its depths even as he caught sight of the tiny babe, wrapped in a bit of white flannel. The blanket had been disturbed by the infant's flailing arms and he saw that dark hair crowned the tiny head, as with openmouthed cries the child demanded attention.

He picked up the small bundle, his eyes searching the surrounding area, hoping for a glimpse of whoever had left this child here in the cold. Holding the swaddled babe to his chest, he rose, standing before the makeshift shed amidst the shepherds, a sheep on one side, the donkey on the other, and looked down into the face of innocence.

Apparently soothed by the hands that held it, the baby snuffled, poking one small fist into its mouth, sucking earnestly on his hand and opening his dark eyes to look up at the man who held him. David caught his breath, recalling with sorrow the last time he'd held a child thusly, the day of his son's birth. The poignant memory scalded his eyes, and tears poured forth, dropping upon the white blanket-wrapped bundle in his arms.

He turned hastily toward the parsonage and as he did so, he caught a glimpse of a figure darting from the side of the church, into the bushes by the road. It had been a woman, a slender form that seemed almost ghostly, yet he knew what he'd seen, and in vain he called out to the woman.

It was cold, the wind picking up, and he quickly carried the baby to his house, opened the door and stepped into the parlor, where he stood immobile for a moment, unsure of his direction. His groceries lay in the churchyard and he placed the baby on his sofa and turned to retrieve the results of his shopping, hastening across the small distance to pick up the bundles of food.

A slight figure walked quickly down the road, heading for the middle of town, and he called out to her, for it was obviously a woman, her skirts swaying as she hurried on her way. Dark hair hung past her shoulders, and a dark cloak was wrapped around her. Yet in the moonlight she cast a glance behind her and he saw the face of a girl, not a woman after all. But a girl with tearstained cheeks, gleaming in the light of the rising moon.

His groceries at hand, he bent and picked them up, then returned with haste to the parsonage, there to hear the wail of the child who lay on his sofa. He dropped the foodstuffs he'd bought onto the kitchen table and returned to the babe, bending to unwrap the blanket, the better to see the infant he'd rescued.

Wrapped in the folds of the blanket was a diaper and a bottle, filled with milk, a nipple attached to it in readiness should the child require feeding. And from the sounds of things, David decided that food was essential, for the cries were louder, the small face redder, and the arms and legs had kicked off the blanket, exposing small limbs and bare feet that did not measure nearly as long as his index finger.

Gathering the baby to himself, he held it cradled in his left arm and offered the bottle to the tiny mouth, a mouth that opened wide to accept the rubber nipple, apparently accustomed to being fed in such a way.

His heart was gripped with an emotion unlike any he'd ever experienced, a pouring out of his need, the memory of an infant, buried in his mother's arms, and hot tears fell as the child's face blurred before his sight. His arms tightened as his thoughts soared. If only... And yet there were no such miracles, no such travels back in time in which he might have a taste of the joys of holding his child, a joy that had been denied him.

For these few moments he could dream, and dream he did, his mind moving on to the service he would hold in but an hour. A service of happiness, of joy, of worship. The sight of their pastor carrying in a child to the service might be beyond their ability to understand, and so deciding to spare his small flock the sight, he arose from his chair, discovered that the infant he held needed a dry bottom and tended to that small chore.

Not familiar with such doings, he took much longer than the babe deemed necessary for the task. But in another ten minutes he'd wrapped the tiny form in the flannel blanket, added a shawl he'd hidden deep in a dresser drawer, to provide additional warmth against the winter night, and set off for his church.

Arriving early, he lowered the lamps, lit them and set them in place, then placed the sleeping babe on the back pew of the choir loft, careful to prop hymnals before the tiny form, lest it roll to the floor.

Within a half hour the small church was filling with his congregation, the children excited, whispering among themselves, the adults properly worshipful for this most holy of services in the life of his church.

They sang with uplifted voices, they sang from memory the old carols that told the Christmas story, of Mary and the babe of Bethlehem. They sang of shepherds, of the kings from afar, and then, after the reading from St. Luke, they bowed in prayer. To the faint echoes of "Silent Night" the flock filed from the church, and David stood before his pulpit, watching as one lone woman knelt in the very last row of seats.

He picked up his charge, thankful that the baby had slept throughout the hour-long service, and with the wrapped bundle against his shoulder, he walked silently down the long aisle to the back door of the church. As he passed the last pew, he looked aside to where the young woman knelt, and paused there.

Marianne looked up, knowing that there were eyes intent on her, feeling the warmth of someone's scrutiny. Her eyes were blurred with tears, for she had just committed her small brother into God's hands, not knowing what his future might hold, but trusting that somehow he would find sanctuary this night.

In the dim light of the moon, shining through the church doors, a tall man watched her—the pastor of this church, the man who had lifted Joshua from the manger just hours earlier. Now he held the baby against his shoulder, the white blanket a pale blur against his dark suit.

"Do you need help?" the man asked, his voice deep and tender, as if he knew somehow who she was. "Why don't you come with me and have some tea over in the parsonage kitchen?"

He waited, unmoving, as she looked into eyes that even in the dim light seemed to glow with an unearthly light. There was no question of trust, for she'd known from her first glimpse of him that this man was kind and wore the cloak of goodness on his shoulders. How such a thing could be, Marianne didn't understand, but she felt a trust in him that was without reason. Perhaps he'd been sent to help her; maybe he would be the answer to her prayers.

She rose and left the pew, looking up at him as he ushered her to the door, his hand on her elbow, his head bent to look into her face.

"Are you hungry?" he asked. And she nodded slowly, unwilling to admit her need, but aware that she must have nourishment to sustain her for the night to come.

They walked from the church together, most of the congregation already leaving the churchyard, only a few townspeople lingering to call out their messages of holiday cheer to the pastor.

Marianne walked ahead of him, aware of the watching eyes, the whispers that followed her progress along the path through the light snow that formed patterns on the ground. Janet, the storekeeper's wife, stood near the gate and lifted a hand in greeting.

"Where are you staying, dear?" she asked quietly. "Do you need to sleep at the store tonight?"

Marianne looked over her shoulder at the tall figure who walked just behind her. "I'm going to have tea with the minister and then decide where I'll go," she said softly, lest anyone else hear her words. It would not do for the representative of the church to be spoken of badly should he give refuge to a woman so late at night.

"David McDermott will take care of you. He's a good man," Janet said readily. "You come and see me the day after tomorrow if you need anything. The store will be locked up tomorrow, but you know where I live."

Marianne nodded, smiling her thanks as she reached for her small brother and took him from Mr. McDermott's hands. The small churchyard emptied rapidly, for the parishioners were anxious to return to their warm homes where Christmas celebrations were about to begin.

Together Marianne and Mr. McDermott walked next door to the parsonage and entered the foyer of the small house. Removing his coat and hat, he turned to her, offering his big hands to take the baby, allowing Marianne to take off her cloak and hang it on a hook by the front door before returning her brother to her arms.

She felt awkward, out of place, and knew that her cheeks were red with embarrassment. "I can't thank you enough for inviting me into your home for tea," she said, her voice shaking with emotion, for tears hovered near, and she dreaded shedding them before a stranger.

"I could not leave you out in the cold, young lady," he said kindly. "For I have a dish of chicken and gravy, sent me by one of the ladies of my congregation, and it will go to waste if you don't help me eat some of it. There are potatoes to go with it, and I can slice some bread. Someone sent me a pound or so of fresh butter yesterday, so my kitchen is well equipped to handle a Christmas Eve meal."

Marianne felt her small brother awaken in his blankets, for he wriggled and pushed his feet out, demanding that he be unwrapped from the binding of his blankets. One arm rose from the wrappings and waved in the air, even as he cried aloud, craving attention.

"I think he's hungry again. Would you have the bottle handy that I left with him?"

"So it was you who put him in the manger. I thought as much, when I saw you in the back of the church. I caught a glimpse of you when you walked away from here earlier, and I figured you'd show up sometime tonight. I knew you'd be wanting to check on the baby."

David pulled a chair from under the kitchen table and offered it to Marianne, watching as she sank into its depths, the infant in her arms squirming now, anticipating his next meal. She unwrapped him, delving beneath the blankets to check on the condition of his diaper, and her face flushed as she looked up at the man before her.

"I need to have a bit of privacy to change him, I fear. There are several clean diapers in my bag, if you'll let me use a flat surface somewhere to clean him up a little."

David smiled, his thoughts not altogether above reproach, for this young woman was appealing to him on a level he had not considered for some time. Her scent was fresh, clean and her face was akin to what he thought the young mother in Bethlehem might have looked like. Dark hair hung long, waving and thick, in a veil that almost covered her back. She was dressed in rough clothing, but everything about her was clean. Even the child she carried in her arms had not carried the scent of an unwashed body, but had been as fresh and clean as a babe could be.

Somewhere she had found resources to keep the child well fed and clean, and he admired the courage of a young woman so able to do her duty as she saw it. "How old is your little boy?" he asked, attempting to lure her into conversation, lest she be frightened and flee his house.

"He is three weeks old, sir. But he is not my child, but my baby brother. My mother and father died of the fever and he was born as my mother breathed her last." Her head bent over the baby and a tear fell on the blanket, one he knew she'd tried not to shed, for she had been careful up until now not to show her emotional state.

"Bring him into the parlor," David said, leading the way. "I'll warm up the chicken and heat a bit of milk for his bottle while you change him and make him comfortable."

Marianne followed him, thankful for his help, her stomach rumbling as she considered the meal she would eat at his table. Her bag held the clean diapers she'd washed earlier at Janet's home, and in much less time than David had taken to do the same task she had changed and freshened Joshua's bottom, then she wrapped him again and headed back to the kitchen.

Smells of food were welcome, for she knew she must keep up her strength, and she sat at the table once more, watching as the tall minister worked around the kitchen. Adept at his chores, he stirred the chicken as it simmered on the stove, took plates from the cupboard and found forks in a drawer, all simultaneous moves that astonished Marianne. Her own father had been useless in the kitchen, her mother had often said, for the man was more at home with cows and horses than in the house where the food was prepared.

This young minister seemed to know his way around the kitchen, and in just a few minutes he set a plate of chicken and gravy, side by side with a helping of mashed potatoes, in front of her. A plate of sliced bread and a pat of butter were between them as he settled into a seat across the table, with his own plate of food.

She watched as he lowered his head and spoke soft words of blessing on their food, then she picked up her fork, shamed by the trembling of her hand as she lifted it to her mouth. "I didn't know I was so hungry," she said quietly. The food was good, tasty and nourishing, for there were bits of carrots and peas mixed in with the gravy and the chunks of chicken were hearty and plenteous.

A slice of bread was halved and buttered and placed on her plate, and she smiled her thanks. "I suspect it might be difficult to deal with a baby and butter your bread at the same time," David said with a smile.

Marianne had held Joshua across her arm as she ate, resting his bottle on her breast as he nursed, leaving her free to eat while feeding him. "I usually lay him across my lap and let him sleep while I eat," Marianne told him. "But he's wide-awake tonight for some reason. And until he finishes and gets rid of his burp, he'll be restless."

David smiled and a chuckle escaped his lips. "Probably because he slept all through the service tonight. He was behind me on a pew and I had hopes that I could outtalk him if he woke up before we were finished."

"I didn't see him up there," Marianne said. "I wondered what you'd done with him, for I saw you carry him into the church."

"What did you think would happen to him when you left him in the manger?"

She shook her head. "I didn't know, but I'd decided to watch until someone found him and then thought I might offer my services to help take care of him. I really didn't plan ahead well, but when I saw the empty manger in front of the church, I knew I should put him there and hope for the best."

"You're a brave young woman." He leveled his gaze at her and his voice was soft as he asked her name.

"Marianne Winters. Joshua, as I said, is my brother."

And if she expected him to believe that, he'd do his best to accept her words as truth, David decided. For the child bore a definite likeness to her—eyes widespread, dark hair and a pointed chin that were small replicas of her own. If he was not Marianne's own child, it would be a miracle, for being born in the midst of a typhoid epidemic such as the one running rampant over the county during the past month or so was a death sentence in itself. The child surely would have been exposed to the dread disease upon birth. To live through such a thing would have been a miracle.

"If you would like to stay here for the night, I have a spare room to offer you," David said suddenly. Whether or not his congregation would approve was not an issue as far as he was concerned. This woman needed help and a warm place to sleep with her child, and it would not behoove him as a man of the church to cast her out into the cold. Perhaps she would be willing to work for her keep until she could find a job with enough pay to care for herself and her child.

"I need someone to keep house for me," he began slowly, offering the idea for her to chew on. "Perhaps you would be interested in working here during the day and staying in a nearby home at night. I'd not be able to pay you a lot, but your food would be included in your wage and I don't mind having the baby around."

Marianne looked up in surprise. That such an offer might be made tonight was beyond her wildest dreams. And especially from a man living alone, a man who stood to ruin his good reputation if it became known that he had opened his home to a single woman and a child.

"I wouldn't do anything to damage your name in town," she said quietly. "I'm sure it would cause talk if I were to spend my days here, and even though I need work to support myself and Joshua, I hesitate to accept your offer."

"Stay for tonight anyway, and we'll see what tomorrow brings," David said.

"Thank you, Reverend," Marianne said, her words sincere, for she hadn't expected such a welcome.

"My name is David. Would you mind calling me by name?

It's been a long time since anyone spoke to me without a title. Sometimes I yearn to be an ordinary man, and I fear that my congregation has put me in a box and labeled me as a man of the church, and I miss being just David McDermott."

"Have you never been David to anyone here in town?" Marianne asked, seeking to know more about the man who sat so quietly across from her.

"My wife called me David, and had he lived, my son would be calling me Daddy by now, I think." His eyes grew dark with sorrow as Marianne watched and she rued her words that had caused him such pain. Her hand patted Joshua's back in a rhythmic fashion as he stirred against her shoulder, and she rubbed the length of his back, knowing that the burp he held within was making him restless.

It erupted on a loud note and Marianne laughed softly, bending to kiss the small head, accepting his offering gladly, for without it he would have slept badly. Now the chances were that he would last until morning without food, kept warm and cuddled closely as he seemed to enjoy.

"Thank you for the meal and for your help," Marianne said, looking up at David as he cleared the table. His hands moved rapidly as he put the plates into the dishpan, the silverware with them, and then poured in hot water from the stove's reservoir.

"I'd like to wash the dishes, if you'll show me where to put the baby down," she said, rising and looking about for a hallway that might lead to the bedrooms.

"Follow me," David said quickly. "There are clean sheets on the bed in the spare room and we can leave the door open to let the heat from the stove enter. It's the room closest to the kitchen, so he should be warm enough."

The bedroom was small but clean, the bed covered with a handmade quilt, and two fat pillows were propped at the headboard. "This is lovely," Marianne said, pulling back the quilt to place Joshua in the middle of the big bed.

"I wish I had a cradle to offer you for him, but the one I

made for our son was given away after he and his mother died. I couldn't stand to keep it in the house, and a lady outside town was having her first child and they couldn't afford a bed for the baby. It seemed the right thing to do, so I offered the one I'd made. They put it to good use."

Marianne's heart ached for the loss he'd suffered and her tender heart went out to him, wishing she might have the words to offer that would give surcease to his pain.

"I'm sure your wife would have wanted someone else to use the cradle, David. I think she'd be happy to know that another child slept in it."

"Thank you," he said, avoiding her gaze, as if he hid a trace of tears in his eyes and did not want to share his grief.

Marianne propped pillows around Joshua, making sure that he was well padded so that should he wet his diaper it would not dampen the bedding. Then she went back to the kitchen and found a dishcloth, preparing to clean up the kitchen. It was a small matter, washing and drying the few dishes they'd used, cleaning out the pan he'd warmed the food in and then hanging the dish towel and cloth to dry on a small line he'd strung behind the stove.

She wiped the table clean, swept the floor and lowered the lamp a bit, to save the kerosene for another day. David sat at the table, paper and pen before him, bent over a letter he had begun.

"I'll go on to bed now," Marianne told him, walking to the bedroom doorway, then turning back to face him.

He looked up from his writing, his eyes distracted by her words, then he smiled. "I'm just writing a letter to my folks, back home in Ohio. I'm telling them about you and Joshua and the way you left him in the manger for me to find. I hope you don't mind."

"Will they think badly of me for abandoning my brother that way?"

He shook his head. "They'll understand that you were desperate, that you had no resources to care for him by yourself.

It was a smart move for you to make, actually. You just didn't imagine that I would be the one to find him and take him indoors, did you?"

Marianne flushed uncomfortably, for she had indeed thought just such a thing might happen and her words verified that fact. "I thought perhaps a minister and his wife would care for a foundling like Joshua. I had no idea you were alone here in the parsonage."

David smiled, his thoughts hidden from Marianne. "I think perhaps things worked out the way they were supposed to, anyway. I needed Joshua as much as he needed someone to care for him."

"I'd have spent my whole life tending him if I could, Mr. McDermott."

"I thought we'd gotten past the Mr. McDermott thing," David said quietly. "I liked it much better when you called me by my given name. I felt we were becoming friends, Marianne."

Bravely Marianne spoke her thoughts aloud. "I'd like to keep house for you, David, if the offer is still open. I'll see if Janet will let me sleep at the store, and then I can come here during the day to cook and clean for you. In exchange, perhaps you would consider giving Joshua a home until I can provide for him."

"I'll want to talk to the men on my church board before I make a commitment to you, Marianne. I can't do anything that would reflect badly on my position here, and I don't want any hint of gossip to touch you or Joshua."

"Can you do that? Talk to the men who run the church with you? Do you think they'll object to such a plan?"

"They've known for quite a while that I need help in my home and surely it is an obvious solution to my problem and yours, too. I'll speak to them after the Wednesday-night meeting."

"And for tonight you think I should stay here in your spare room?"

He nodded agreeably. "I don't see that we have any choice.

Tomorrow is Christmas and the town will be closed up tighter than a drum, with folks celebrating with their families and such. Why don't you plan on cooking dinner for me and getting Joshua settled in here? You can walk over and talk to Janet in the morning and sound her out about you staying at the store nights."

Marianne considered the plan, not willing to put David to shame in any way, but the hour was late and the lights were out in the houses around them. It was beyond time for folks to be in bed and she accepted that her fate for this day was out of her hands.

"All right. We'll do as you say, David. I'll go on to bed now and be up early with the baby, then it will be time enough to cook your breakfast and take a walk to see Janet."

He watched as she went into the bedroom, closing the door behind her, and his heart was full as he considered the day to come. He'd been beyond lonely without the companionship he'd come to enjoy with a wife. His years with Laura had been few, but his months without her had seemed an eternity, so quiet had been the house, so empty his heart.

For a moment he thought of another plan that might work, and decided to seek out Marianne's thoughts in the morning. Should she be agreeable, they might be married and share the parsonage together, thus satisfying any gossip that might arise in town concerning her presence here. She was a lovely girl, with pleasing ways about her, and he didn't doubt that she would be more than capable of running his home as his wife.

Whether or not Joshua was her own child or her brother, as she claimed, he was willing to accept her as she was, without any guarantees, and he might find an end to the long days and nights he'd spent alone.

He went to his bedroom and closed the door, aware that even through that stout panel he would hear should Joshua awaken during the night.

Chapter Three

The rooster in his neighbor's chicken coop sounded his usual early-morning call, and David pulled the quilt up over his head, unwilling to leave the warmth of the dream he had enjoyed for the past few minutes. A dark-haired girl, her form slender yet pleasingly curved, had been featured throughout the night hours, and his sleep had been broken, his eyes opening suddenly several times as he awoke from nocturnal thoughts that were far from dignified.

He sat up suddenly, recalling the heated dreams he'd indulged in, and his heart stuttered within him as he considered the woman in the next room. Even as he thought of her, he heard the movement beyond his bedroom wall as she arose, heard the small, soft sounds of a baby's cry as Joshua awoke, announcing his hunger aloud.

His trousers were on the bedpost and David slid into them quickly, made haste to don his shoes and stockings, tucked his shirt into his pants hurriedly and went to the kitchen.

He found Marianne there before him, intent on heating milk for Joshua's breakfast. She'd put on a small pan, warming an amount of milk from his pantry that would be sufficient to fill the baby bottle she was washing in the sink. He watched her from the doorway, noting her quick movements, the soft curves of her arms as she worked the pump ha[...] of her hips as she turned back to the stove to resc[...] lest it be too hot for the baby.

"Good morning," he said quietly, not wanting to startl[...] Her head turned quickly to where he stood and a rosy flus[...] covered her cheeks, as if she had been trying to be quiet and had still disturbed his sleep.

"I tried not to wake you," she said, and he smiled, aware that he had read her aright.

"That's all right. It was time for me to be up and about anyway. The rooster always sounds his alarm at dawn, and I find it a good time to begin my day."

She poured the warmed milk into the bottle, careful not to spill any on the stove, and he watched her graceful movements, his breath coming quickly as he bent his appreciative gaze on her. The nipple was snapped into place and she turned her attention to him quickly.

"I'll just go and get Joshua and feed him before I make your breakfast," she said, heading for the spare room.

"Why not bring him out here and let me feed him and you can go ahead with breakfast. We'll kill two birds with one stone, so to speak."

Her smile was quick and ready, and he basked in the warmth of it. "I'll wait here in the rocking chair." And for the first time in months he sat in the rocker he'd bought for Laura during her pregnancy, pressing his foot against the floor in a slow fashion, allowing the chair to perform as it had been constructed to do.

Marianne came back from the bedroom, Joshua wrapped securely in his blanket, and collected the bottle from the table as she approached David. Her arms were extended to him and he took the small bundle from her, feeling an emotion akin to sorrow as he held the tiny mite against his chest. So might he have held the child Laura had borne months ago, and he caught his breath quickly, lest Marianne think he did not want to feed Joshua as he'd offered.

44 ... eyes ... damp with tears that he refused to shed. Not ... matter of manliness or masculine pride, but he ... that it w... make her uncomfortable with his spasm of sorrow. ... would was no longer fresh, and he found that he spent hours ... bout its presence in his heart. Now he had the opportunity ... holding a child, though not his own, yet in a sense he felt a kinship to Joshua.

That he had found the child in his manger in the midst of the Nativity scene he'd constructed with his own hands was certainly part of his feeling of ownership of the child. Though children could not be possessed as might a dog or cow or some other belonging, he felt that Joshua was meant in some distinct way to be a part of his life. He had had a wife, never treating her as a possession, but as a partner in the wonders of marriage. They had been happy together, her cheerful demeanor giving him joy each day, her loving arms filling him with the satisfaction of a relationship that went beyond friendship, and hovered on the edge of love.

He'd made the mistake of not speaking his love aloud to Laura, assuming that she knew of his devotion to her, and had spent long hours of regret after her death, that he had never declared his heart aloud. Should he ever have the opportunity again to share such a relationship with a woman, he would not make the same mistake, he vowed silently.

And then he cuddled the baby against him, testing the warmth of the milk in the palm of his hand as he offered the nipple to Joshua's rosy mouth. With gusto the baby attached himself to the rubber nipple and nursed. The span of eight hours or so had made him hungry and he clung tightly to the source of nourishment, almost choking on the abundance of milk he consumed.

Finally he released the nipple and his burp was loud and long, Marianne turning from the stove to laugh at him.

"He has no manners to speak of," she said with a joyous light in her eyes. "I've never enjoyed anything so much in my life as I have tending him over the past weeks. He keeps my grief at bay somehow. Even though I miss my parents terribly, he manages to soothe my heartache." Her words were soft, almost whispered, but David heard them clearly, knowing the truth in what she said, for she did not seem to have any sense of protecting herself from him. She was open and her heart was clearly involved in the child he held.

He watched her as she sliced bacon and placed it in his skillet, cracked eggs and whipped them to a froth with a turning fork, then poured the mixture into a second skillet. Bread was sliced and she slid it into the oven, lifting a stove lid to check the flames within. She was efficient, capable of tending to the making of a meal, and she'd obviously been well trained in her skills in the kitchen.

"Did you cook for your mother and father?" he asked, and she nodded, as if unable to speak of it aloud. He thought her shoulders trembled as she faced the stove and then she uttered words of regret, making him sorry he'd asked his question.

"I used to think it was a chore to cook sometimes, but my mother was not well when she carried Joshua and I had the full load of tending the kitchen and keeping the house clean. I thought if I were cooking for a family of my own it might have been more enjoyable, but I could foresee years ahead of helping with my parents and the child that came so late in their lives. They had not expected to have more children after I was born, for my mother bore several infants born too soon and they were not able to survive. There were four graves beyond our orchard, and she was not happy when she discovered that Joshua was on his way, for she was certain that he would share a similar fate with those who had come before."

"How fortunate that he was a survivor," David said softly, looking down at the sleeping child he held. The bottle was almost empty and the baby had bubbled a drop of milk from his mouth, making David yearn to bend low to kiss it away.

"My mother would have been heartbroken had he not lived. I like to think that she knew somehow that he was a healthy child even though she died in birthing him. It wasn't the birth that caused her death, but the fever she had suffered with for two days. The doctor said it was a miracle that Joshua hadn't succumbed to it himself, but he didn't ever show signs of sickness, right from the first. I think he was meant to live."

"I agree with you, Marianne. He has a purpose in life to fulfill, as do we all. Your mother's may have been in bearing him and giving him life. We have no way of knowing what lies ahead for a child, only that we must do our best to raise him in such a way that he be a good man and a credit to his parents."

"I'll do my best to fulfill my mother's dreams for him, David. She and my father were so looking forward to his birth, and it seemed I was bitter and angry with God for taking their lives just when it seemed happiness was in their future."

"We don't know why things happen the way they do, Marianne, but I'm sure Joshua will be a good man, with you to raise him and provide for him."

She put two plates on the table, steam rising from the scrambled eggs, and then retrieved the bread from the oven, where it had toasted golden-brown. "Let me take Joshua now," she said, moving toward the rocking chair, her arms outstretched. She took him carefully in her arms, bent to press her lips on his forehead and carried him to the bedroom.

Within moments she was back, taking her seat at the table, across from where David awaited her presence. He bent his head and spoke brief words of thanks for the food, asking a special thanksgiving for the joyous blessings of Christmas, and then lifted his eyes to meet her gaze.

"Eat while it's hot, Marianne. We have things to tend to this morning. I haven't found it in my heart to celebrate Christmas this year, but I find that there is reason to rejoice today. I'm going to speak to our mayor this morning. I don't want to interrupt his holiday with his family, but I think he will understand the reason for my concern."

"Will you stay here while I go and see Janet first?" she asked, needing to make arrangements for a place to sleep should Janet be agreeable to the plan she had concocted.

"Of course. Let Joshua have his morning nap while you go, and I'll clean up the breakfast things."

Her face lit with a smile, and he thought once again that she was a lovely girl. A woman really, for she was certainly of age to be married and have a child, at least almost out of her teens. And to that end he asked a question that had gnawed at his mind.

"How old are you, Marianne? Perhaps it's none of my business, but I don't want anyone to think I'm taking advantage of a young girl, asking you to work for me with little in the way of payment."

"I'm eighteen," she answered. "I might have been married and expecting a family of my own by now, but the young man who had been courting me contracted the fever and was buried just before my parents died." Her eyes were dark with the additional sorrow of that loss and he felt a pang of pity as he considered the grief she must bear.

"I'm sorry for your pain. It may be that we can comfort each other in our grief, Marianne. For if my plans go aright, I'm going to ask my church board their opinion of a marriage between you and me. I think it would work out well for us, and I want you to know that I would not expect you to fill the role of a wife before you felt ready for it. Joshua would have a home and I would have the advantage of a wife in the parsonage, a helpmeet for me in my work. Can I have your permission to ask such a thing?"

She looked up at him, surprise alight in her face. "I hadn't thought of such a thing, David. I'd only thought of working here and having a chance to give Joshua a good life, with enough food and more clothing as he grows. The thought of marriage hadn't entered my head."

"I realize that," he told her, "but I spent a lot of hours last night trying to find a solution to your problems. This seems to be the answer for both of us. I'd hoped you might be agreeable."

Marianne was quiet for a few moments as if she must assimilate all he'd said. Her head was bowed as she considered David's words. She'd not thought of marriage, for having Joshua to care for made her somewhat of a burden for a young man just starting out in his life. Whereas David had been married, knew the ups and downs connected with a relationship with a woman and, much to her surprise, he was willing to take her on, along with her brother, and make a home for her here in the parsonage. She felt a thrill of delight that such a man would be interested in her, that he found her attractive, for surely he would not marry a woman who did not appeal to him.

She donned her cloak, watching as David cleared off the table and rinsed the plates in the sink. He was obviously used to washing up after a meal and she could not help but notice his skills as he wiped off the table, put the dishes into the pan and readied them for washing. He would be a husband to be proud of, she decided, hoping that his plan might bear fruit, that their marriage might be welcome to the townspeople who supported his church and paid his salary.

"I'll be back shortly, once I talk to Janet," she told him, opening the back door and stepping onto the porch. "Joshua will sleep for an hour or two—at least he usually does in the morning after he eats. I'll give him a bath when he awakens and do his washing. I hope you won't mind if I use the line behind the stove to dry things on."

"You are welcome to do as you please while you're with me, Marianne. I enjoy your company, and having Joshua here is a bonus for me. I feel attached to him already. I hope you'll truly consider what I've asked of you. I've only proposed once before, when I asked Laura to be my wife, so I probably didn't do a very good job of it, but I want you to know that it is the desire of my heart to take care of you and Joshua and give you a home where you'll be safe and happy. I think I should make it clear that you may have your own bedroom, for I have no intention of pushing you into an intimate relationship. If and when you are ready to truly be a wife, I'll expect you to let me know, for I'm more interested right now in getting to know you better and finding out how we get on together."

She smiled, standing in the open doorway. "That's quite a speech, David. You've made me an offer I can hardly refuse. I hope you won't find any dispute to your proposal from the board of your church, for this will be the answer to my prayers, if all goes as you have planned."

She blushed as his scrutiny swept her from head to toe, and his smile was approving as he walked toward her. His hands rested on her shoulders and he bent to her, pressing his lips against her forehead.

"Talk to Janet about it if you like, Marianne. See if she gives her approval. I honestly think she will, for she is a sensible lady, one who will see the obvious advantages for both of us." He held her apart from him and his smile was warm, his lips curved in a look of pure happiness. "Merry Christmas, my dear. I hope this day will be a happy one for both of us."

Marianne walked quickly to the house next to the general store, rapping once on the door and waiting as she heard footsteps approaching, the sound vibrating on the porch. Janet opened the door wide and welcomed her inside.

"Merry Christmas, Marianne. I wondered what had happened to you last night. I left the store unlocked in case you wanted to sleep there, but I noticed this morning when I went over to put wood in the stove that you hadn't been there."

"I slept at the parsonage," Marianne admitted quietly. "David felt it would be better for Joshua to be in a warm house where there was everything available to tend to him. He's sleeping now in the spare bedroom. And that was where I spent the night, Janet. I hope you don't think there was anything out of order going on last night. David gave me a place to stay and I got up and made his breakfast."

She slid her cloak from her shoulders and sat in the chair Janet offered, nodding her head as she offered Marianne a cup of tea, a gift received with a grin.

"Thank you. David prefers coffee apparently, and I didn't ask if he had any tea. My mama used to always have a cup for breakfast or in the middle of the morning. I miss sitting at the table with her and talking of what we would do during the day and what work needed to be done."

"What have you and Mr. McDermott spoken of, Marianne? I think from the look on your face that you have something to talk over with me. Am I wrong?" Janet sat across the table, lifted her teacup and sipped at the warm brew, waiting till Marianne should decide to speak.

"He wants to marry me," she said softly. "He asked if I would live there and keep house for him and cook and do the laundry and all that is entailed in being a wife."

"All?" Janet asked quietly, her brow rising as she posed the query.

"All but the sleeping in his bedroom part," Marianne said, feeling awkward as she explained the circumstances David had suggested. "He said he would not expect that of me, for we barely know each other, having met but yesterday. I think he's willing to give me as much time as I need to become accustomed to his company before he makes a change in our relationship."

"And how do you feel about it?" Janet asked, as if she were feeling her way, trying to negotiate a rocky path. "Would you be comfortable living in the parsonage and answering to the ladies in town, for surely you know they will watch you like a hawk."

"I hadn't thought of that," Marianne told her. "I suppose they feel somewhat protective of David, given the circumstances of his wife's death and the loss of his child."

"It could well be the best thing that could happen for both

of you," Janet said slowly, as if her mind must catch up to her words. "I assume you've had a good upbringing, Marianne, and your parents were no doubt strict with you. Have you had a gentleman friend in your life before this?"

"A young man in our neighborhood wanted to court me a couple of years ago and my father told him he could come calling so long as he didn't see me alone, without a chaperone. He talked about marriage for the past few months, and I had just about agreed to the idea, for he was a good man, with good prospects."

Janet eyed her, obviously noting the tears that threatened to fall as she spoke. "What happened? Did you change your mind?"

"No. He came down with the fever and died just before my parents became ill. A lot of the folks in our part of the county fell ill and many of them didn't make it. There are a lot of homes without mothers, some without a breadwinner, and the winter looks to be a sad one for several families who are grieving for loved ones."

"Is that why you left home with Joshua?"

"My neighbor said her sister lived here in town and I might be able to stay with her while I found work. You know how that turned out, once her husband got wind of the idea. I don't think my old neighbor is aware of the situation in her sister's home."

"Well, you didn't need that sort of problem anyway," Janet said bluntly. "What you've been offered is far and away the better choice for you."

"David said he's going to speak with the mayor today, even though it's Christmas. He's anxious to get someone else's approval of his proposal."

"The mayor is head of the church board, and if he gives his okay, David has clear sailing," Janet said with a grin. "I'll bet he's anxious to get things in motion. I wouldn't be surprised if you're not a married lady by tomorrow."

Marianne almost choked on her tea. "So soon? Do you really think he'll want to do things that quickly?"

"He can't keep you in his house without marrying you, Marianne. You're old enough to know folks will talk if such a thing were to be going on. It's better for you and David both if you speak your vows right away."

Marianne stood, gathering her cloak up from the chair and tossing it over her shoulders. "I think maybe I'd better get back to the parsonage and let David do his business with the mayor, hadn't I?"

Janet smiled, her eyes beaming with anticipation. "I can't wait till tomorrow. Every lady in town will be in the store before the day is over, wondering what is going on. You'll have their eyes glued on you, I'll guarantee it."

Marianne felt a flush creep up her cheeks. "I don't know if I'm looking forward to that. I'd thought maybe we could keep it very quiet if we decided to do this, sort of just make it a private thing."

"Not a chance," Janet said with a hoot of laughter. "Everyone in town will be wanting to give you a pounding."

"A pounding?" Marianne's eyes widened as she considered the word, wondering at its meaning.

"A pounding is where each family brings a pound of this or that to the happy couple's home. A pound of coffee, or flour or maybe sugar or butter. Quite often it's more than just a pound, for folks think highly of Mr. McDermott and they'll want to welcome you into the parsonage as his wife in fine style."

David left the house as soon as Marianne returned, heading for the mayor's home, leaving Marianne with a smile, and his expression speaking of his pleasure at the circumstances. He obviously was pleased at the idea of gaining a wife so readily, Marianne decided. It was likely that he was weary of taking care of himself, although the parsonage did not show neglect in any way. He apparently had taken good care of his home, keeping it clean and caring for his belongings.

She spent an hour preparing dinner, first finding a piece of smoked pork in the pantry, then placing it in a baking pan, sliding it into the oven and deciding on a kettle of green beans and potatoes to go with it. Most men enjoyed their big meal of the day at noontime—at least her father had, and her mother had said it was the usual circumstance to have a large meal at noon, then just soup or some such thing for supper later on in the day.

She heard Joshua's cry as he awakened and she made haste to wash her hands and set a pan of warm water on the table for his bath, then gathered him up from the bed and stripped him of his clothing so that she could give him a fresh start. He was a pleasure to tend, contented to allow her to wash his head, using a cloth to wipe his arms and legs and then his back. He shivered as she finished the task, and she wrapped him in a clean towel she'd found in David's bedroom. His small head smelled sweet, she thought, just as an infant should, and it was with joy that she diapered him and found the last clean gown for him to wear.

The laundry must be done soon, for he was almost out of diapers, having only just a few more than a dozen to his name. A washtub on the porch offered her a place to soak his clothing, and she put it in front of the stove, half filling it with warm water from the reservoir.

His bottle ready, she held him in her arms in the rocking chair and sang to him as he ate his meal, his hands clutching at her fingers, his nose nuzzling her as he searched out the nipple she'd carefully washed and readied for his use.

He was warm and soft and she felt an overwhelming love for the mite as she rocked him, holding him close, humming a lullaby she'd heard her mother sing as she worked around the house, one she remembered hearing as a child.

When David returned from his jaunt across town, she had

just put Joshua down on the bed, knowing that he would sleep again for at least two hours. He was a good baby, her former neighbor had said, quickly accustoming himself to the schedule of eating and sleeping. Marianne had not spent much time with children up until this point in her life, but tending to her brother was a chore she accepted as her due.

David had good news. "The mayor seems to think it would be a good idea for us to be married. He said every man needs a wife, and a preacher especially so. The parsonage is usually the place where people come with their problems, and it is better if there is a true family living there. I understand what he was saying, for it isn't a good idea for a man of the church not to have a wife of his own. He said I've been the object of several young ladies' attention of late, and I suspect he is right. For I feel sometimes like I'm on display."

Marianne nodded at his words. "What do you think we should do?" she asked.

"Did Janet have any ideas?" David wanted to know. "I thought she might speak her mind to you."

Marianne nodded, looking down at her hands, clenched tightly in her lap. "She thinks it's a good idea, our getting married. I just don't want you to jump into something you may be sorry for later on. What if you find that you don't like me well enough to share your life with me?"

The expression on David's face was almost comical, for he'd apparently not thought of that possibility. "I see no reason why we couldn't make a good marriage. You're a woman who would appeal to any man with eyes in his head, and I'm not immune to the allure you offer."

"Me?" She was stunned by his words. "I didn't think you had looked at me that way, David."

"You don't know much about men, do you?" At the quick shake of her head, he continued, his voice soft, his gaze upon her seeming as warm as a spring breeze. His words were genuine, spoken from his heart, and he felt the pace of that organ in his chest vibrating in a mysterious rhythm. "You are slender and most appealing, Marianne, with curves that speak of feminine form and beauty. Your eyes are lovely, your hair looks like pure silk. It makes my hands itch to touch it and run it through my fingers. Altogether you are a woman any man would be proud to marry. Best of all, your demeanor is modest, your upbringing obviously that of a girl with a good background. I'll bet your folks were strict with you, weren't they? I doubt they allowed you to be alone with any young men, did they?"

He halted, watching her with a warmth in his eyes that made her wonder at the many charms he had described, made her stomach swim in a delightful manner. She shook her head in bewilderment. "No one has ever spoken to me this way before. I don't know what to think, David. I look in my mirror every morning when I wash my face and brush my hair, and I swear to you I don't see the woman you have described."

"Perhaps I look with the eyes of a man who is attracted to you, Marianne. Maybe my viewpoint is so different than yours because it is one of masculine interest. Know that I am being as honest with you as I know how. I would never tell you an untruth or exaggerate my feelings. You are a tempting woman and I would find it no hardship to put my ring on your finger and claim you as my wife."

Chapter Four

"Is this what you told the mayor? That you were ready to speak vows with me?"

David nodded silently, then awaited her answer. It was not long in coming. "I've decided to do as you've asked, David. I'll marry you and take up the reins in your home and do my best to make you happy and make your life as easy as possible. I'll keep your house clean and your clothing in order and in all ways act as a minister's wife should when the occasion warrants it."

His hands found hers, long fingers clasping smaller digits, warmth sheltering small chilled fingers, and his smile was enough to warm the entire house, she thought. "You've made me a happy man, Marianne. The circuit judge will be making a stop here tomorrow morning to make a ruling on a man the sheriff is holding in jail. I'll visit him early in the day and ask for his assistance in this matter. I'm certain he'll arrange to marry us before the day is over. Will that please you?"

She was speechless. That her whole life could so quickly change, that her position be elevated to that of wife in less than twenty-four hours was something she had not believed could happen. Yet if David were to be believed, that would be the plan for the morrow. And she knew, somehow, deep inside, that

David did not make plans without the intent of carrying them out in full. And so she smiled up at him, nodding her agreement.

And as if he was tempted beyond his ability to refrain, he surrounded her with his arms and held her against his body, lowering his head and tilting it just so, until his lips were hovering over her own and his breath warmed her mouth. "Am I being too bold, asking a kiss from you, sweetheart? I ache to hold you and know that you will be mine tomorrow, and I need to know that you are not averse to kissing me and allowing my caresses."

Marianne tilted her face to his. "I've only been kissed twice before, from the man who wanted to marry me, so I'm probably not very good at it, but I'm willing to learn, David."

In a few long moments she discovered that the whole exercise was an experience of true delight, that the man's lips were soft, yet demanding, that his heartbeat was strong and rapid against her breast and she was more deeply involved in the brushing and pressing of lips than she'd thought possible. A thrill of surprise ran through her body, her arms developed gooseflesh and her legs felt weak, as if she were standing on limp noodles.

"David?" Her voice had even developed a strange lassitude, for she could not seem to speak aloud, only murmur his name. "David," she whispered again, and his eyes were lit with discovery, his cheeks flushed with a line of ruddy color over his jawline.

"I think kissing you will fast become a habit," he said softly. "You are a lovely woman, Marianne. I'll enjoy very much being married to you."

His arms tightened their grip on her and she was pulled tautly against his long frame, the powerful lines of his chest cushioning her breasts, his long legs surrounding her more feminine lines. Her hands moved from his shoulders to his hair, to that dark, waving mass of silky stuff that invited her fingers to investigate and caress the fine threads that seemed to be as soft as dandelion fluff in the spring.

She tilted her head back and looked closely at his face, the straight nose and dark brows over blue eyes that glowed with a strange light even now. His jaw was firm, with just a trace of whiskers to mar the surface, and her hand went there, feeling the roughness of his beard, which was so much a part of a man. She was held tightly against him, and his legs were taut with a strength she had not realized—his very body seemed coiled and ready, as if he would move on to another phase of this courting he'd undertaken. For surely that was what he had set into motion. An accelerated courting that would last only a day, for on the morrow they would be wed.

"I don't know much about what goes on in a marriage, only that my mother and father were happy together, and worked together to make a home. I know she loved him and cared for him, and he felt the same way about her. They touched frequently, his hand on her shoulder or her hand reaching to touch his fingers at the table. And I know there was a connection between them that defied my imagination, for they were very close, very loving when they thought I didn't notice."

"It sounds to me as though you had a good pattern to follow, Marianne," David said with a broad smile. "My own parents had just such a marriage. We always knew that they put each other first in all things, that we children were loved, but that their marriage was important to them."

"That's what I want in life," she said quietly. "I need a man to care about me and my brother and always take care of us."

"And is he your brother, Marianne? I know that the ladies in town have spoken in the general store and the mayor asked me outright if Joshua was indeed your brother or if he was your own child."

"I haven't told you any falsehood, David. It is exactly as I said. My mother died just minutes before he was born. He's my only relative, my brother. I'm sworn to care for him and provide him a good life."

"All right. I don't want you to be upset, sweetheart. It's just that folks have noticed he holds a close resemblance to you, and that fact alone made the ladies suspicious. I'll be sure that they know the truth of it."

"I can't prove it, David, unless I write to my old neighbor and ask for a letter of verification from her."

"It may come to that one day, but for now I'm satisfied with what you've said."

And yet a pall hung over Marianne's mood, for if there was the slightest doubt in David's mind that she was not what she claimed to be, she would not be happy in this marriage. It was with a heavy heart that she retired that night, the loneliest Christmas of her life, for there had been no gifts to exchange, no words of celebration, only the dinner she'd cooked and a second reading of the Christmas story from St. Luke.

She slept better than she'd expected, Joshua being well fed at bedtime and sleeping throughout the long night hours. The rooster from next door awoke them again at dawn and she rolled from the bed and dressed quickly, carrying Joshua to the kitchen to feed him. In minutes she had warmed his milk and filled his bottle, and she was settled in the rocking chair when David came from his room.

"Good morning," he said quietly. "You haven't changed your mind about today, have you, sweetheart?" He watched her closely from his place by the stove, one hand holding the stove lid, the other a chunk of wood he was planning to lay within the black cave, where it would provide enough heat to cook breakfast.

"No, I've not changed my mind. I was wondering the same about you, though."

"I don't make an offer I'm not prepared to follow through on, and my offer of marriage to you is firm, Marianne. I'm waiting anxiously to hear that the judge has arrived in town, and when he does we'll walk over to the sheriff's office and I'll introduce you to him. I'm sure the mayor will make it his business to do the honors when we get there, for he'll be on hand for the occasion. I'd thought you might ask Janet to stand by your side during the ceremony, and the mayor will stand with me. Does that suit you?"

"Of course. I'm sure Janet will be agreeable to the notion. I'll stop by and ask her early on so's to give her time to get ready. And in the meantime, I'll stop by at the general store and see if there is a dress there I may purchase to wear myself. I haven't anything fit for such an occasion, David. But I have enough money to purchase a dress, I think."

"If you haven't enough, I'd be happy to buy you a dress, sweetheart. May I go along?"

"Will the store be open early, do you think?"

"Janet is generally there by eight o'clock. Let's eat quickly and take a walk over."

"If you'll finish feeding Joshua, I'll fix breakfast," Marianne offered, and with a grin, David switched places with her, holding the baby in his arms and presenting the nipple to the tiny mouth. It was an eager little boy who ate his breakfast, almost as though he knew there were plans afoot that included his presence. By the time his bottle was empty and he'd been properly burped over David's shoulder, Marianne had made gravy from the leftover dinner, and along with fresh biscuits from the oven and the savory mixture of meat and gravy, they sat down to a veritable feast. David ate quickly, obviously anxious to be on his way, but strangely enough, Marianne seemed to have lost her appetite this morning, for she ate but half the food on her plate.

"I'm nervous," she explained, donning her cloak, then wrapping little Joshua warmly and carrying him beneath the thick woolen garment she wore. "The wind is brisk and I don't want him to get colic from the cold air. And I keep feeling chills down my back. Do you suppose I'm coming down with something, David?"

His grin was wide. "I think you're having bridal nerves,

Marianne. You'll be fine once we get together with the judge and things start rolling. Just don't change your mind on me, will you?"

She shook her head, a quick firm movement that fully expressed her thoughts, for she'd decided in the long hours of the night that living in David's house with the handsome man as a husband might just be the best fate that could have befallen her.

They headed to the sheriff's office, made their arrangements and then walked across the street to the general store. With a great deal of whispering and laughter, Janet and Marianne sorted through several boxes of clothing and finally selected a dress both thought would be suitable for a wedding. A session in the storeroom with David holding Joshua at the front of the store, warming them both by the potbellied stove as he waited, ended with Marianne emerging from the curtained area garbed in a shimmering white dress dotted with golden daisies and sashed with a wide ribbon of the same color.

"You look beautiful," David said in a hushed voice, his eyes warm with a tender emotion as they scanned her form. "Just as a bride should look, Marianne. Have you spoken to Janet about what we discussed?"

Janet spoke up quickly. "Yes, she surely did, and I'd be so proud to stand by her side while she marries you, Mr. McDermott. This is the finest thing that could have happened here in Walnut Grove. What a wonderful ending to a delightful Christmas."

It was almost noon when the small group trooped across the street to the lawman's office and appeared at his door. The familiar figure of Judge Pearson stood from his position behind the sheriff's desk and extended a hand toward David. "Mr. McDermott, I understand we have a happy occasion to celebrate today. I'm honored to officiate at your wedding, sir. And is this the bride?" he asked, peering down at Marianne, whose blushing countenance had assumed a look of confusion.

"Yes, sir, I'm Marianne Winters. I'm new in town, for my family, all but my small brother, died of the fever over in the next county early in December. Janet over at the general store let me stay there for a bit and then on Christmas Eve when Mr. McDermott found my little brother in the Nativity scene, he was kind enough to give me shelter and has decided I would make a good addition to his home. I plan to be his wife, cook for him and keep things up over at the parsonage. In return, he will care for me and my brother and be responsible for our well-being."

"Well, that's quite a speech for a young lady. Sounds to me like you've got your plans all lined up well, ma'am. And how do you feel about this situation, Mr. McDermott?"

David grinned widely. "I'm feeling on top of the world, sir. Being a married man was a most wonderful thing when my Laura was alive, and I have every hope that Marianne will be as fine a wife as Laura ever was. We seem to have hit it off well, and she is a lady through and through. She even comes equipped with a little boy, her brother, Joshua." With those words he reached to Marianne and took the baby from her arms. "Between the three of us, I think we'll make a good marriage and have a fine home together.'

His words stunned Marianne with their forceful enthusiasm, for she had no idea he was so motivated about this marriage to be performed today. She'd felt his approval of her and Joshua, had known he was a good man, willing to put forth any effort to help her, but to have him so thrilled over the wedding itself was a surprise to her.

The judge eyed them for a moment, glancing at Janet and the figure of the mayor who stood next to David, and then began his task. Opening a small book from his pocket, he began reading the familiar words of the marriage ceremony. They floated over Marianne's head like so many bumblebees, the sound but a buzzing in her ears, and when the judge looked at her pointedly and cleared his throat, she realized he was waiting for a response from her.

"I will," she said, hoping that those words were the proper ones to have uttered at that point. They seemed to have been what he'd waited for, for he turned to David and asked questions that David listened to intently, and then nodded and repeated the words Marianne had spoken. "I will."

A brief prayer was spoken then and in a sonorous voice, with great dignity, the judge announced that they were to be considered husband and wife, in the eyes of the Almighty and the laws of this Territory. "You may kiss your bride, sir," the judge said with a smile.

David gripped Marianne's shoulders and bent to her, his lips touching hers with a light caress that offered his troth in a simple gesture. He'd slid a narrow gold band onto her finger during the ceremony and it weighed heavily there as she curled her fingers and held it tight, lest it fall to the floor, for it felt a bit large for her.

David apparently had noticed it, for he whispered a message in her ear. "We can go over to the store and pick out one just a bit smaller, if you like. I'm sure Janet has a selection we can look at."

Marianne nodded, holding Joshua firmly against her breast, watching as David shook hands with the judge, then the mayor and the sheriff, who had been standing by with a wide smile on his face. The judge approached Marianne and spoke kindly words.

"I'm sure you'll be a happy bride, Mrs. McDermott. You have a good husband, and David will take good care of you and your child."

Her mouth opened to deny Joshua's belonging to her, for she wanted to make it clear that he was her brother, not her son, but the moment passed and David ushered her from the building, across the street to the general store, where Janet's husband was busily tending his customers. He sent a bright smile in their direction as they entered his domain, and hugged his wife as she walked close to where he stood.

A tray of rings from the counter lay before them then, and Marianne lifted one very similar to the ring she had been wearing for the past fifteen minutes or so. "Will this one fit, do you think?" she asked David, offering it to him.

"Well, let's find out, sweetheart," he said, sliding the first from her finger and replacing it with the one she had chosen. "How does that fit?"

"I think it will stay on better," she said quietly. "I feared I would lose the first one, for it slid on and off too easily. I plan on keeping this ring for a long time, David."

"And so you shall," he said, laughing and nodding at Janet, watching as she returned the tray of rings to the cabinet. "Shall we have our dinner at the restaurant at the hotel?" he asked Marianne.

Behind her, Janet was nodding in a secretive manner, flapping her hands at them, as if she knew of some great secret involving their wedding day. The walk to the hotel was but a short one and they were seated ceremoniously at a white-draped table and accorded the courtesy due a newly married couple. Janet had taken Joshua from Marianne's arms as they left the house, and over her protests had claimed him for the rest of the day.

"Go enjoy your wedding luncheon," she'd said with a laugh. And so they had.

A roast beef dinner appeared before them, the gravy and vegetables steaming hot, the savory scent of spices used in roasting the meat giving Marianne an appetite. They ate well, enjoying the meal prepared for them, surprised by the number of townsfolk who gathered around to congratulate them on their marriage.

By the time they left the hotel, they were surrounded by a crowd of well-wishers and escorted to the parsonage by a large group of David's parishioners. The front door of the parsonage was thrown open as they approached, Janet standing to one side with Joshua in her arms, a roomful of people behind her.

The crowd shouted congratulations, crepe paper was draped over the kitchen, from one corner to the other, and the table was covered with piles of foodstuffs and wrapped gifts. Marianne was overwhelmed by the welcoming crowd, and her eyes overflowed with tears of joy.

"We didn't mean to make you cry, ma'am," the school-teacher said, offering a pristine hankie for her use. "We just wanted to let you know how happy we are for our pastor, finally finding a good woman to fill the parsonage. It's been empty for ever so long, since Laura passed away, and he's been one lonesome fella."

"I hope you'll all be satisfied with me," Marianne said. "I'll do my best to be a good wife and a good addition to Walnut Grove."

She was pressed into a chair at the table, David beside her, and they were presented with a stack of gifts to open. Embroidered pillowcases, a set of glistening white sheets and hand-crocheted dishcloths were soon piled before them, packages of coffee, flour and sugar surrounding the tinned goods that centered the display. Cans of peaches, Mason jars of beef and fish, vegetables in a bright array, put up in pint jars, and a string of red onions atop a huge burlap sack of potatoes made up the bulk of the gifts offered.

"I've never seen so much food in one place in my life," Marianne declared, her eyes wide as she scanned the largesse before her. "I can't believe you people did all of this for us."

"They're good folks," David said quietly, standing up and drawing Marianne to his side. "We can't thank you enough, and we want you to know that your help and affection for the parsonage family is much appreciated."

The group surrounding them broke into applause and with a general exodus, they left the house, leaving David and Marianne alone. A small cradle stood in one corner of the kitchen and in its depths, Joshua slept amid all the excitement.

"Where did that come from?" Marianne asked, bending to brush her fingertips over the shimmering wood that formed the small bed.

"Looks like something Tom Frent might have put together. He's the best carpenter in town, and I've seen his work in other homes."

"We'll have to be sure to thank him. I never thought Joshua would have so fine a bed to sleep in."

"We'll have to order a larger crib for when he outgrows this one," David said, bending to pull the blanket up over the baby's shoulder. The tiny hand slid with unerring precision toward his mouth and Joshua latched onto his thumb as they watched. Soft laughter erupted from both man and woman as they gazed down at the tiny mite they were committed to love and care for.

By the time Marianne had put away all the foodstuffs and stored the linens away in the big dresser in David's room, she was weary. She'd changed her dress, hanging her new gown in the spare room and dressing in a warm housedress. "Do you want something for supper, David?" she asked.

"Not a whole lot," he answered. "I'm still full of roast beef and gravy. But maybe you could fix something for dessert later on."

"Are you fond of apple pie? Or maybe fruit cobbler?"

His eyes lit with delight. "My mama used to make cobbler with apples and brown sugar and cinnamon. Do you know how to fix something like that?"

"I'm a whiz at such things," Marianne said blithely. "My mother taught me cooking from an early age and desserts were always my father's favorite thing. I'll make you the best cobbler you've ever eaten."

"That's a deal, if I ever heard one," David answered, his hands full with the last of the gifts from the table. "We have enough coffee to last for six months, I think. And someone even brought you a tin of tea, honey. Somebody must have put a bug in some lady's ear."

"I'll bet it was Janet. She knows I enjoy a cup of tea. I had one with her just yesterday." And that seemed like a long time ago, Marianne thought. So much had happened, so many changes had been made in her life over the past forty-eight hours that her head was spinning.

When they sat down to eat the apple cobbler she'd put together, the sun had set and the surrounding homes were dimly lit from within, the inhabitants of Walnut Grove apparently being early to bed. The night ahead loomed before her and Marianne felt apprehensive as she thought of what might take place. That David would expect a physical relationship tonight was not likely, but sometime in the near future he would want to take her to his bed, and she felt totally inadequate to allow such an intimate thing to take place.

Her mother had not spoken of marriage, at least not in the physical sense, and yet Marianne knew that there was a bond between husband and wife that made them a single unit, that gave them the strength to face the world as a couple, as a married team. She yearned for such knowledge to be hers, and yet she feared the actual act that would unite her with David in such a way.

She needn't have feared such a thing on this night, though, for when the kitchen was cleared and the dish towel hung to dry, he simply carried Joshua's small cradle into the spare room and she followed him in, watching as he placed it beside the wide bed. He approached her then, bending to her and enclosing her in his warm embrace.

"Good night, Marianne. Sleep well, my dear. I know you're weary, for the day has been long and your whole life has undergone a lot of changes. I'll be nearby if you should need anything. And if I have it figured right, Joshua should sleep through the night. He's had a long day, too." With a final touch of his lips on hers, another kiss that brushed her forehead and a tightening of his embrace, he left her, reluctantly it seemed, but with a finality that assured her that he did not plan on sharing her bed tonight.

Chapter Five

Marianne undressed and slid into her bed, listening as she heard David's footsteps in the kitchen, heard the bolt sliding in the back door, then the clink of the lantern as he blew out the light over the table. Her bedroom door stood open and he halted there in the opening, looking within, as if he might speak to her, and then walked on to his own room, next to hers.

He was alone and guilt rose within her, knowing that he needed affection from her, needed whatever a wedding night entailed, for he was a man who'd been married, who'd shared his bed with a woman and had been privileged to know the joys of sleeping with the warmth of a willing woman beside him. He'd told her that he would wait, that he would not rush her into an intimate relationship, but that she should let him know when she was ready for such a thing to come into being.

She thought of him alone in his big bed, on his wedding night, the sheets cool beneath him, his body alone beneath the quilts and his heart empty of the affection she could offer him. For affection was what she felt for the man—not any great love, for she barely knew him, but she admired him, appreciated his gentle kindness with Joshua and her. His heart was yearning for the love of a woman, of that she was certain, for he was a lonely man, and it was within her power to give him what his body craved tonight.

David rolled to face the window, unable to lower his eyelids, for his only thoughts were of the girl who lay in the room next to his. Not for the world would he force his attentions upon her, for he'd given her his word that she must come to him when the time was right for a relationship to be formed between them.

He'd slept alone for so long, each night a lesson in patience, for David had known the love of a woman, had shared his bed with a willing wife and now faced more long nights alone, for surely the young girl in the next room was not ready yet for the sort of marriage relationship he craved. He heard her turn in the bed, heard her cough once and then listened as she rose from the bed and crossed the room to the door.

"Marianne, are you all right? Do you need something?" he called softly, not wanting to awaken Joshua.

She appeared in his bedroom doorway, a pale vision in white, her nightgown made from yards of flannel, falling about her slender form like a tent that might hold three women within its seams.

"Your gown is too big for you," he said with a trace of good humor in his voice. "It looks like it would fit Mrs. Henderson over at the post office, and she's a good-sized lady."

"It was my mother's gown," Marianne said softly, her voice quivering. "I came to see if I might sleep in your bed, David. You said I should tell you when I was ready to be your wife, and if you want me, I'd like to spend the night in here with you."

Her courage was weakening as she spoke, for her voice faded as her words came to an end. What if he'd changed his mind and she was about to make a fool of herself, making such an offer? But her fears were stilled in moments, for David sat up quickly, reaching his hand to her, speaking rapidly, the words the cry of his heart.

"I'd hoped you might come to me, sweetheart. I didn't want to push you into anything that might frighten you, but if you'll come lie with me, I'll be the happiest man on earth."

She flew across the room, and he lifted the sheet and quilt to allow her room beside him. His arms enclosed her quickly and drew her next to his masculine form, his need for her already apparent. She was soft in his arms, her curves gentle yet generous, for her bosom was full and lush. He felt fulfilled for the first time in nearly a year, like a man whose wildest dreams have come true, a husband who has been granted the joy of a willing, warm woman in his bed.

His kiss was tender against her mouth, his lips skating across the side of her face to spend warmth on her eyelids and then her temple. He discovered the curl of her ear, the soft vulnerable place beneath her lobe, there where her life's blood beat at a rapid pace.

"Don't be frightened of me, love," he begged, his hands careful not to intrude too quickly against her feminine body. Her breasts were pressed firmly against his chest, her narrow, chilled feet touching his shins, and he encircled her with one arm, drawing her body ever closer to the heated length of his own.

"I'm not frightened, only anxious that you'll be pleased with me. I don't know anything about this, David. Only that there will be some sort of union between our bodies and there will be pain for me in the process."

"I'll try my best not to hurt you," he vowed, and knew that should she truly be Joshua's mother, there would be no pain in her introduction to his body. Her gown was easily pushed up, exposing her lower form to his hands, and his touch was gentle as he explored the soft skin of her belly and thighs. One hand slid to capture a breast and he caught his breath at the shapely treasure he held. The gown was lifted higher yet, and he touched his mouth to her breast, seeking to taste the sweet essence of woman he scented there. She wiggled against him as he suckled the crest he'd uncovered and he rejoiced that she responded to his touch.

"It feels so strange," Marianne whispered. "I didn't know you could make me feel so good, so warm all over."

"It's the way it's supposed to be," David told her. "There should always be pleasure between a man and wife when they come together in their bed at night. Or in the morning, or afternoon. Whenever they seek each other out for the comforts of marriage."

"In the daylight?" she asked, her voice hushed and filled with surprise.

She had much to learn, he decided, looking forward to teaching her all he had learned over the past years as it related to the intimacy between man and woman. She would be an avid learner, for she was eager to do as he asked, even now.

Her leg rose at his bidding and he slid his hand between her thighs, his fingers careful, and he sought out the plush secrets of her feminine parts. She was small, feeling almost untried, and he hesitated a bit as he shifted his body over hers, forming her to his will as he held her beneath him.

"You're not frightened, are you, sweetheart?" His words were soft, his query meant to soothe her, and she responded as he'd hoped.

"No, I'll do whatever you say, David. I want to please you."

His kisses prepared her, his caresses delivered a message of desire that would not be appeased but by his possession of her body, and he loved her well, with a heated rush of kisses and touches that seemed to make her head swim, for she sighed and whimpered against his ear. No part of her was secret from him, for he wanted to know her body as well as his own, and even her toes and fingers received accolades of praise from his lips.

And then he was over her, his legs between hers, and Marianne held her breath, knowing that she was about to become a wife, no longer an innocent girl or a blushing bride, but the wife of a man who was determined to complete the act of marriage.

He pushed that hard part of himself against her and she felt a slickness that was new to her, an ability to accept his body part within her own, and she inhaled deeply as he pressed forward, filling her until she thought she might burst. For a moment he seemed to find some barrier to his progress and then with a sharp, small pain, his way was eased and he slid deeper within her with apparent ease. She wiggled beneath him.

"David, I'm so full. It's so tight."

"Umm…" His voice uttered a sound of deep contentment and she relaxed beneath him. He moved then, a steady rhythm that seemed to bring small jolts of pleasure to her body, deep within her, there where that part of him was contained. Her arms circled his shoulders and he kissed her throat, her forehead and then her mouth, his tongue pressing within, imitating the movement of that other part of his body within her depths.

His words were broken and she heard her name spoken, then he called her his sweetheart, a word she was fast coming to cherish, and from her deepest inmost parts a rush of warmth encompassed her, a flush of heat that seemed to enclose her in the fire that he had set there where no one had ever ventured before tonight. She caught her breath, the feeling so overwhelming, so filled with shivers of ecstasy, she could hardly bear it. And she called out his name, even as her body convulsed in spasms of joy.

"Sweetheart." Again he spoke it as if it were her name. "Ah, sweetheart." And again he whispered that treasured word in her ear. And then he moved over her, his movements thrusting deeply within her, and a groan escaped his lips. For a long moment he was quiet, and then he breathed a sigh so heavy, it washed her throat with the warmth of his breath. His big body was heavy on hers, his head buried beside hers on the pillow they shared.

"Are you all right, Marianne? Did I hurt you too badly? I wasn't sure before that you were a virgin, and I fear I didn't take long enough before I came inside you. I know it was your first time, but honestly, I tried not to hurt you, honey."

"You knew I was a virgin, David. I told you I was."

"I know you did, but I wasn't certain. I'd heard the women in the store talking and I wondered if I had been foolish to believe your story about Joshua being your brother."

She pushed at him, scooting from beneath him, and her heart ached with pain at the words he'd spoken.

"You believed the women in town before you would believe me? How could you, David? How could you think me a liar?" Her tears came readily and she slipped from his bed, gathering up her nightgown, for he'd somehow taken it from her body and dropped it on the floor. With hurried steps she ran from the room and back to her own bed. Her nightgown went over her head and she fell heavily onto the mattress, turning to bury her face in the pillow, where she wept hot, bitter tears of regret. Regret that she had offered herself to a man who did not trust her, who had doubted her words.

Behind her, David entered the room and sat on the side of her bed, his hand on her shoulders, attempting to turn her to face him. "Please, Marianne. I'm so sorry I've hurt you. I never meant to say those words to you. I suppose I was so pleased to know that you were chaste as you'd said you were that I spoke without thinking. Even if Joshua were your son, I'd have married you anyway. I want you for my wife, sweetheart. I need you to fulfill my life and make this place a home again for me."

"Wouldn't any woman have done as well?" she asked, brushing away her tears.

"No. You're the only woman I've looked at since Laura died, the only female that has meant anything to me. The only female I've been able to imagine in my bed. Please listen to me, Marianne. I want our marriage to begin well, and already I've made a mess of things. I'm so sorry. Please forgive me, sweet-heart."

His hands lifted her against his chest and Marianne heard the rapid beat of his heart as he nestled her head over that place on his body. She felt the soft brush of dark hair against her face, caught the scent of masculine flesh and turned her mouth to kiss the hair-roughened skin beneath her face.

His voice was but a harsh whisper. "Can you ever forgive me? Can we begin again? I'm so sorry, love. I wouldn't have hurt you for the world. I spoke before I thought, a common failing of many men, I fear."

"I'm your wife, David. You've seen to that and I can't be sorry, for you were kind and gentle with me. You've given me a happiness I didn't think I would ever find, and I find I can forgive much knowing that you accept me as I am."

He held her close and his sigh was deep as if he'd shed his fears and was at rest. "Thank you, sweet. Let me lie here with you, with Joshua nearby. We'll hear him if he awakens and take care of him together. Will you let me sleep with you?"

"Of course." Marianne moved over in the bed, a more narrow piece of furniture than the one in David's room, and one that did not allow for them to be apart during the night. They lay in the middle of the bed, arms around each other, David's hands wandering where they would, as he became better acquainted with the lovely curves and hollows of his wife's form. Before dawn, before the rooster crowed from the henhouse next door, he once more found his place within her lissome body, and found the same warm welcome there when she responded to his embrace and welcomed him.

It was with joy that they awoke a short time later to face a new day, and the beginning of their lives together.

Chapter Six

The days passed rapidly as David and Marianne learned the joys of life lived within the walls of the small parsonage. Their first Sunday in church was a happy time, with the congregation welcoming them with jovial words of congratulation and even a smattering of gifts from those who had not appeared the day of the wedding.

Only the whispers of several of the ladies speaking behind their hands as Marianne walked past their small circle marred the tranquil happiness of her day. She heard the sounds of gossip clearly as she was meant to, for their words insinuated that she was not fit to grace the parsonage, indeed was not fit to be a pastor's wife, so dark was her past. The words *illegitimate child* reached her ears more than once, and even though the vast majority of the womenfolk were warm and welcoming, Marianne felt a deep sense of shame as she thought of the words she'd heard spoken by those who bore her ill will.

David waited until she'd put Joshua down for his nap before he began quizzing her. His arms encircled her waist and he bent his head to touch her temple with warm lips. And then his voice coaxed her into his confidence.

"What happened? What did you hear that upset you so?"

She turned her face against his chest, then clung to his tall body, her arms around his neck, her tears falling in a deluge that surprised him. Marianne was not one to cry unless there was a very good reason; in fact, not since their wedding night had she shed a tear. Her words were faltering, but she spelled out carefully the words she'd heard from the lips of three of the ladies of his congregation.

"They didn't care that I heard them, either," she sobbed. As if her heart would break, a deluge of tears fell upon his white shirt and he was angered as he thought of the pain the cruel women had visited upon his bride.

"We'll be all right," he said finally. "Things will work out, Marianne. I'll do something to make amends. I don't know yet just what I can figure out, but I'll do something."

"I don't want you to get in the middle of this. It might hurt your standing in town," she said.

"If my standing in town is damaged because I defend my wife, then I don't belong here," he said angrily.

And to that end, he slammed from the house, his feet moving almost at a run as he went to the house of the man who was the most powerful figure on his church board.

"Mr. Mayor, I need to speak with you," he said, his tone harsh, his voice strident as he faced the man on his porch.

"What's the problem, Reverend?" the mayor asked, his gaze apprehensive as he noted David's obvious anger.

His face dark with the emotion he seldom allowed to control him, David punched his hands into his pockets and spoke words that he knew might rob him of his livelihood, and the house he called home.

"My wife has been insulted for the last time. I won't stand for it happening again. There are several *ladies* of the congregation, and I use that term with a total lack of courtesy, I'll admit, who have made it their business to speak cruelly of Marianne. She has been badly hurt by their barbs, and the thought that she could be so badly treated puts me in a precarious position. Either there will be an apology from the women involved, or I will quit my post here and find another line of work. I cannot tolerate my wife's pain any longer."

"What was said to Mrs. McDermott?" the mayor asked as his wife appeared in the doorway behind him.

"She was discussed as being unfit to grace the parsonage, accused of having an illegitimate child and treated as an outcast by several of the women who sit in the pews in our church. I will not abide such cruelty. My wife is indeed the sister of the child in our home. She was a virgin bride and Joshua has been the center of her life since her parents died from typhoid fever. Either something has to happen to make amends or I will be moving from Walnut Grove within two weeks."

The mayor's wife clutched at his arm, speaking in a low tone, words that her husband apparently did not approve of, for he turned to her and shouted an accusation that brought her to the brink of tears.

"Do you hear what you and your lady friends have caused, Hazel? This man is the most loyal pastor, the most patient man we've ever been privileged to have here in Walnut Grove, and now he's threatened to leave our town and the church because of the harassment his wife has undergone at the hands of our fine Christian ladies."

His wife flushed an unbecoming red, and her voice faltered as she answered his accusations. "I heard what Mr. McDermott said, Joseph, and I'll do all I can to make amends with his wife. Gossip is so easy to listen to when a woman hears the same story from different sources, but—"

"I don't care how many sources of gossip we have in this town. This is inexcusable, and I expect you to be making the rounds of your sewing circle and setting the record straight. I can't make it any plainer than that."

He was shouting by the time he'd finished his diatribe, and David backed from his porch, unwilling to watch as the mayor's wife dissolved in tears.

As he walked away, he heard her penitent voice as she did

her best to soothe her husband's ruffled feathers. "Yes, dear. I'll walk over to Gladys's place right now and then stop by Mrs. Hobson's to speak with her. We'll make things right—I'll see to it."

His footsteps were heavy as David let himself into the house minutes later, and Marianne met him in the middle of the kitchen.

"What have you done, David? I hope you haven't made the church board unhappy with you."

"Just the opposite, my dear. I'm fuming at the lot of them. There are several women who will be in a peck of trouble by tonight, unless I've read the mayor wrong. I think he'll take care of things."

He hugged her against him and then pulled a chair from beneath the table and lowered her into it, taking a seat across from her. His words were tender even as he spoke in a firm, determined tone. "What was your neighbor's name—the lady you were staying with after your parents died?"

She told him, recalling Mrs. Baker's kindness when it seemed that Marianne's world had collapsed beneath her. She told him that when that lady's sister, here in town, had not been able to offer any help, she had not wanted to let Mrs. Baker know how bad things had become for her sister.

"I should have written her before now, David, to let her know that I'm all right. And I should have told her about her sister's circumstances. She needs to know."

"I'll see to it," David said shortly. "Don't worry about it anymore, sweetheart. Things will work out."

Her faith in the man she'd married eased life considerably for Marianne over the next weeks. Sleeping in his arms each night, wakening to his kiss each morning and spending her days by his side seemed to her to be a glimpse of heaven. For his care of her and little Joshua were all she could have asked. He gave her leave to buy whatever she needed from the general store, offered her freedom to do as she wanted in his house and did his best to make her life one of ease and contentment.

She found herself falling in love with the man she'd married. Indeed, she wasn't even sure what she should call the emotion she felt for him, for it was akin to no other she'd ever known. Her love for her parents had been absolute, and the adoration she felt for young Joshua was a given, for she couldn't have cared more for him had he been her own son. Indeed, he was as close to a son as she might ever get, she decided. But for David, there was an overwhelming rush of feeling she could not describe. A tender emotion she could not put a name to, only that she loved him, body and soul, with all her heart and mind.

She refrained from telling him of her feelings, not wanting to make him feel compelled to reply in a like manner, for surely men did not have this sort of emotional attachment to a woman as did a female for a man of her choice. So, wisely, she kept her thoughts to herself, only spending the wealth of her love upon his body during the night hours when he claimed her as his wife.

Two more weeks passed quickly after their speaking of Mrs. Baker and her sister. Marianne spent her days working in the house, washing the kitchen windows and ironing the curtains during a warm spell late in January.

During the days that passed, she was visited by the ladies who had so crushed her with their words after church that memorable Sunday morning. Each of them made it known that they had totally misunderstood her situation and were apologizing for the gossip they had helped to spread. Even though her pain had gone deep, she was happy to know that her position as the minister's wife was again on an even keel, and she began to gain back her naturally sunny disposition.

She rose early one morning, feeling a burst of energy, for the weather seemed mild and she had cleaning to be done. The small parlor was first, that rug being thoroughly swept and the furniture polished. Then she scrubbed the kitchen cupboards and washed the floor with the water left over from doing David's laundry.

She hung his clothes outdoors on a line strung from the porch to the outhouse, and with a brisk westerly wind, they were dry in short order. Once she'd sprinkled his shirts and trousers, she set up the ironing board and heated the irons on the stove. This tending to a man's needs was powerful stuff, she decided, making her feel needed and appreciated, for David never failed to tell her of his joy in finding clean clothing in his drawers, hot food on the table at night and a warm, willing woman in his bed after the sun went down.

They had developed a schedule that pleased them both, David visiting those of his congregation who were ailing or hurt in some way, then working at the church to keep the wood box full of lengths of cordwood for the Sunday services and the floors clean, the windows sparkling. It was all part of his job, and he enjoyed the chores that took so much of his time. He spent Wednesday evenings with a smaller crowd, an hour of singing and praying with his people, an hour Marianne shared with delight, sitting in the front pew with Joshua in her arms.

It was late one evening in March when a knock came at the front door of the parsonage, and when Marianne opened it wide it was to see Mrs. Baker standing there, arms outstretched. "I heard you were married, girl, but I had to come and see for myself. Are you doing all right? Are you happy? And how is that baby brother of yours? Can I see him?"

Her questions rang out loud and clear, and David came from the parlor to greet her. "I'm so glad to see you, ma'am. I assume you got my letter."

"I surely did, young man, and I'm here to set things right for this girl."

"I don't know what you're talking about," Marianne said, her eyes alight with questions.

"Your husband here tells me that there's talk going around town about you, how you're not fit to be a preacher's wife, what with you having a baby when you arrived here and all."

"The ladies have tried to set things right, but I know there are still those who have little faith in me," Marianne said quietly. "But you know about Joshua, Mrs. Baker. You know that the stories that were told about me were not true."

"I surely do, Marianne, and I know your mama would roll over in her grave if she heard such things being said about her girl. I'm here to set things straight and give these ladies in town an earful."

"Oh my, I'm afraid you've started something, David." Marianne's eyes filled with tears as she considered the mess that was about to unfold in Walnut Creek.

"I only asked Mrs. Baker to set things right for us, sweetheart. I know what a wonderful woman you are and I want the whole town to know the truth about Joshua. If they can't believe me, then perhaps they'll listen to Mrs. Baker. She was there, after all, when he was born, and if anyone can set these gossiping females straight, it'll be Mrs. Baker."

"Thank you, Reverend. I'll surely do my best." Mrs. Baker puffed up her bosom, tilted her chin in an arrogant manner and shook David's hand, an assurance of her willingness to lend a hand.

"Now, let's see what we can do," she said, settling at the kitchen table. Marianne made a cup of tea for her and they began to talk. The result was a walk early the next morning, as soon as the general store opened. Mrs. Baker, accompanied by the Reverend McDermott, entered that establishment, primed to set the town's ladies aright.

Mrs. Baker spent three hours visiting with the women who came and went that morning, Janet by her side throughout, David McDermott sitting by the potbellied stove with several of the menfolk, who through careful questioning heard the truth from the lips of their minister. Without making any blunt statements he assured the men around him that his wife had been as pure as the driven snow when she came to him, child in arms.

Mrs. Baker told the story of the Winters family and the tragedy of their deaths due to the typhoid epidemic early in December, and the ladies of Walnut Grove were properly abashed as they heard the message of Marianne Winters's courage and her yearning to make a life for herself and her infant brother.

"I'm just so happy that she's found a good home here in Walnut Grove," Mrs. Baker gushed, speaking loudly enough that her voice carried to where David sat, his grin wide, his fingers busy on the checkerboard as he played a rousing game with old Mert Conners.

"I know all you people are happy to have such a good girl in the parsonage, for she'll be an ideal wife for your minister, bring raised by such good folks and all. Her mama's no doubt looking down from heaven even now and sending down blessings on all you good women for taking her daughter to your bosoms like you have."

If the ladies were shamefaced or embarrassed, Mrs. Baker simply ignored them, speaking long and loud about the blessings Marianne Winters had bestowed on all who knew her as she grew up. "A right nice girl, she was. Couldn't have asked for a better daughter. And work! My, did she work on that farm, milking cows and making butter and tending the hens—just like a farm woman, she was. Her folks were so proud of her. And so am I, proud to have known her. I just know you folks will treat her well and give her your love and respect same as the folks back home did."

The ladies flocked around Mrs. Baker, somewhat subdued but willing to speak well of their preacher's new wife. And it was with a wide smile that David McDermott led her from the store in time for the dinner Marianne had cooked at the parsonage.

They ate voraciously, as if they hadn't had a good meal in weeks, David summing up the morning with a long tale of Mrs. Baker and the ladies gathering around her like a flock of biddy hens.

Marianne laughed aloud at his tale, pleased beyond words as he described the happenings in the store. Janet dropped in as they were finishing up their meal, and Marianne poured her a cup of tea, settling her at the table next to Mrs. Baker.

"We had ever so good a time this morning," she said cheerfully.

"I've heard all the details from my husband," Marianne said with a laugh.

"Well, you should have been there. Your friend here let all those ladies in on a few home truths, gave them chapter and verse about you and your family and how Joshua was born and how your folks died and left you with the burden of caring for a newborn child."

"He's no burden," Marianne said, denying the words Janet spoke. "He's been a real blessing for me. For he's helped me conquer my grief and given me something to look forward to."

"And how about me?" David asked quietly. "Have I been of any help?"

Marianne's eyes filled with hot tears as she looked up at him. "You've been the best thing that ever happened to me. I'll forever be thankful for the day I came by the church and saw the Nativity scene out in front."

And then they were coaxed into telling Mrs. Baker of the scene on Christmas Eve when David rescued Joshua from the manger and carried him into the parsonage. "It was the most important night of my life," David avowed. "For it marked a new beginning for me, and for Marianne, too. Joshua is truly a Christmas child, a baby meant for great things, for his beginnings were humble but his future is guaranteed to be filled with wonderful promise. With Marianne to love him, and with a daddy who dotes on him, he'll be a fine man one day. And if I have anything to say about it, he'll have a houseful of children to share his life with."

"But he'll always know from whence he came," Marianne said softly. "For I want him to know that his mother and father loved him dearly and looked forward to his birth, and even though they never saw him, they may even now be his guardian angels, watching over him."

"He has a lovely heritage indeed," Mrs. Baker said, "and I'm proud to have been a small part of it."

"Now that you're here, do you suppose you can do anything to help your sister?" Marianne asked somberly.

"I stopped by there on my way into town and told her she can bring her children and come home with me if she wants to. Your husband told me in his letter that her situation was bad and that if ever a woman needed rescuing, it was my younger sister. My husband is agreeable to taking her in, and if things go well, she'll hitch up her wagon and go home with me."

"I've spoken to the sheriff about it already," David said. His voice was firm and filled with a controlled anger, but Mrs. Baker and Marianne both seemed to understand that he would be behind such a venture wholeheartedly.

"The sheriff said to let him know when you plan to leave and he would be out there to help you get things organized and get her free of that brute she married."

"I can't thank you enough, Mr. McDermott," Mrs. Baker said, tears flowing freely as she thought of what this day had wrought. "We have room and enough for all of them in our farmhouse, for our own children are grown and gone but for one still with us, and we have four empty bedrooms—more than enough for Sarah and her brood."

The days passed quickly and Mrs. Baker made several trips to visit her sister, making plans for their leaving. In less than a week, a wagon was found at the livery stable where Marianne had left her swaybacked mare. The mare was tied to the back of the wagon and preparations were made to return her to her owners as the wagon was piled high with enough hay to cushion the children, who would be riding thereupon for the trip back to the Bakers' farm.

With the sheriff in attendance, the wagon was filled with

bedding and clothes for the four children, and the belongings Mrs. Baker felt her sister might need. By noon the two ladies and four children were on their way, intent on traveling without ceasing until they reached the Baker farm.

Chapter Seven

"I feel that we've helped someone in a roundabout fashion, in a way that will bring about good results for that lady and her children," Marianne said as she lay beside David in their bed that night. She'd been quiet since crawling beneath the sheet, her mind working over the unhappiness to be found in a bad marriage, her thoughts wending upward as she felt true thanksgiving for the man beside her.

"I need to tell you something, David. I've not said anything up until now, because I wasn't sure you wanted to hear these words, but my heart is full with love I have for you. You've changed my life totally, given me the opportunity to be a good sister to Joshua, and I hope a good wife to you. I want you to know how important you are to me and how much I look forward to each day we spend together."

He was silent as if he mulled over her words and then in a quick move that startled her, David rolled to face Marianne, his arms encircling her, his lips touching her face where they would, brushing her eyelids, her cheeks and finally finding the soft curve of her mouth, where he once more found the nourishment for his soul that had been long missing from his life.

His words sounded almost rusty, Marianne thought, as he

spoke her name, then offered his thoughts to her, in broken phrases and whispers that touched upon her ear as music.

"I love you, Marianne. I've loved you almost since that first night, on Christmas Eve, when you left Joshua for me to find and I called out after you when you ran off down the road. When I saw you in church, my heart sang, for I knew I would once more have the opportunity of talking with you, of learning to know you.

"Your presence during the days and weeks, here in this house, have healed my heart, for I ached for the warmth of arms to hold me, of a love that would sustain me through the days and nights of my life to come. I've been doubly blessed in my life, first with Laura, who shared this home with me for such a short while, and then with the joy of finding you, and making you my wife.

"I ache to tell you what you mean to me, and I vowed when Laura died without my words of love in her ears that I would never again withhold those words from a woman, should I find one who would win my heart.

"You are that woman, Marianne. I love you with all that is within me. All the affection my heart can hold for another person has been heaped on you. You are my life's companion, and I'm thankful every day when I open my eyes in the morning that I can turn and see you beside me in our bed."

Marianne reached to hold him close, lifting her face for his kiss, her body pressed close to his long length, her heart overflowing with the bounty of love she bore for this man.

"I never thought that living in a parsonage could feel so close to heaven," she said with a warm chuckle. "Or perhaps it's just being in your arms that makes me think I've received a blessing like no other. I love you, David, more than I ever thought I could love a man, more than I can tell you."

His arms tightened around her, his kisses grew warmer, his hands caressed her slender form and his words spilled out upon her as he assured her of his love, his devotion and the pleasure he found in her.

The sun was rising in the eastern sky when the rooster crowed at his usual time the next morning. Joshua awoke but minutes later, making soft sounds in his cradle, waving his hands in the stream of sunlight as it shone through the bedroom window across his hand-hewn bed.

And in the wide bed beside him, where two lovers lay entangled in each other's arms, love reigned supreme. For Christmas had come and gone, yet its magic remained. Spring was even now covering the meadows with its glory, blossoms creating a wonderland for those who walked there.

And in the hearts of two lovers the wonder of their first moments together remained as a memory of everlasting joy. One that would serve to forever remind them of the union of two hearts and lives, pledging themselves, each to the other, in an unending paean of devotion.

* * * * *

THE CHRISTMAS DOVE

Victoria Bylin

Dear Reader,

Do you have a favorite Christmas memory? I have dozens that involve family and friends, but my most vivid memory is of silence and snow. It happened on Christmas Eve. We were living in Pine Mountain Club, a small town in the Los Padres National Forest. We lived among ponderosas and Jeffrey pines, the trees that smell like vanilla if you scratch them.

It had snowed all that day. At dusk I went outside for a breath of air. Everywhere I looked I saw blue snow. Not pale blue, but a royal blue that reminded me of new denim. Snow clung to the upturned branches. A breeze stirred and flakes swirled in a silver mist. I felt renewed and strengthened, ready for two days of music and crackling paper, the aroma of turkey and the excitement of two small boys who'd soon be playing video games. When I think of Christmas, I remember that beautiful blue day.

I hope you enjoy Maddie and Dylan's story. Like me, they found something special in the midst of a storm.

Merry Christmas!

Victoria

To my aunt and uncle, Katie and Gary Hailey. Thank you for the wonderful Christmas memories.

Chapter One

December 1890
Crystal River, Wyoming

Dylan McCall didn't know what to make of the noise at the back of the livery stable. He'd come to sell Jesse a horse, but the owner hadn't been in the shed he used for an office. Dylan didn't have time to wait around for the older man. He'd come to town late yesterday, gone to a Christmas social at the parsonage and bought supplies. With a storm brewing, he had to get home to his ranch.

Eager to speak with Jesse, he'd stepped inside the barn where he'd heard rustling in the straw.

"Hello?" he called.

Someone gasped.

If Jesse had a thief on his hands, Dylan intended to haul the fool into the street. He liked Jesse. The old man had given Dylan a break with an offer to buy three horses. He'd also given him a lecture he'd never forget. A year ago, the livery owner had hauled him out of the saloon and dunked his head in a water trough.

You can be a loser like your old man, or you can prove your worth. Take your pick.

Dylan had decided to prove his worth. He'd sobered up, worked to buy his own place and dedicated every breath to earning respect for the McCall name. He'd even started going to church. He liked the stories, but mostly he wanted a wife, and church seemed a smart place to look. This morning Reverend Taylor had talked about Christmas. Dylan had been touched by the story of Mary and her baby. The way the reverend told the story, Joseph had put everything he owned, including his good name, on the line for the girl he loved.

Dylan understood that call. He'd loved a girl once. He'd have walked on hot coals for Maddie Cutler, but she'd treated him like the good-for-nothing he'd been. Dylan envied Joseph. He'd had the pride of a good name and the means to care for a wife. Dylan had neither. In a year or so, he hoped to build a new house. By then, he'd be ready to get married. As things stood, the cabin leaked cold air. He owned a few horses and some cattle, but he lived on bacon and beans.

His belly growled at the thought of food, but right now he had other concerns. He wanted to know who had invaded Jesse's stable and why.

"Come out or I'm coming in," he called.

Silence.

Maybe the intruder was a kid, someone hiding out as Dylan had done when his father drank. That's how he'd got to know Jesse. Of all the possibilities, that one made the most sense. Who'd steal a bale of hay? As for the horses, a thief would have struck a ranch, not Jesse's stable of nags.

The intruder, Dylan figured, had to be someone in need. He made his voice friendly. "I know you're in there. Come on out."

Peering into the barn, Dylan thought of the hawk he'd found downed on his ranch. Fear had made the animal unapproachable, but food had made him Dylan's friend. He'd nursed the creature back to health and set it free. If a boy needed help—a meal, a kind word—Dylan wanted to give it to him.

He walked through the barn, looking into each stall. Most

held horses, but a few were empty. As he neared the back wall, he heard the rasp of human breath. Low and fast, it rattled with fear and guided him to the far corner where he saw a woman huddled on a pile of fresh straw.

She'd bent her neck to hide her face, but he saw a tangle of brunette hair tumbling from beneath her fancy hat. The curls called to his fingers and jarred his memory at the same time. Maddie Cutler had sported a head of wavy hair that exact color. He could still feel the silkiness of it, the softness of her lips teasing his. The game had started the summer he'd worked on her father's ranch, a huge spread called the Castle. The name fit. Lord Albert Cutler had money, British blood and a princess of a daughter.

Except the princess hadn't been happy. She'd run off with a gambler named Brodie Jones. Fool that he'd been, Dylan had tried to stop her. He knew men like Brodie. They cheated and lied. When he'd seen Maddie carrying her satchel to the train station, he'd hauled her into an alley and spoken his mind. She'd slapped his face and called him two-bit trash. Not a day passed that Dylan didn't think of her. Had Brodie married her? He doubted it. Knowing the gambler, he'd used Maddie and cast her aside. Dylan feared that she'd fallen hard.

He had the same feeling about the woman in the straw. Looking down, he saw a hat that looked as if someone had broken off the feathers. A black cloak hung from her shoulders and spread like a lake at midnight. Her dress, red taffeta trimmed with black lace, draped her ankles. Dylan hadn't visited the upstairs rooms at the saloon in a while, but he knew a soiled dove when he saw one. Like the hawk at his ranch, this bird had broken wings. He prayed Maddie hadn't met the same fate.

He made his voice gentle. "Miss?"

She tucked her chin into her cloak. "Please, leave me alone."

"I can't do that."

"I'm fine."

"You don't look fine."

She answered with a shiver.

"You look cold," he said. "Hungry, too."

"I'm not."

Dylan didn't believe her. When he'd been hungry as a boy, Jesse had reached out to him. He felt that call for this woman. He'd buy her lunch and take her to Mabel's place, a respectable boardinghouse for women. If Mabel didn't feel charitable, Dylan would pay for a week's room and board. It seemed fitting for the season…a bit of Christmas charity. Hoping to appear friendly, he dropped to a crouch. "Looks to me like you need a friend."

She curled into a ball. Had she been abused? She hadn't looked up, but he kept his hands loose and in sight. "I mean no harm, miss. I can't leave you alone if you're in need."

"I'm not." The cloak muffled her voice even more than before. "I'm waiting for someone."

"Who?"

She said nothing.

"Why not wait at the café?" He put a smile in his voice. "Alice makes great hot cakes. Coffee's good, too."

As the woman shook her head, Dylan heard a sound that sent chills up his spine. He didn't know much about babies, but he recognized the soft smacking of an infant at its mother's breast. As his gaze dropped to the front of the woman's cloak, a pink bootie popped into view. The cloak gaped wide, giving him a view of a baby latched to her mother's breast. Dylan knew about nature's way between a man and woman. He enjoyed it quite a bit, but he hadn't thought much about the end result. Looking at the child in her mother's arms, he felt an awe he'd never known.

He didn't realize he was staring until the woman gasped. Frantic, she covered herself. "Get out of here!"

Dylan deserved the rebuke. A mare with a foal would have kicked him for getting this close. He pushed to his feet and looked down. Against the golden straw, the woman's dress looked Christmas red. Blinking, he thought of Reverend Taylor's sermon.

Christmas is about second chances. We can all start over, anytime and anywhere.

Had the woman at his feet come to Crystal River for that reason? Was she hoping to pass herself off as a widow? With a baby, she'd have a hard time. The locals could be both kind and cruel. Dylan knew from experience.

He took a step back. "I'll wait outside."

"No!"

A chill ripped down his spine. Without the cloak muffling her voice, she sounded just like Maddie Cutler. He dropped to one knee. Craning his neck, he took in the woman's down-turned profile. Her cheek had a dimple he'd never forget.

"Maddie?"

She huddled in the cloak.

He touched a stray curl. "It's you, isn't it?"

"Go away!"

How could he? He'd kissed this woman. He thought about her every day and prayed for her at night. He wished now that he'd punched Brodie in the nose and hauled her back to the Castle. Instead he'd watched her leave, his cheek stinging where she'd slapped him. He wouldn't repeat that mistake. Pushing to his feet, he blocked her in the stall. "I won't leave you."

"Dylan, please—" She bit her lip.

"What?"

"I need privacy."

He'd forgotten about the baby. "Of course."

He left the barn with one thought in mind. Maddie had come home and she'd brought a child. Respectable women didn't nurse their babies in a stable. Maddie Cutler, the belle of Crystal River, had come home in a cloud of shame.

Dylan shook his head at the irony. He'd been born a McCall,

a family known for fighting, cussing, drinking, whoring and then some. The McCall name got no respect at all. Maddie's life had been the opposite. Lord Albert Cutler, the third son of a duke, had come to America and made a fortune. The man had more polish than a silver teapot, but Maddie had still run away. Even before she'd left Crystal River, she'd tarnished the Cutler name. A spoiled rich girl, she'd bossed shopkeepers as though she owned the town. With a bastard child in her arms, she'd be a target for scorn. Not even Mabel would welcome her.

Where could she go? Had Lord Albert sent someone to meet her? Dylan had been in town for nearly two days and hadn't seen a soul from the Castle. The last he'd heard, Lord Albert had banned the mention of his daughter's name. Maddie had no friends. From the looks of her, she had no money.

The wind gusted from the north, bringing a chill that promised snow. Dylan stared at the gray clouds. He had to get home before the breeze turned into a blizzard, but it wasn't the weather making his belly churn. He'd just found a wounded bird, one that had fallen from the sky and landed hard. He knew what happened when he nursed a bird back to health.

It fought, but he helped it anyway.

It scratched, so he wore gloves.

No way would he leave Maddie to fend for herself. She'd said someone was coming for her, but who? Dylan looked at the heavy sky. Only a fool got caught in bad weather. He had to leave town now. If Maddie didn't come out soon, he'd go inside and get her. He'd promised to feed her and a gentleman always kept his word.

Butterflies beat against Maddie's ribs. She'd recognized Dylan's voice the instant he called into the barn and had prayed he wouldn't come inside. With her daughter latched to her breast, she'd listened to his boots come down the aisle. She'd recalled his blue eyes and dark hair. She knew how he smelled—clean in a Sunday kind of way. She'd felt the strength of his arms and the intent of his lips.

She also remembered calling him trash. Maddie owed everyone in Crystal River amends, but Dylan deserved them more than anyone else. An hour before she'd run off with Brodie, he'd cornered her in an alley.

Don't be stupid, Maddie. He's using you.

You don't know anything!

I know men.

She'd answered by slapping his face. Maddie shut her eyes to fight the memory, but she couldn't block the picture of Dylan's disgust. She'd expected to face him, but not today. Not in the red dress that marked her as a fallen woman. Not with Cora fussing in her arms.

"All right, baby girl," she crooned. "Let's switch sides."

As she moved the infant to her other breast, cold air pebbled Maddie's skin. Cora turned her head in a greedy search, found her mother's nipple and latched on.

The sudden pull filled Maddie with a bittersweet truth. A baby had to be selfish. An infant had needs and no way to meet them. In a grown woman, selfishness had no place. Babies took. Mothers gave. Maddie had become a mother. The road had been steep and full of stumbling, but she'd left her old self in San Francisco. She would have left the red dress, but her other gowns had been more risqué and she didn't have the money to buy something new. She knew what she wanted, though. Something in gray with a high collar.

Sighing, she thought of the clothes she'd left in her wardrobe at the Castle. Even if the dresses fit, she didn't want to wear them. She'd changed, and wanted people to know it, especially her father. Coming home for Christmas was a calculated risk. Lord Albert gave a lavish celebration for everyone at the Castle. Would he welcome Maddie or send her away? She didn't know.

Thoughts of her father triggered the worry she'd had when

she first stepped off the train. Before leaving San Francisco, she'd sent a wire to Riley, her father's foreman, asking him to meet her. Maddie loved Riley like a grandfather and he loved her back. She'd been certain he'd help her, but he hadn't come to the station.

"Maddie?"

"I'm almost done," she called to Dylan.

She didn't want his help, but maybe he'd seen Riley. As soon as Cora's mouth went slack, Maddie tugged the dress over her chest, stood and brushed off the straw sticking to the velvet cloak. Bending at the knees, she picked up the satchel and walked through the barn.

As she neared the door, she heard Dylan humming a Christmas carol. It took her back to Christmases as a child—the tree in the front room adorned with glass ornaments, the cookies shaped like angels. She'd taken it all for granted. If her father didn't take her back, Maddie didn't know what she'd do. She had no skills except flirting. She spent money but didn't know how to earn it. Brodie had called her his good luck charm, but he'd started to lose and she'd lost her shine. He'd considered her pregnancy the worst luck of all. Maddie didn't. Cora hadn't ruined her life. She'd saved it.

Strengthened by her daughter's needs, Maddie stepped into the light, where she saw Dylan standing a few feet away. The past year had changed him. Instead of a cowhand with a bristly jaw, she saw a clean-shaven man dressed in a leather coat. His Stetson looked new, but she recognized the snakeskin band. He'd been wearing it the first time he'd kissed her.

What a tease she'd been…. She'd been riding alone and had caused a stir by not coming home for supper. Her father had sent Dylan to look for her. He'd found her napping in the shade. Fearing she'd fallen and hit her head, he'd jumped off his horse and raced to her side. Brat that she'd been, she'd stayed still. He'd touched her shoulder, called her name in a panic and stroked her cheek. She'd opened her eyes and laughed.

I should kiss you for that.

I dare you.

With his eyes glinting, he'd put Maddie in her place. It hadn't been her first kiss, but it had been the one to make her wise. It had also made them friends. He'd been right about Brodie and he deserved to know it.

She set down the satchel. "Hello, Dylan."

"Hello, Maddie." He tipped his hat. "Welcome home."

His eyes darted from her face to the front of her cloak. "You've got a piece of hay—"

She wiped it furiously. "I'm a mess. You must think—"

"I think you have a baby."

"A daughter," she answered. "Her name's Cora."

"I don't suppose Brodie married you?" Dylan asked.

"No."

"I figured as much."

"You were right, you know."

"It doesn't matter now." His voice sounded bland. "How are you getting to the Castle?"

"I sent a wire to Riley."

Dylan's brow furrowed. "Don't you know?"

"Know what?"

"He died."

Maddie felt the same shock she'd experienced when the doctor said she was with child. "That can't be true."

"It is."

"But I sent a wire," she murmured. "He's supposed to meet me. I—" Her throat closed with a rush of memories. Early in the morning, she'd find Riley in the barn and they'd talk. *You're as pretty as a picture, Miss Maddie. But a woman needs more than looks to be beautiful. She needs a good heart.* Maddie hadn't understood at the time, but she did now. Having Cora had changed her. Riley would never see her beautiful baby. He wouldn't know the woman Maddie had become. She'd been counting on his friendship.

Now she had no one. She bit her lip, but tears still blurred her vision.

Dylan's voice came through the pain. "I know you liked the old man. I did, too."

"When…" She couldn't finish.

"This summer. He passed in his sleep."

The wind plastered her skirt against her legs. She had no one to help her, no way to get home.

Dylan shoved his hands in his pockets. "I'm sorry."

"Me, too."

"Maybe your father sent someone else."

"He doesn't know I'm here."

She had enough money for a night in a boardinghouse, maybe a meal or two, but then what? Shivering, she looked back at the stable. For a moment, she considered stealing a rig and driving herself to the Castle. Thievery…could a woman go any lower? The answer, she knew, was sadly yes. Tears filled her eyes. Embarrassed, she bent her neck and wiped them with her sleeve. A blue bandanna fluttered below her nose.

"Use this," Dylan said.

When she shook her head, he wiped the tears for her. "Don't cry, Maddie. I'll take you home."

Home.

Did she have one? Riley had called home a place where people loved you no matter what. Maddie didn't deserve to be welcomed at the Castle, but she desperately needed food for herself and shelter for Cora. The thought of facing Lord Albert made her mouth go dry, but she had no choice. She hadn't eaten since yesterday morning. Her stomach felt so empty she feared losing her milk. With Cora snug in her arms, she looked into Dylan's eyes. Light glimmered in his blue irises. What had she been thinking to call this man trash? He had every right to turn his back, yet he was offering kindness. She felt so unworthy she could barely hold up her head.

"It's so far," she said. "Are you sure?"

His expression hardened. "It's not as far you think. I bought the Gridley place."

Maddie flashed to the last time she and Dylan had snuck off together. Instead of kissing by the stream, he'd taken her to a stretch of land south of her father's place. It had belonged to Warren Gridley.

I have dreams, Maddie. I want my own land. This place isn't much, but someday…

She'd turned up her nose. *It's nothing compared to the Castle.*

He hadn't mentioned the Gridley place again. A week later, she'd met Brodie and pushed Dylan out of her life. Except for cornering her in the alley, they hadn't spoken again. She knew now that she'd belittled his dreams. She wanted to apologize, but they had a long ride, one best made without dredging up the past.

Dylan lifted the satchel. "My wagon's at the feed store."

Bolton's Hay and Feed was six blocks away. Maddie cringed. She'd have to walk through town with Cora in her arms. She considered asking Dylan to bring the wagon to the livery, but the request struck her as selfish, the kind of demand the old Maddie would have made.

He must have seen her hesitate, because he lowered his chin. "Are you all right?"

"I'm fine."

"I could bring the wagon around."

"No," she said. "I'll walk."

With her chin raised, Maddie headed for the heart of Crystal River. Welcome or not, the prodigal daughter had come home.

Chapter Two

By the time they'd walked two blocks, Dylan wished he'd fetched the wagon. Maddie had wrapped Cora with the cloak, but everyone they passed took a long look. The town had grown and so far no one had recognized her. A few smiled, especially women. No one seemed to notice the broken feathers on her hat or the hem of her red dress.

The instant Dylan spotted Sylvia Hollister, he knew everything would change. A glance at Maddie told him she'd noticed Sylvia and would have crossed the street if it weren't for a wagon blocking the way. Dylan didn't keep up on town gossip, but even he knew the women didn't care for each other. A few years ago, they'd had a fight in the dress shop. People still talked about the hissing over a particular hat.

Dylan didn't care for Sylvia at all. Before he bought the Gridley place, she hadn't given him the time of day. Since then, she'd taken to batting her eyelashes at him. At last night's Christmas social, she'd stood under the mistletoe long enough to grow roots. He found her annoying at best.

She spotted him and smiled. "Hello, Dylan."

He tipped his hat. "Sylvia."

Her eyes shifted to Maddie. Dylan saw the moment of recognition and braced for hissing.

Sylvia squared her shoulders. "Well, look who's home."

"Hello, Sylvia," Maddie answered. "How are you?"

"Fine, thank you."

"I'm glad to hear it." Maddie sounded sweet, even shy.

Cora heard her mother and cooed. Keeping her eyes on Sylvia, Maddie patted her daughter's back. "This is Cora."

Dylan saw no guile in her expression. No pleading. He admired the dignity of her direct approach.

Sylvia, however, saw a downed bird and pounced. "You have a baby."

"Yes, I do."

The blonde raised an eyebrow. "Is your *husband* with you?"

Maddie didn't flinch. "I'm not married."

Dylan smelled blood. Knowing Sylvia, she'd go in for the kill. He wanted to step in, but the fight belonged to Maddie.

"I'm so sorry." Sylvia raised one brow. "You must be widowed."

"I'm not," Maddie said simply.

"So Brodie left you."

"I left him."

Dylan had heard enough of Sylvia's snide tone. He'd behaved himself this past year, but he was still Blackie McCall's son. He had an Irish temper and he felt it now. He stared hard at Sylvia. "Any other nosy Parker questions?"

"Just one."

"Ask it," he said.

"Why are you speaking to her?" Sylvia spat the words. "You've changed, Dylan. You're too good for her."

He raised one brow. "You think I'm *good?*"

"Well…yes."

"Sylvia, honey." He made his voice a sexy drawl, the one he'd used with whores. "I raised hell in this town and you know it. Sure, I've changed. But so what? When someone's down, you don't kick 'em."

Maddie looked at her feet. He hadn't meant to embarrass her, but he'd spoken the truth.

Sylvia glared at him. "My mistake, Dylan. You haven't changed *at all.*"

He felt the barb but didn't care. As long as he respected himself, the opinion of a woman like Sylvia Hollister meant less than spit. He looped his arm around Maddie's waist. "Let's go."

He took a step, but she didn't move. He figured she wanted the last word. Good, he thought, Sylvia needed to be taken down a peg or two.

Maddie squared her shoulders. "This is long past due, Sylvia. But I'd like to apologize."

What?

Sylvia looked more surprised than Dylan.

Only Maddie seemed composed. He glanced to the side and saw a new softness in her expression. Instead of tilting her chin up, she lowered it. "Before I left Crystal River, I treated you terribly. I'm sorry. I hope you'll forgive me."

Sylvia sneered. "You used to be important, Maddie. But not anymore. Take your bastard baby and run home to papa. If you're lucky, he'll let you sleep in the barn."

Dylan saw red. "Now wait just a—"

Maddie broke in with a surprising gentleness. "Like I said, Sylvia. I'm sorry."

Dylan wanted to fight but held his tongue. *Turn the other cheek... Do unto others as you would have them do unto you.* He'd learned the words from Reverend Taylor, but today Maddie brought them to life. At that moment, he admired her more than ever. He also felt her quivering and tightened his grip on her waist. With an exaggerated tip of his hat to Sylvia, he guided Maddie down the boardwalk.

"That woman's a nuisance," he said.

Maddie sealed her lips.

Her sad eyes pained him, so he tried to joke. "She's a bigger pain than you used to be."

"You shouldn't have done it." Her voice quavered.

"Done what?"

"Defended me."

"Why not?" He'd expected praise, even gratitude.

"Sylvia's right." She clipped her words. "I was Brodie's mistress and Cora's a bastard."

Dylan tugged her into an alley, dropped the satchel and pinned her against the wall, making a cage of sorts with his arms. He'd caged wounded birds before. Sometimes they tried to fly before they had their strength. Cages kept them safe. Maddie needed one now.

"Listen to me," he said.

Tears welled in her eyes. "I wish I'd listened before. I wish—" She sealed her lips.

Dylan saw that pucker and nearly lost his mind. Kissing her would have been as natural as breathing. Not the passionate kind his body remembered... She didn't need that kind of touch. He wanted to kiss her with a tenderness that would heal her wounds. Brodie Jones had used this woman. He'd lied to her as surely as the serpent had deceived Eve. Dylan had once believed the same kind of lies about himself.

You're no-good trash, McCall.

You're just like your old man...a drunk and a loser.

Dylan knew how it felt to live with shame. He couldn't stand the thought of Maddie hating herself. He honed his eyes to hers. "Don't you dare call yourself names."

"It's true."

"It's the past."

"Yes, but I have to live with what I did." She kept her chin high. "I can handle the shame for myself. I earned it. But my baby—" She kissed Cora's head through a pink knit cap. The child peeped like a baby chick.

Dylan swallowed a lump the size of a rock. "So help me God, if anyone calls that sweet child a foul name, I'll—"

"You'll do nothing," Maddie insisted. "I'm not your concern."

"Who says?"

"I say."

Dylan didn't like being told what to do. "I'll do whatever I please." He'd have said *damn well please,* but he'd stopped cussing. Sort of.

Maddie's eyes filled with pity. "You'll regret it, Dylan. Sylvia said you've changed. I can see it, too."

He wanted to feel proud, but her tone put distance between them. "I haven't changed *that* much."

"Yes, you have." She laid her palm on the front of his coat.

He'd bought the jacket last week. It smelled new and didn't have a single stain. He'd never owned anything so nice. The coat made him feel good, but only on the outside. Deep down, he still felt like trash.

Maddie's eyes misted. "You shouldn't be seen with me."

"Why not?"

"People will think ill of you."

"I don't care." Dylan meant it. He hoped to redeem the McCall name, but what good was the respect of others if a man didn't respect himself? When push came to shove, Dylan answered to his gut. He always had, always would. He stared hard into Maddie's eyes. "I don't give a damn what people think and you know it."

"You should." She raised her chin. "You shouldn't be seen with me. Now go on. I'll meet you at the feed store."

"Not a chance."

Her lips trembled. "It's for the best."

"Who says?"

"I do."

No way would he let her walk through town alone. The best way to win the argument was to turn the tables on her. Stepping back, he put his hands on his hips. "Let's see if I understand. You're too good to be seen with me. Is that it?"

"No!"

"So what's the problem?"

Maddie looked mad enough to spit. Good, he thought. He knew how to deal with Maddie in a rant. Her tears made him weak.

"Don't be coy," she said. "You know what I'm saying."

"You're saying you don't want to be seen with me."

"No," she said, dragging out the word. "I don't want *you* to be seen with *me*."

Hoping to rile her more, Dylan smirked. "You're as bossy as ever, aren't you? Telling me what to do, giving orders."

"I'm trying to protect you!"

"You're being a brat."

"I am not!"

He grinned. "Don't worry about it. I like brats."

Her mouth gaped.

Dylan hadn't chuckled in a long time, not since he and Maddie had fooled around on her father's ranch. It felt good to be with her again. Too good, he reminded himself. He had nothing to offer this woman except hard work. The one time he'd dared to hint at his dreams, even his feelings, she'd stomped him like a bug. Dylan still burned with the embarrassment of that day. A woman like Maddie Cutler played with two-bit trash, but she didn't take it home to supper.

The truth sobered him. "Come on," he said. "We have a long ride." He stepped back and lifted the satchel.

The wind made her cloak flap, but Maddie didn't budge. She looked frail and broken, like a bird that wanted to fly but didn't have the strength. He wondered when she'd had her last meal.

He cupped her elbow. "Let's eat. I'm hungry."

"Me, too," she admitted.

He guided her to the street, where they walked another block to the Cattleman's Café. Dylan liked the place. It catered to cowboys and working folks, though the high-and-mighty of Crystal River paid an occasional visit. With a little luck, no one would pester Maddie.

As they passed the window, she glanced inside and stopped. "You go in," she said. "I changed my mind."

Dylan peered through the window, saw Mayor Hooper and his wife and knew why Maddie had lost her appetite. Mrs. Hooper was the sweetest woman in town. In spite of Maddie's snobby ways, she'd invited her to join the Women's Guild, a group dedicated to charity. Maddie had snubbed her badly.

Maddie looked at Dylan with a plea in her eyes. "I can't face Mrs. Hooper. Not yet."

After the scene with Sylvia, Dylan felt the same way. He guided Maddie to a bench on the far side of the restaurant. "Wait here."

"Where are you going?"

"To get food."

He set the satchel at her feet, then he walked into the café. At the counter he asked the waitress to wrap up sandwiches. While waiting, he surveyed the people at the tables. Would anyone welcome Maddie back to Crystal River? Reverend Taylor and his wife would. They had a story of their own and judged no one. But everyone else—shopkeepers, clerks, the four women in the corner—would recall her superior ways. As for Maddie's father, Dylan had no idea how Lord Albert would react.

His mind flashed to Reverend Taylor's sermon about Joseph and how he'd stood by Mary. Dylan wanted to give that protection to Maddie, but how could he? She'd been born a Cutler. He was a McCall. She'd grown up in a mansion. He owned a one-room cabin. He'd earned a bit of respect, but not enough to shield Maddie and Cora from foul names. Never mind that he loved her… After the way she'd laughed at his hopes for the Gridley place, he'd keep that secret until his dying day.

What he couldn't do was abandon her. She needed a friend and he intended to be that person.

"Here's your food," said the waitress.

Dylan turned to the counter, saw the wrapped sandwiches

and remembered that Maddie was eating for two. He took six bits out of his pocket. "Would you add a jug of milk?"

"Sure," the waitress said. "A quart?"

"Make it two."

She sent a boy in an apron to the icebox, then turned back to Dylan. "Anything else?"

He scanned the trays behind the counter. Someone had decorated cookies for Christmas. The bright colors charmed him and made him melancholy at the same time. This year Christmas meant something to Dylan. He felt profoundly grateful for the changes in his life. He also felt a bone-deep loneliness that came with sleeping alone. As soon as he had a real home, he wanted a wife to share his bed, children who'd make noise in the morning. Christmas cookies offered a small consolation. He nodded at the silver tray. "I'll take six sugar cookies and six gingersnaps."

Gingersnaps were Maddie's favorite.

The waitress bagged the cookies, took Dylan's money and counted his change. He picked up the milk and sandwiches, put the cookies in his pocket and left the café. As he turned to the bench, he saw empty wood. Maddie had fled.

Cora started to fuss the instant Maddie sat down. To calm her daughter, she picked up the satchel and paced back and forth along the boardwalk, each time going farther until she ended up in front of Regina Vincent's dress shop.

The dress in the window stopped her in midstep. Dove-gray with a white collar, it had a modest neckline and a column of buttons that made it perfect for a nursing mother. A year ago she could have walked into Regina's shop and charged the dress to her father's account. Now she could only stare through the glass.

"There you are."

She turned and saw Dylan striding down the boardwalk. He'd always been handsome, but the past year had broadened his shoulders. He had confidence now, an air of authority that

Maddie admired. Judging by his tone, he'd had a moment of worry.

"I hope you weren't looking long," she said.

"Long enough."

"Cora started to fuss. Walking calms her."

"Are you ready?"

She forced a smile. "As ready as I'll ever be."

Maddie took a last look at the dress, then turned away from the window. She didn't want to face her father wearing the red gown, but it would have to do.

She took a few steps, but Dylan didn't move. She turned and saw him looking at the gray dress.

"It's pretty," he said.

"Yes."

His lips quirked up. "What size to do you wear?"

"Dylan, no."

"It's Christmas. I'm buying you a present."

"Clothing is too personal."

"Who says?" He looked her up and down—not in an ugly way, not the way Brodie had ogled her—but as if he were taking her measurements. "I know how tall you are. What's your waist size?"

She sealed her lips to stop from telling him.

His eyes honed to hers. "If you won't tell me, I'll ask the clerk. I bet Regina has records."

True, but Maddie's waist had thickened a bit. She desperately wanted the dress, but she had no way to pay for it. "Please don't. I can't repay you."

His eyes darkened. "It's a gift, Maddie. Something from a friend."

"But—"

"What size do you wear?" He sounded gruff.

Maddie could feel the wool on her skin. Warm and soft. Clean. Modest but still pretty. She whispered two numbers, her bust size and waist size.

Dylan stepped closer. "I didn't hear you."

She said the numbers again.

He bent his neck. "It sounded like you said 34-26."

"I did."

What was she thinking? She couldn't permit him to buy her a dress. Regina would gossip. The town would talk and Dylan would be tarnished by her reputation. When he turned to go into the shop, she grabbed his arm. "I said no."

"Too late." With a glint in his eye, he shook off her grip and walked into the store.

Maddie watched through the window as the clerk, a girl she didn't know, made eyes at Dylan. When he smiled back, she felt a pang of jealousy. She had no right to feel possessive of him, but she did. She knew how he kissed, what made him laugh. If she'd been smart, she'd have stayed in Crystal River and shared his dreams.

When the clerk went to the back room, Dylan turned to the window and winked. Maddie felt as if they'd never been apart. What a fool she'd been to run off with Brodie…. At the time, she'd felt trapped on her father's ranch. The gambler had offered freedom, even adventure. Maddie had been like a child gobbling candy. Later she'd learned the truth about his motives, but it had been too late to come home. Cora had already been conceived.

The clerk came out of the back room. As Dylan opened his billfold, a lump pushed into Maddie's throat. She hadn't appreciated him when she'd left. She'd been a rich girl playing with a cowboy. That cowboy had become his own man. He had pride. A future. Independence. Until she'd had Cora, Maddie hadn't known how much security mattered. Now she did.

She also knew Dylan. The times he'd kissed her had been magic. He'd made her laugh and had listened to her silliness. He'd also cared enough to warn her about Brodie. Looking at his broad shoulders, she touched the glass and murmured, "I wish I'd listened."

She owed Dylan an apology and vowed to make it before they reached the Castle. As for the way she'd dismissed his dreams for the Gridley place, she wished now that she'd given him respect. She couldn't think of anything better than owning a home of her own. Maddie kissed Cora's cheek, then stepped back from the window. With tears in her eyes, she waited for Dylan to come out of the shop.

Chapter Three

The wind blew from the north with an unchecked fierceness. Dylan didn't mind the chill for himself, but he worried about Maddie and Cora. Before they'd left Crystal River, he'd tried to give her his coat but she'd refused to wear it. Short of wrestling her into it, he couldn't have won the argument. He'd settled for wrapping her in a wool blanket he kept under the seat in case of bad weather.

They'd been on the road over an hour. Maddie had eaten her sandwich and downed half the milk. Dylan reached inside his pocket and gave her the bag of cookies. "You still look hungry."

She peeked in the bag. "Gingersnaps! My favorite."

"They're all yours."

She lifted a cookie, took a bite and sighed with pleasure. Then, as if she remembered her manners, she took out a cookie decorated with green sugar crystals and gave it to Dylan. "This one's pretty."

As he lifted it from Maddie's fingers, he glimpsed a new consideration in her eyes. In the old days, she would have eaten the cookies and not given him a thought. Today sharing the goodness made the cookies even sweeter.

He smiled at her. "They're tasty. Have another one."

"I think I will." She grinned. "I'm eating for two, you know."

He knew, all right. When Cora woke up, she'd want to nurse. With a storm threatening, he couldn't stop the wagon and take a walk to give Maddie privacy. He'd hear every sound and want things with Maddie he couldn't have. Dylan expected to reach the Castle in three hours or so. He planned to leave her at the door, then take a back road to his cabin. The last time he'd taken that trail had been the day she'd called the Gridley place a dump.

She'd been right and she still was. Dylan had added stock and built a corral, but he hadn't done a thing to improve the cabin. He glanced to the side and saw Maddie staring straight ahead. In spite of the focus in her eyes, she looked distracted.

"Warm enough?" he asked.

"I'm fine, but I have to say something."

She'd already scolded him for the purchase at Regina's shop. In addition to the gray dress, he'd asked the clerk to include plain underthings and a night rail. The unmentionables had been a bold purchase, but he wanted Maddie to feel brand-new when she faced her father. She'd complained about the extra packages, but she had them tucked at her side.

Dylan kept his voice light. "If it's about the dress—"

"It's not." She took a breath. "It's about the day I left…what happened in the alley."

He didn't want to recall that day. It still hurt. "It's in the past."

"Not for me," she replied. "I owe you an apology."

"Forget it."

"I can't. You were right about Brodie."

His blood boiled at the memory of Maddie's last days in Crystal River. The gambler had played her like a poker chip. She'd been foolish for running off with him, but Dylan laid the blame on Brodie. The man had conned her. Dylan felt certain he'd been using Maddie to get to Lord Albert's money. Maddie had learned a painful lesson.

"I wish I'd been wrong," he said.

"And I wish I'd listened," she answered. "I had no right to slap you. As for what I said—"

"It's over."

"I was wrong to insult you," she insisted. "We were friends."

Dylan flashed to the stream where they'd lazed on a blanket, kissing and touching through their clothes. They'd been more than friends. They'd almost become lovers. Maddie had been that daring. He'd been that selfish. He'd stopped for one reason. He didn't measure up and he knew it.

His mouth hardened. "It's over and done."

"Even so," she said. "I hope you'll forgive me."

"Of course."

He'd forgiven her the instant he'd recognized her voice in the stable. Maybe the instant she'd slapped his face. Dylan didn't hold grudges, but neither could an apology span the gap between them. Tarnished or not, Maddie still had a silver spoon in her mouth.

She sat straighter, as if a weight had come off her shoulders. "I'm glad that's settled. I hope we can be friends again."

"Sure."

Except he knew the taste of her, the feel of her arms around his neck. He knew she'd arch her back if he nuzzled her ear. He pushed the memories aside but they pushed back, stirring him in ways he didn't want. He needed a wife, not another go-around with Lord Albert's daughter. He'd take her to the Castle and head home to his ranch. There would be no visits on lonely afternoons. No rides to the stream where they'd played with fire.

A mewling broke into his thoughts. He glanced to the side and saw Maddie huddled over Cora.

"Is she all right?" he asked.

"She's hungry."

Dylan's neck hairs prickled. "I'd stop but—"

"I know," she answered. "We'll manage."

She scooted to the far side of the wagon and turned her back. Dylan stared down the road, but he heard the rustle of her taffeta dress. Cora made eager sounds, then went silent. Maddie hummed the tune of "Greensleeves." Dylan filled in the words to "What Child Is This." This morning, he'd sung the song in church. Not once had he imagined a real child at rest, feeding in Maddie's lap.

A mile passed without a word between them. With as little motion as possible, Maddie switched Cora to her other breast. As the wind gusted, Dylan looked up at the sky. A raindrop hit his cheek. Another splashed on his boot. He reached under the seat for a slicker. As he handed the oil cloth to Maddie, the sky let loose with a torrent.

"Use this," he said.

"I will in a minute."

Why wait? Dylan risked a glance to the side and saw pink booties on Cora's tiny feet. Holding the reins in one hand, he opened the slicker and tried to cover Maddie's lap. The baby wasn't the least bit distracted, but Dylan was. Maddie had always been pretty. Today she had an inside glow that made her beautiful. Feeling tender, he lifted the hood of her cloak and covered her head.

She smiled. "Thank you."

Rain turned the air into gray mist. The muted light made Maddie's lips cherry red and her eyes twice as brown. Looking at her filled him with crazy thoughts about wedding rings and bedsheets. They had five miles to go. Soon the temperature would drop and the rain would turn to snow. If a blizzard hit, he'd be stuck at the Castle. Dylan didn't mind staying in the bunkhouse, but he had to get home to his ranch. Expecting to be gone one night, he'd left his horses in the pasture. With the storm coming, he wanted to put them in the barn.

Thinking of home, he nudged the horses into a faster walk. Maddie sat straight. Dylan glanced to the side and saw her put

Cora against her shoulder. While patting the baby's back, she scooted across the seat. Their feet touched, then their hips. She moved back an inch, but Dylan still felt her warmth.

Using one hand, she spread the slicker over his knees. "You're getting wet."

"I'm fine," she insisted.

"Don't be silly."

As she reached across his lap, her breast grazed his ribs. He raised his arm to give her room, but he couldn't escape her nearness. He saw the shell of her ear and recalled kissing it. The scent of her reminded him of summer grass. As she tucked the oil cloth under his leg, he gritted his teeth.

"Now we can both stay dry," she said.

Staying dry was the least of Dylan's problems. He had to stop noticing her, but how could he? He had to protect her from the cold. As she sat straight, he put his arm around her shoulders. He hadn't bothered to button his coat. With the leather gaping, he felt her warmth like a caress. It gave him thoughts—both loving and lustful—until Cora nudged him in the ribs. He had no business thinking about Maddie in his bed. Not now. Not ever.

Just as Dylan feared, the rain turned into wet snow. As they neared a fork in the road, he peered at a distant ridge, faint because of the white flakes. To the left, the Castle lay beyond the hills. To the right, his cabin sat like a wart in a meadow. It lacked class but offered shelter. He didn't want to take Maddie to his house, but he couldn't risk the ride to the Castle. The valley dipped like a man's hand. Snow would fill the bowl and erase the road. He reined the horses to a halt. "We're not going to make it."

"Then where—"

"My place," he said. "It's a mile down this road."

Maddie bit her lip. "I hate to impose."

Dylan stifled a snide remark. A person couldn't impose on a man living in a hovel. "It's no trouble."

As he loosened the reins, the horses smelled home and picked up their pace. He wished he shared their excitement. The thought of Maddie seeing his cabin made him irritable. The thought of spending time with her—days, maybe longer—made him feel an excitement he had to deny. Gritting his teeth, he vowed to do the right thing. She'd be his guest, nothing more. To the extent of his abilities, he'd treat her like the Queen of England.

As they neared Dylan's ranch, Maddie peered through the snow. She saw the barn first. It needed paint but looked large. To the side she saw a fenced pasture where four horses stood together for protection from the wind. She flashed to the last ride she'd taken with Dylan.

I'd like to breed quarter horses. They're fast and smart.

Like me?

Exactly.

What a brat she'd been…. No way would she be selfish today. She wanted Dylan to know she admired him. "You've worked hard."

"Yep."

Looking across the yard, she spotted a log cabin near a stand of pines. The logs had chinks in the mortar and the porch sagged. The rock chimney stood tall, but the roof was missing shingles. She judged it to be one room, a rectangle with two windows and a plank door. Dylan, she knew, would give her his bed while he slept on the floor.

He steered the wagon close to the porch. "As you can see, it's not the Castle."

"It's cozy."

He grunted. "You're being polite."

"That's not true," she insisted. "I see four walls and a roof. What more do you need?"

"You'll know when you see the inside."

His tone angered her, but she said nothing. He jumped down

from the seat and went to the back of the wagon where he lifted her satchel. He took it inside and came back to help her out of the wagon. She handed him the clothing first. She'd been protecting it under the slicker. "I don't want anything to get spoiled."

He put the packages in the cabin, then came back and offered his hand. Holding Cora in one arm, she clasped Dylan's fingers, hopped down from the seat and landed in a puddle.

"Oh!"

He saw her fancy shoes and grimaced. "I'll set them by the fire to dry."

"I can do it."

"No," he said. "Let me."

Maddie thought of her father's butler and frowned. Charles had a bald head and a cold heart. She didn't like him. Ignoring Dylan, she walked into the cabin and looked around. The shuttered windows kept out the light except for cracks that glowed silver. In the shadows she saw a cookstove and cupboards, a table with two chairs, a rock fireplace, a wood box and a rocking chair with a sagging cane seat. Against the back wall she saw a rope bed covered by heavy blankets, including one made of rabbit fur.

Small things made the cabin Dylan's home. He'd left the Montgomery Ward catalog open to a page showing tools. On the stove sat a tarnished pot that smelled of old coffee. She looked again at the back wall and saw his clothing hanging from nails. Maddie envied him. He had a home. No one could close the door in his face. Her father's ranch had been dubbed the Castle, but Dylan had a castle of his own.

"It's very tidy," she said.

He grunted.

She felt condemned. "What did I do?"

He waved his arm to indicate the room. "Tell the truth, Maddie. It's a dump."

"I *am* telling the truth."

"No, you're not."

She bristled. "I don't appreciate being called a liar."

"Then open your eyes."

She'd heard enough. "You *own* this place. You have a warm bed and enough food. You have *clothes* that aren't embarrassing. What more do you need?"

His eyes turned dark and protective of her. He'd had that look the times they'd kissed. It had sent shivers down her spine then, and it did now. Dylan knew what he wanted and how to get it. He'd wanted this house. Not so long ago, he'd wanted *her*. But not anymore. She had a bastard child who would shame him. He had a ranch to run, and she couldn't boil water. Another woman could have lit the stove and made coffee. She'd have started a fire and cooked supper. Maddie had no such skills. She turned her back to hide the sadness in her eyes.

Dylan lit a lamp. As the wick flared, Cora fussed. She needed a clean nappy and they all knew it.

He walked to the bed and turned down the covers. "I have to see to the horses before we're in a white-out. I'll light the fire as soon as I can. In the meantime, stay under the blankets."

Maddie didn't want to take his bed, but she very much wanted to lie down. Two days on the train, always sitting and holding Cora, had made her ragged. "Thank you."

He studied the ceiling. "I'll hang a curtain for privacy. A few nails ought to hold it."

She thanked him, again.

"You'll need a wash bowl."

"*Thank you.* I'll be fine."

She hadn't meant to sound dismissive, but his tone embarrassed her. She wasn't worthy of being a guest. Frustrated, she went to the satchel to retrieve a diaper.

Dylan headed for the door. As his boots thudded across the porch, Maddie thought of all the things she couldn't do. The list shamed her until her gaze landed on the fireplace where she saw a triangle of shavings, kindling and logs already arranged in the hearth. If she struck a match, the shavings would catch and Dylan would walk into a warm cabin. The thought filled her with pleasure.

After changing Cora's diaper, she covered the baby with the fur blanket. Startled by the texture, Cora cooed.

Maddie tickled her chin. "I'll be right back, baby girl."

She walked to the fireplace and found a box of matches. Thanks to experience with a few cigarettes, she had no trouble striking a match against the rocks. She held the flame to the shavings until they blazed to life. Her cloak felt damp, so she crossed the cabin and hung it by the door. Pleased with herself, she took off her wet shoes. As she bent to pick them up, she smelled smoke. Gasping, she whirled toward the hearth. Instead of orange flames, she saw black smoke billowing into the cabin.

Cora shrieked, then coughed.

Maddie ran to her daughter, lifted her along with the blanket and raced for the door. She needed the satchel for Cora, so she grabbed it off the table. Her eyes shifted to the packages from the dress shop. It broke her heart to leave the gray dress, but she didn't have an extra hand.

What had she been thinking when she'd tried to light a fire? If the cabin burned down, Dylan would lose his home, his possessions. Blinded by snow and tears, Maddie ran into the yard and shouted for help.

Chapter Four

Dylan dropped the pitchfork and ran out of the barn. The instant he saw smoke coming from the windows and not the chimney, he knew Maddie had lit a fire without checking the flue. He didn't expect the cabin to burn down, but the smoke would leave a mess. Adults could handle the dirty air, but he worried about Cora.

Halfway to the cabin, he met Maddie. She'd had the sense to grab a blanket for the baby, but she'd taken off her cloak. He took in her bare shoulders and the curve of the bodice. Red suited her. Aware of his own humanity, he forced his eyes to her face.

"I'm so sorry," she murmured.

"Wait in the barn." He didn't care about the smoke or the mess. He cared about *her*.

She bit her lip. "I should help you."

"You can't."

She winced.

He hadn't meant to sound angry, but he felt raw inside. If he'd had a decent house, she would have seen a handle and opened the flue. In his falling-down cabin, he had to reach into the chimney and prop the flap with a metal rod. Cora's wailing tore at him. He couldn't build a house in the next two minutes, but he could keep Maddie and her baby warm.

He yanked off his coat. "Take this."

"But—"

"Don't argue." He hung the jacket on her shoulders. "There's clean straw inside the door. Flop down and wrap up in the blanket."

As Maddie hurried through the snow, Dylan headed for the cabin. He took a breath on the porch, held it, then strode to the fireplace where he opened the flue. As the chimney pulled the smoke, he opened the shutters, then put on the old coat he kept for working in the barn. He'd owned it when he'd worked for Lord Albert. Putting it on now reminded him of who he'd been.

With light coming through the windows, he went back to the hearth to shovel the mess into the ash bucket. As he worked, he thought of Maddie. He didn't care that she'd lain with Brodie. He'd whored around and had no right to judge her. But others would. She had a tough road ahead of her. So did Cora. Dylan knew from experience. As Blackie McCall's son, he'd been taunted until he'd bloodied every nose in town.

Who would fight for Maddie?

As he carried the ashes outside, Dylan considered Lord Albert. The Englishman had white hair and a ramrod spine. He made men, including Dylan, as nervous as little girls. If he'd take Maddie back, she'd have a powerful ally. If he didn't, she'd suffer.

As he dumped the ashes on the snow, Dylan saw the black smear and acknowledged a sad truth. A person could clean up a mess, but stains lingered. So did bad smells. The cabin would reek for hours. Until it aired out, Maddie and Cora would be more comfortable in the barn. He still had to bring in his horses, so he set the ash bucket on the porch, crossed the yard and entered the barn. He saw Maddie lying in the straw with Cora. As she lifted her head, he thought of the hawk he'd nursed. She looked just as broken.

"Dylan?"

"Everything's fine."

"What did I do wrong?" She sounded like a mouse.

"You forgot about the flue."

"Oh."

He lifted a lead from a nail. "The cabin needs to air out. You'll be warmer here until I build a fire."

She settled back into the straw. "I feel like a fool."

"Don't. You're used to fine things."

"It's common sense. I should have known."

He didn't want to hear excuses for his lowly cabin. "Are you warm enough?"

She curled under the blanket. "I'm fine. So's Cora."

Dylan strode into the yard. Squinting through the storm, he headed for the pasture where dark shapes indicated the horses. If the storm kept up, he and Maddie would be trapped together for several days. She'd be here for Christmas. The thought gave him a rush. It also sobered him. He'd seen the Castle on Christmas Day. Lord Albert served up a feast and passed out greenbacks to the hands as though they were newsprint.

Dylan's plans for the day had been far more humble. He'd expected to go to church, share a meal with Jesse and head home. The storm had changed everything. Maddie and Cora would be his guests. Staring into the storm, he glowered at the emptiness. What did he have to offer? Canned stew for Christmas dinner…fancy that!

"Damn fool," he muttered.

With the rope in hand, he headed for the pasture. He took the horses to the barn, then went to the cabin where he lit a fire and hung a blanket to give Maddie privacy. The blanket wouldn't block the rasp of her breath, but at least he wouldn't have to fight the urge to watch her sleep.

He glanced at the fire. Confident the flames were steady, he went to the barn to fetch his guests.

"Wake up, Maddie."

Dylan's voice broke into her dream. She'd been in San

Francisco running from her hotel room with Cora in her arms. The hallway had gone dark and she'd felt Brodie grab her from behind. As a whimper escaped from her throat, she startled awake. She jerked her head to the side, saw Dylan and felt safe.

He dropped to a crouch. "I've got a fire going in the cabin. Hot coffee, too."

"That sounds good."

"Let me help you up." He stood and offered his hand.

Maddie shifted Cora to her shoulder. As she sat upright, the blanket slipped and bared her shoulders to Dylan's eyes. She hated the red dress, but there hadn't been time to change when she'd fled San Francisco. Shivering, she tugged the neckline as high as she could, then struggled to put on the coat Dylan had left for her.

As she wrestled her arm into the sleeve, he reached behind her back and held the coat. When his fingers brushed her shoulder, a tingle raced to her fingertips. Warm all over, she fought the sudden heat. She and Dylan had been kindred souls, but the past had to be forgotten. Maddie had ruined her life. She refused to drag Dylan down that road.

After shifting Cora, Maddie wiggled into the second sleeve. Shivering, she stepped on the cold floor.

Dylan looked down. At the sight of her bare feet, he scowled. "Where are your shoes?"

"In the house."

"You came out here *barefoot?*"

She felt stupid enough without his anger. "I thought the cabin was going to catch fire. I grabbed Cora and ran."

Maddie had never seen Dylan look angrier. He muttered something about the blasted flue, then looked at the barn door. She followed his gaze to a white rectangle of light. Earlier she'd noticed trees and a fence. Now she saw blowing snow and the faint outline of the cabin. It looked a hundred miles away.

Dylan lifted the blanket. "Give me the baby."

"Why?"

"I'll take her inside and come back for you."

Maddie hadn't set Cora down in three days. Her arms ached, but she couldn't bring herself to hand her daughter to Dylan. He'd be tender, she knew that. The fear came from the longings trapped in her heart. Once she saw Dylan holding Cora, she'd never get the picture out of her mind.

"It's not far," she insisted. "I can walk."

His brow furrowed. "It's worse than you think. If you keep a grip on Cora, I'll carry you both."

"No!"

The thought of Dylan holding Cora would haunt her dreams. Feeling his arms around *her* would fill her every thought.

"All right," he said. "We'll do this another way."

He went to a workbench, cut two lengths of cord, then took two empty feed sacks from a rag bag. Using his chin, he indicated a stool by the work bench. "Have a seat."

As she positioned herself, Dylan dropped to one knee. With his neck bent, he lifted her foot with his gloved hand, wrapped it in the burlap and knotted the rope around her ankle.

Maddie felt like a child who couldn't button her own shoes. She hated feeling helpless. She was also ticklish and Dylan knew it. A year ago he would have tortured her toes. Today he efficiently wrapped her other foot, stood and steadied her as she hopped off the stool. Mindful of Cora, he draped the blanket over her shoulders, lifted the satchel and guided her to the door.

When she stepped into the yard, snow pelted her face. The wind whipped at her skirt and pushed her back. Close to a foot of snow had fallen. In places it had drifted higher.

Dylan latched the barn door, then hooked his arm around her waist. "Lean into the wind."

Hunching over Cora, Maddie slogged into the drifts. Everywhere she looked, she saw white velvet. Dylan's cabin looked perfect and bright. Behind it, a row of pines had changed from spikes to feathery angels. There wasn't a speck of mud in sight. If only her life could be made this new ... With Dylan supporting her, she trudged forward. Halfway through the yard, the burlap came loose and she stepped out of it. Her bare foot landed in the snow. She bit her lip to stop from crying out, but Dylan looked down and saw the rag. He set the satchel in the snow.

"Hold tight to Cora."

Before Maddie could speak, he slipped his elbow behind her knees and swept her into his arms. "Put me down!"

"Not a chance."

"But—"

Dylan scowled. "Do you know what frostbite looks like?"

"No."

"Your toes turn black."

Maddie had never felt so helpless in her life...or so relieved. She wanted to rest her head on his shoulder, to hear the thunder of his heart and feel his strength. For just a moment, she wanted to lean on him. But she couldn't. She had a baby in her care. She had to stay strong.

Dylan plowed through the snow and up the porch. Using his elbow, he opened the door and carried her to the fireplace. Robust flames filled the room with orange light. As the logs crackled, heat touched her cheeks.

Dylan set her down. "Here you go."

"Thank you."

Cora cooed her appreciation.

Maddie glanced at Dylan and saw a light in his eyes that made her yearn for the life she'd sacrificed for Brodie's lies. He'd be a good father, she was sure of it.

He broke his stare and went outside. A minute later he came back with the satchel and put it behind the curtain he'd hung around his bed.

He stepped back into the room. "Coffee?"

It sounded wonderful, but she didn't want Dylan to wait on her. Babies needed people to feed them. Maddie wanted to fend for herself. "I'd love some. What can I do?"

"Not a thing."

That, she knew, was sadly true.

While Dylan poured, she slipped behind the curtain and changed Cora's diaper. He'd made the bed and fluffed the pillow. He'd also left a flannel shirt and a pair of his wool socks on top of the sheets.

"Maddie?"

She jumped. He was on the other side of the blanket, just inches away. "Yes?"

"I have sugar, but no cream. Is that all right?"

She didn't give a hoot about cream. She was grateful to be warm. "Sugar would be nice."

"Do you see the shirt?"

He'd spoken as if she were a child. "I do."

"You can wear it over your dress. Put on the socks, too. I'll put your shoes by the fire to dry."

"I can do it."

He paused. "Just don't put them too close."

I'm not stupid!

Except she felt as helpless as Cora. As she opened the satchel, Maddie's mind buzzed with her own needs, all of them irritating. She needed the outhouse but didn't know where it was. Tonight he'd cook supper because she didn't know how. She couldn't stand the thought of Dylan waiting on her like a servant. She had to find a way to be useful.

Even a fallen woman had her pride. Maddie couldn't cook, but surely she could find a way to make the meal nice.

Chapter Five

Dylan dumped flour in a bowl, added baking powder, salt, shortening and canned milk. He beat the mixture with a wooden spoon, dumped it on the counter and flattened it with his hands.

"I could do that," Maddie said hopefully.

"No, thanks."

He didn't want her help, but Maddie seemed determined to give it. After putting Cora down on his bed, she'd come out wearing his shirt over the red dress. The flannel covered her shoulders, but he'd already glimpsed bare skin in the barn. Tonight he'd see that skin in his dreams. He needed to put air between them, but Maddie stayed at his side. Earlier she'd offered to peel a potato. Dylan didn't have one. She'd mentioned carrots. He didn't have those, either.

She stepped back from the counter and looked around the corner he called a kitchen. He figured she'd never seen such poor digs.

Out of the blue, her face brightened. "I know what I can do."

He scowled. "What?"

"I'll set the table."

"Good idea."

He'd have agreed to anything that put distance between

Maddie and his nose. His shirt smelled like him and her dress smelled like her. Sugar and spice, like the Christmas cookies. No, he reminded himself, she smelled like money and he didn't.

"Where's your silver?" she asked.

He had three forks, two spoons and four knives, including one with a broken handle. If he'd needed a reminder that Maddie outclassed him, being asked about his "silver" would have done it.

He pointed to a box on the counter. "Look in there."

She riffled through the utensils, then carried the items to the table he'd moved close to the fire. She set them down with care, as if she were at a fancy tea, then came back to the kitchen. "Where are the dinner plates?"

At least she hadn't asked for his "china." With the biscuit pan in hand, he aimed his chin at a stack of dishes on the shelf. "Use those."

He'd bought a set of plates when he'd moved to the ranch. He'd been proud to own them. Now they looked cheap.

She carried plates to the table, set them across from each other, then stood back to inspect the arrangement. Dylan ladled the stew into a chipped bowl the Gridleys had left behind. As he carried it to the table, Maddie slipped behind the curtain blocking his bed. He set down the bowl, then went back to the kitchen to fetch the biscuits. Hot and golden brown, they should have made his mouth water. Instead he thought about the lack of butter. He put them on a plate and carried them to the table where he saw Maddie standing behind her chair.

As he set down the biscuits, he noticed a white rectangle with scalloped edges under his fork. He'd seen linen napkins before. He'd even used one at Lord Albert's Christmas supper for the hands. The cloth on the table wasn't a napkin.

"What's that?" he asked.

Maddie grinned. "It's table linen."

The fabric looked ridiculous with his tin forks. Dylan snorted. "Isn't that nice."

"I thought—"

"I know what you thought."

She liked fine things. He didn't have them. He moved to hold her chair, but Maddie sat before he could help her. He took a seat, spooned stew onto her plate, then his.

She put her napkin in her lap, then looked him in the eye. "You said you knew what I was thinking."

Dylan frowned. "It's obvious."

"Not to me."

"Then you're blind." He held up the handkerchief. "You put out *table linen* because I've got rags."

Her eyes clouded. "I wanted to make things nice."

"What for?"

"Because I—" She lowered her head.

When firelight revealed a single tear, Dylan felt a knife to his heart. He'd hurt her but didn't know why until she picked up the hankie. As she dabbed her eyes, he thought of Mrs. Taylor's Christmas party and how she'd set the table with her finest things. She'd decorated the parsonage with candles and holly. The men barely noticed, but the women had admired the pretty things.

Too late, Dylan understood Maddie's heart. The napkins had been a gift, the best thing she had to offer, and he'd been snide. He regretted hurting her, but he'd spoken the truth. He made his voice gentle. "I didn't mean to hurt your feelings."

She sniffed.

"The hankies were a nice idea." He meant it. "But we both know the truth. This supper isn't good enough for you."

"*Good* enough?" Her voice shook.

"That's right."

She indicated the stew with her hand. "If you think this isn't good enough for *me,* you're crazy."

Dylan frowned. "What do you mean?"

Tears flooded her eyes. "You don't know what I've done, where I've been. Brodie—" She bit her lip.

Dylan knew exactly what she'd done with Brodie. He wanted to kill the man. "Maddie, don't."

She burst into tears.

Dylan saw stars and they weren't pretty. Brodie had been a snake in the grass. He'd bitten Maddie and filled her with poison. To heal, she needed to bleed out. Dylan knew, because he'd done his bleeding with Jesse. Truth had a way of washing a man clean.

He dragged his chair closer to hers, then took her hand. "Tell me what happened."

She lifted the hankie to her eyes. "I'm so ashamed."

"Of what?"

She grimaced. "Isn't that obvious?"

"You're not the first woman to fall, Maddie. You won't be the last." He stroked her fingers. They felt small, birdlike. "Want to know a secret?"

"Sure."

He let his eyes twinkle. "My slate's not exactly clean."

"But—"

"But nothing," he insisted. "A mess is a mess. We've all made them. With a little help from the Lord, we mop up and move on."

Maddie wanted to share Dylan's faith in second chances, but she couldn't. She dabbed at her eyes. "This isn't a puddle of spilt milk."

"No," he said gently. "It's your life."

"And Cora's."

He squeezed her hand. "Trust me, Maddie. You can start over."

She wanted to believe him, but he didn't know how far she'd fallen. In the beginning, she'd felt no shame. Living as Brodie's mistress had been a game to her. Even knowing he probably wouldn't marry her, she'd gone willingly. Cora—and a woman named Lula Hughes—had changed everything.

Maddie would forever be grateful to Lula, but the facts stood. Maddie hadn't been an innocent victim. Riley had warned her.

Be careful, Miss Maddie. You can't unring a bell.

Oh, but she wished she could…. She raised her gaze to Dylan's face. This morning he'd been clean shaven. Now he had a bristle that reminded her of the past. She wanted to touch it—not to tease him but to feel the innocence they'd once shared. But she couldn't. She'd rung a bell and had Cora to prove it.

Her cheeks flamed. "I'm so embarrassed."

"Why?"

Why did he keep asking that question? He'd seen the red dress. He knew what she'd been to Brodie. She tried to pull back her hands.

Dylan squeezed tighter. "Don't be embarrassed, Maddie. I know where babies come from."

She felt even worse. "I love Cora."

"Of course you do."

"She's innocent…. I'm not." Maddie looked into his eyes. "I knew what I was doing when I left home. I can't blame Brodie."

"*I* can."

"But—"

"He used you, Maddie. He took what he wanted and left you to deal with the mess. That's not right."

Her throat burned. "Cora's not a mess."

"No, but your life is."

He stood and poked the fire. Sparks crackled up the chimney. Maddie's stomach churned. "I want to make things right."

"And you will." Dylan put down the poker and sat. He pushed the chair back to give her room, but they were still eye to eye. "What do you know about rattlesnakes?"

"They bite."

"They inject poison."

She shuddered.

Dylan kept his voice low. "The bite hurts, but things get worse. The victim can't move, can't breathe. He's trapped in his own body. Not all rattlers slither. Some have two legs and cripple their victims with lies."

Maddie trembled anew. After Cora's birth, she'd felt paralyzed by her circumstances. She'd wanted to leave, but she'd had no money, no friends. That last night, when Brodie had ordered her to come to his room in the red dress, she'd gone because she'd had no choice.

Dylan held her gaze. "You need to kill the snake, Maddie."

"What do you mean?"

"Brodie… Tell me what happened."

"No!"

"You've got to," he said. "The poison's still in you. I know, because I was snakebit, too. Jesse cut me open and I bled all over him. Don't walk around with Brodie in your head. Kick him out."

"I can't."

"Then *I* will." Dylan pushed to his feet. She felt his eyes on the top of her head, burning a circle on the crown of her head. His voice dropped to a growl. "That *bastard* conned an innocent girl. He told you what you wanted to hear, kissed you until you were stupid and took what he wanted."

"Stop!"

"Am I right?"

Maddie couldn't stand being a victim. She raised her face and stared hard. "I *let* him touch me! *I* made a choice."

Dylan put his hands on hips. "I don't give a damn what you did."

"But—"

"But nothing." His voice went deep. "We *all* have dirty laundry. Do your own, but don't do Brodie's."

The thought stopped Maddie cold. She'd been taking the

blame, but didn't Brodie deserve some of it? He'd been older and worldly wise. He'd told her they'd get married in Denver, but they hadn't. He'd seduced her with pretty words that had all been lies.

Dylan pulled the chair close again, sat and reached for her hand. "You made a mistake, sweetheart."

Tenderly he lifted her hand to his lips and kissed her knuckles. She felt the silk of his mouth and a warmth that raced to her heart. Dylan had called her "sweetheart" before. It had been a game between them, a taunt more than an endearment. Tonight it sounded real. Tears rushed to her eyes.

He tipped up her chin. "I need to know something."

She cringed. "What is it?"

"Will Brodie come after you?"

"I don't think so."

"But you're not sure?"

The last night in San Francisco came back to her in a flood. She couldn't stand the thought of reliving it, so she sealed her lips.

Dylan touched her cheek. "I have to know, Maddie. If he's on his way to Crystal River—"

"He's not."

"How do you know?"

She gave a dry laugh. "Because Brodie only loves himself."

Dylan's eyes narrowed. "What about Cora?"

Memories of that last night swarmed through her mind. She saw the note delivered by a maid, informing her that a nurse would stay with Cora for the night. He'd told her to wear the red dress and silk underthings.

Don't deny me, Maddie. I've waited long enough.

She'd gone to his room to bargain for her escape. To keep his temper from flaring at the sight of her, she'd worn the red dress but not the fancy undergarments. Brodie hadn't been kind. He'd listened to her pleas, pushed her down on the bed and taken what he wanted.

Tears ran down Maddie's cheeks. After Cora's birth, she'd felt brand-new. She'd imagined being a virgin again, untouched by Brodie and his lies. For weeks she had wanted to leave him. She'd almost written to her father for help, but she'd feared his response. That last night, when Brodie called her a whore and Cora a bastard, the truth had entered her bones.

Dylan squeezed her hand. "Maddie?"

She sniffed. "You don't need to worry. Brodie cares less about Cora than he does about me."

"Then he's a fool." His eyes lingered on her face. "What happened to make you leave?"

He raped me.

She couldn't say the words, but she managed to raise her chin. "Lula helped me."

"Who's Lula?"

"She's the midwife who delivered Cora."

Maddie warmed at the thought of her friend. During her recovery from the birth—a wretched experience that had lasted for two days—Lula had stayed by her side. She'd brought baby gowns and assured Maddie she'd be a good mother. She'd sounded a lot like Riley. When the labor pains had become excruciating, Lula had prayed for God's mercy.

Dylan's lips curled into a smile. "Birthing a baby… I can't imagine it."

Maddie groaned. "*I* can."

"You had a rough time."

"The worst." But the rape had hurt even more, inside and out. "Lula saved my life…twice."

He looked terrified for her. "First with Cora?"

"That's right. She also paid for my train ticket." A smile crossed Maddie's lips. "When she gave it to me, she said 'Merry Christmas.' Until then, I didn't know what day it was."

"I like her," Dylan said.

"Me, too."

He honed his gaze to hers. "What made her give you the money?"

She'd hoped to distract him with talk of Lula, but he'd always been savvy about the truth. Maddie hung her head. "I can't talk about it."

"It'll hurt more if you don't."

"I said no!"

She jumped to her feet, then realized she had nowhere to go. The cabin walls were her only protection from the cold. Feeling trapped, she paced to the shuttered window, leaned against the wall and pressed her face to the crack. She gulped fresh air, but her mind stayed in a fog. She didn't see Dylan approach, but she felt his warmth at her back. If she turned, she'd be in his arms. Just like in the alley, he'd trapped her.

Dylan clasped her shoulders, anchoring her in place. "I'm not moving until you talk to me."

"Then we're in for a long night."

"Fine by me," he drawled.

Maddie sucked in cold air, but her head didn't clear. Instead she imagined a snake slithering toward her feet, touching her toes, going up her leg. She *hated* that snake. She hated Brodie and wanted to see him die. Her skin crawled with memories she couldn't bear.

A shriek escaped from her lips. Whirling, she faced Dylan. "All right!" she cried. "I'll tell you. He raped me. That last night, he did unspeakable things."

"That son of a—"

"Don't!" Maddie pressed her hands to her face. "I want to forget."

The next thing she knew, she was sobbing and Dylan had her in his arms. She felt his lips on her temple, his hands pressing her tight against his chest.

"I tried to run," she sobbed. "But I couldn't get away."

She'd fought, though. At least until Brodie had pinned her

down. Then she'd begged for mercy. She'd pleaded that Cora needed to be fed, but he'd ignored the milk leaking from her nipples. The next time she'd nursed Cora had been on the train, and she'd wept.

Dylan's breath brushed Maddie's ear. "Brodie should die for what he did to you."

"It was my fault," she sobbed. "I ran off with him. I let him touch me."

"Don't you *dare* blame yourself!"

"I went with him. I—"

"Stop it, Maddie." Still gripping her shoulders, Dylan stepped back with his eyes blazing. "You made a mistake. That's all. Brodie committed a crime."

She felt the truth of his words, but she couldn't stop crying. She was back in the San Francisco Hotel. She'd never forget those terrible hours. Her insides had been sore and torn. She still hadn't bathed and felt dirty inside and out.

Dylan looked murderous. "How did you get away?"

"I took Cora and went to find Lula."

"And she helped you."

"Yes." Gratitude welled in Maddie's chest. "Someday I'll pay her back."

She'd reached the end of her story, but she had something to say to Dylan. Trembling, she forced herself to look into his eyes. "I want you to promise me something."

"What?"

"Don't *ever* say that you're not good enough for me. *I'm* not good enough for you."

His eyes glinted. "Oh, yeah?"

"Yes."

"You're wrong, Maddie." His voice dipped low. "And I'm going to prove it to you."

Chapter Six

His breath rasped in the same rhythm as hers. She recognized the slackening of his jaw, the intent in his eyes. He understood her in ways no one else did. She loved him. She'd been too foolish to know it before she'd left with Brodie, but she knew it now.

His eyes drifted to her lips, lingered, then bounced to her eyes. She saw the same fierceness she'd seen the day he'd first kissed her, the day she'd pretended to be hurt and had scared him. This time, though, she wasn't pretending. She *was* hurt. She felt dirty and used.

Dylan leaned closer.

If she raised her chin, he'd match their lips and remind her of the innocence she'd lost. Desire made her cheeks burn. Shame made her look at the floor. The combination stung like salt on a wound.

He stepped back. "Put on your shoes."

Startled, she raised her chin. "Why?"

"We're going outside."

She craved air that didn't smell like Dylan, but she wouldn't leave her baby. "I can't. Cora's asleep."

"We're not going far."

He turned to the hearth, where she'd left her shoes. He picked them up, then pulled out a chair. "Sit down."

"What for?"

He handed her the fancy boots. "Put them on or I'll do it for you."

I dare you!

The thought came from the spirited girl she'd once been. The glint in Dylan's eyes belonged in the here-and-now. They'd changed, yet they hadn't. When he lowered his chin, Maddie raised hers. "You're a pain."

His eyes twinkled. "So are you."

While she buckled her shoes, Dylan put on his boots and fetched the coats. He held the new one for her. As she slipped into the sleeves, she felt small. With clumsy fingers, she worked the buttons and looked up. "I have to check Cora."

"Sure."

She peeked behind the curtain and saw her daughter sleeping soundly. Maddie wanted to hide with her under the blanket, but Dylan had been right about bleeding out Brodie's poison. She felt better. She also trusted Dylan. If he wanted to go outside, she'd follow. She let the curtain fall back in place and turned back to the room. Dylan opened the door and motioned for her to pass.

She stepped on the porch, looked up and gasped. The clouds had broken into silver bands. Between the jagged strips, she saw black velvet studded with diamonds. Moonlight rained down on the yard, turning the snow into white satin. The beauty filled her with awe but saddened her, too. The night, like her life, was black and white. She looked down at her toes.

Dylan put his arm around her waist. As he looked up, she felt the tug of his arm urging her to look at the sky. He hummed with pleasure. "It's awesome, isn't it?"

Look up.

The voice in her head belonged to Riley. Maddie wanted to lift her eyes, but she felt unworthy of such beauty.

Dylan released his grip, lifted something off the porch and then hooked his arm around her waist. "Let's go."

"Where?"

"It's a surprise. Follow me."

She saw a tool in his hand but couldn't make out the details. "Cora—"

"If she cries, we'll hear it."

Maddie wanted to resist, but he'd piqued her curiosity. She also welcomed the cold air. It had cleared her mind of Brodie and frozen the last of her tears. When Dylan tugged her down the steps, she enjoyed the crunch of the snow. He took the lead, kicking a path to smooth her way. More than two feet of snow had fallen. In spite of the break in the clouds, she expected more to come. December storms came in waves. They weren't over until the sky turned bright blue from west to east. She could be stranded with Dylan for days.

Maddie didn't know what to think about that possibility. Right now, she felt pleasantly numb. That feeling turned to a childlike glow when they rounded the cabin and she saw a stand of pines.

"I know your surprise," she said to Dylan.

"What is it?"

"You're cutting down a Christmas tree."

He looked over his shoulder and grinned. "You pick and I'll chop."

Dusted with snow, the pines ranged in size from massive to miniature. Maddie thought of the trees her father put up in the Castle's front room. This year's spruce would be covered with ribbons, paper cut-outs and glass ornaments that had belonged to her mother. Maddie's grandparents had brought them from Germany, and her mother had carried them to America as a bride. Young and lovely, she'd died giving birth to her only daughter. Maddie treasured the ornaments. Someday she'd pass them to Cora…if her father forgave her. Tears threatened to spill down her cheeks again. She didn't deserve her mother's ornaments or even a Christmas tree.

When they reached the closest pine, Dylan touched the branch. "Do you know what I like best about Christmas?"

"Cookies."

"You're right, but that's not all."

Her heart stirred. "What else?"

"Until this year, I'd have said nothing." He looked at the stars. Maddie looked at *him*.

"What changed?" she asked.

"I got sick of myself."

Maddie knew the feeling.

He tugged on a branch and let go. Snow exploded in a mist. Watching it, he spoke in a wry tone. "There I was, twenty-three years old with nothing to show for it. Jesse sobered me up and dragged me to church. I'll never forget that day. I looked like hell, but Reverend Taylor shook my hand like I belonged. God touched me, Maddie. For the first time, I felt…good."

Silence settled like a bird. She wanted that touch in her own life but couldn't imagine it.

If you've got a need, say a prayer.

The voice belonged to Riley, but she heard echoes of Lula's alto. She had so many needs she didn't know where to start.

A roof for Cora.

Her father's mercy.

A husband… She had no right to want Dylan's love, but she couldn't deny her heart. Tonight he'd touched her soul, but the facts stood. He needed a wife who could cook and sew and make him proud. She wasn't the brat who'd left Crystal River, but neither had she proven herself worthy of Dylan's love. With her eyes fixed on the stars, Maddie thought of Riley and Lula and prayed for God to make her brand-new.

She wanted to feel something, but the sky stayed black. The stars burned whiter than ever. Ahead of her stretched a silver meadow, a perfect blending of snow and night. The beauty filled her with longing, but she felt no different.

Dylan broke into her thoughts. "Which tree do you like?"

"I don't know."

He pointed to a six-foot pinyon. "How about this one?"

Maddie nodded, but she felt numb again.

Dylan crouched at the base of tree. "I'll cut. You hold it steady."

"Okay."

She gripped the trunk with both hands. Dylan swung the hatchet. The whack shot up her arms. He swung again, harder this time. Snow exploded off the branches and filled her nose and eyes, stealing her breath and blinding her.

"Hold tight," he said.

Over and over, he struck the trunk. Maddie felt each blow until the tree tore apart with a slow crackle. The weight of it pushed her back and she stumbled. Dylan tried to grab the tree, but he fell on top of her. They landed chest to chest, breath to breath. The coats protected her full breasts, but she could feel Dylan's legs tangled with hers, the bend of his knees and a maleness that confessed desire.

He wanted her. She wanted him. But not now…not like this. Not when she felt as worthless as a soiled table linen.

Dylan stared into Maddie's eyes. Did she want to be kissed as much as he wanted to kiss her? He heard the pant of her breath and the silence of the stars. In her pretty eyes he saw both longing and shame.

The longing pleased him.

The shame had to go.

He knew, because Maddie's makeshift napkins had stripped him of his embarrassment about his circumstances. While he'd been fretting about cheap spoons, she'd been fighting for her dignity. Supper had opened his eyes. When a man gave his all to a woman, it included more than the beans he put on her plate. He'd fight for her. He'd die for her. Dylan loved Maddie with that intensity, but he had to be honest about his ability to provide. He had nothing to give her except hard work and hope. If her father took her back, she'd have a far easier life.

Common sense told Dylan to stand up, but he couldn't tear his gaze from Maddie's face. Moonlight turned her cheeks to silver and made her lips a dusty pink. She needed to know how he felt. He didn't give a hoot about Brodie and the past. He loved her for the girl she'd been and the woman she'd become.

With their gazes locked, he slipped off his glove and touched her cheek. Her lids drifted shut and her lips parted. He knew that look. With the confidence of an experienced man, he matched his mouth to hers. The rush took him back to their first kiss, circled to now and shot him into the future. He wanted to lie with Maddie and make her his. He wanted to marry her.

A whimper jarred his thoughts. So did the stillness of Maddie's lips. She felt dead in his arms. Dylan cupped her face between his hands, warming her cold skin with his work-warm palms. He made his voice deep, forceful.

"Listen to me, Maddie. *You're a good woman.*"

"Don't say that."

"It's true." His heart pounded. "I have feelings for you. I—"

"Stop." She put her finger on his lips, hushing his declaration of love. "I can't be the woman you need."

Can't. Not won't.

He saw a difference. The hawk had wanted to fly but couldn't. Maddie wanted to love him but didn't think she'd be a good wife. The hawk had flapped its wings in the cage to strengthen them. Maddie needed to do the same thing. She had to gain strength so she could fly. When that day came, she could face her father without fear. Once she made peace with the past, she'd be free to choose her future.

Shivering, she pushed against his chest. Dylan stood and pulled her upright. "It's cold," he said. "Let's get the tree inside."

Maddie wrinkled her brow. "I don't care about Christmas."

"I do."

Cora's cry shattered the night. Maddie gasped and ran for the cabin.

Dylan lifted the tree with one hand and followed her. When he stopped to adjust his grip, he saw the mark they'd left in the snow. Time would erase the place where they'd fallen, but he'd never forget having Maddie in his arms. He intended to make sure she didn't forget, either. *She* didn't care for Christmas, but he did. Whether she liked the idea or not, he intended to celebrate.

Two days later, Maddie thought she'd explode with anger. As she'd expected, the storm had dropped another foot of snow. It stopped and started, teasing her with the possibility of escape. But escape to where? She had no assurance that her father would open his door to her.

Even so, she had to escape Dylan's cabin. They'd finished breakfast and he'd gone to the barn. Maddie had nursed Cora and put her down for a nap. The room smelled of bacon and pine from the tree in the corner. Twice Dylan had mentioned decorating it. Last night he'd made a show of eating the leftover Christmas cookies for dessert. If he hummed "Greensleeves" one more time, Maddie would scream.

She wanted to feel the Christmas spirit, but she'd left her soul under the stars. She'd prayed to Riley's God, but nothing had happened. She felt as dirty as ever. That's why she hadn't yet put on the gray dress. The only bright spot had been helping with chores. Dylan had been generous with his teaching.

Here's how you light the stove.

She'd boiled water and washed Cora's nappies.

I'll wash. You dry.

She'd stacked the supper plates as if she'd done it a hundred times.

She liked being useful but feared her feelings. Dylan's kiss burned in her mind and wouldn't stop. She cared for him, deeply. But she had to be wise. He needed a wife, not a ninny who'd never cracked an egg.

Maddie looked again at the tree. She couldn't stand the sight of the bare branches. If her father shunned her, she'd never again see her mother's ornaments. The pine scent assaulted her nose. Under her dress, she still smelled of Brodie's cologne. The tree stood for goodness, a purity Maddie would never again feel. A cry burst from her throat. In a rush, she clutched the tree and dragged it out the door and across the porch. The woodpile was on the side of the house. She intended to find Dylan's ax and use it.

Instead she found Dylan.

As she rounded the corner of the cabin, she saw him placing a round on the stump he used for splitting wood. Her gaze went to the ax in his hand, then rose to his eyes burning blue and hot in the gray light. Wordless, he raised the ax and hit the round. The wood splintered but didn't break.

He nudged the round with his boot. "So you don't like the tree."

She swallowed hard. "No, I don't."

"Why not?"

I feel dirty and used. I'm not worthy.

Instead of confessing, she raised her chin. "It's crooked. I'm used to *much* bigger trees."

"That's a crock and you know it."

He raised the ax over his head. The blade flashed silver as it fell and split the round in two. The wood didn't stand a chance against a determined man wielding the right tool. Neither did Maddie. Dylan knew her in ways no one else did. Her battle wasn't with the tree. It was with herself and he knew it.

He set the ax head on the stump, raised one boot and rested his hands on the handle. "You can chop the Christmas tree to bits, but it won't help. They way I see it, you have a choice."

Tears welled. To fight them, she raised her chin. "Is that so?"

His eyes burned into hers. "You can dwell on the past, or you can start over. As for the tree, it's God's creation…just like you. It's beautiful and I intend to enjoy it."

A retort died on her lips. Had he called her beautiful? She felt ugly.

He held out the ax. "Here, cut it up yourself."

When she didn't move, he set the blade on the stump and walked away.

Maddie felt like a child left at the table to eat her peas. She hated peas, but she hated feeling like a brat even more, and that's how she'd behaved. *She* didn't want to celebrate Christmas, but Dylan did. After all he'd done for her, decorating a Christmas tree was a small thing to ask, and she had the ability. She thought of her red dress. The tree belonged to Dylan, but the dress belonged to her. She could do whatever she wanted with it. Right now, she wanted to cut it to ribbons.

She carried the tree back inside the cabin, then opened the packages from the dress shop. She saw the unmentionables first and blushed. Leave it to Dylan to think of something so personal. She set them aside and unwrapped the gray dress. Holding it by the shoulders, she stood and let the wool unfurl. Back at the shop, she hadn't noticed the silver ribbon trimming the cuffs, nor had she taken in the rosettes lining the hem. She'd owned fancier dresses, but she'd never had a prettier one.

The dress was perfect.

Too perfect.

Too good for her.

She almost put the gown away, but she couldn't let Dylan down. No matter how she felt—about herself, about Christmas—she wanted to give him a holiday to remember.

She slipped out of the red dress, then removed her underthings. Using that morning's water in the washbowl, she wiped her arms and face, working downward until she'd cleaned herself for the first time since leaving Brodie's room. Damp and chilled, she slipped into the new underthings. The cotton clung to her like new skin, but the gray dress scratched as she lifted it off the bed. She held it up to her chin, looked down and wondered if she'd ever feel deserving again.

Before she lost her will, she put on the dress, fetched scissors from a kitchen drawer and carried the red dress to the rocker by the hearth. Warmed by the fire, she started to cut.

Chapter Seven

Dylan spent the next six hours doing chores in the barn. The mindless tasks gave him a chance to consider the future. He wanted to ask Maddie to be his wife. He'd spent hours framing the words in his mind.

I love you, Maddie. I'd be honored to marry you and claim Cora as my own.

His heart pounded with the desire to be a family. He wanted Maddie in his bed and Cora in his arms. Twice he'd offered to rock the baby to sleep. Both times Maddie had said no. What would it take to win her heart? Dylan didn't know, but he understood her insecurity. Sometimes in church, he still felt like an impostor.

He'd done every chore imaginable but didn't feel ready to face Maddie. Desperate to keep busy, he approached the pile of junk in the back of the barn. As he moved a bag of empty feed sacks, he saw the cage he'd built for the hawk and recalled the day he'd set it free. He'd left the door open and walked away. The bird had soared over Dylan's head, circled once and disappeared.

Looking at the cage, he thought of Maddie. He didn't want her to disappear from his life, but she needed to soar. Until she found wings of her own, she wouldn't be truly free.

"Dylan!"

Her voice startled him. He strode out of the barn and looked across the yard. On the porch he saw Maddie. Instead of her red gown and his flannel shirt, she'd put on the gray dress. Slightly darker than the snow, it gleamed silver.

She waved at him. "Supper's ready."

Supper?

"Hurry up! The biscuits will get cold."

Biscuits?

His mouth watered. Even more urgent was the desire to hold her in his arms. Was the gray dress a sign she'd found her wings?

Maddie went back inside. Dylan tromped through the snow, kicked his boots clean, then walked into the cabin. Everywhere he looked, he saw candles. He knew where she'd found them. He had a crate where he kept odds and ends. He'd known poverty. Hoarding candles, even stubs with just an hour of life, made sense to the boy in him.

The man in him liked the amber glow. The fireplace burned with the intensity of a summer sun. A log popped. Embers shot up the chimney like the Fourth of July. His gaze shifted from the flames to the wall, where he saw the Christmas tree covered with red ribbons. The taffeta gleamed in the firelight. Velvet bows looked as soft as skin. He recognized the shreds of Maddie's dress.

"What do you think?" she asked nervously.

"It's beautiful."

"I want to apologize for this morning. I had no right to take the tree down. It's yours."

But he wanted it to be *theirs*. He turned to her, wanting to share his thoughts, but her expression trapped the words in his throat. Her brown eyes were as hopeless as mud. In the gray dress, she looked like a ghost of herself. He fought a wave of disappointment. Maddie had laid her old self in the grave when she'd cut up the red dress, but she hadn't climbed out. She still felt useless and unworthy. He could see it in her eyes, the way she stood with her hands folded at her waist.

She motioned to the table. "Please, sit down."

He didn't want to sit. He wanted to breathe life into her body, the kind that lit a woman from the inside. Dylan knew what got *his* blood going. After six months of celibacy, just looking at Maddie made him crazy. He wanted to kiss her, but she looked timid. His hopes crashed. She'd taken a step, but she wasn't ready to fly with him. Tonight she needed to feel safe.

To do the job right, he needed to be at his best. He indicated the curtain. "Mind if I wash up?"

She blushed. "Of course not."

"I won't wake Cora. I promise."

He left his boots by the door, then headed for the kitchen, where he filled a pitcher with hot water from the reservoir. Maddie stirred the pot of stew. As she put on the lid, their elbows brushed.

"Sorry," she said. "I'm in the way."

Not hardly.

He wanted to share every corner of his life, every hope and memory.

With the pitcher in hand, he slipped behind the curtain, looked at his bed and saw Cora sleeping in a nest of blankets. He touched her cheek. When her mouth made a rosebud, he smiled. He knew how loud Cora could cry. He knew other things, too. Maddie mumbled in her sleep. The baby ate every three or four hours and her mama never complained. Cora, like her mother, could be impatient but settled down when she got what she needed.

After today, he'd never see his bed in the same way. Dylan filled the washbowl, laid out his shaving tools, then took off his shirt and the top of his long johns. With cool air touching his skin, he shaved his face, washed his arms and chest, then added a splash of bay rum. Satisfied, he reached for his best shirt.

Cora coughed.

Maddie called from the kitchen. "Is she all right?"

He looked down at the sleeping child. Her mouth was moving like a tiny flower, but she'd stayed asleep. "She's fine."

Before he could put on the shirt, the baby started to cry. He dropped the garment and picked up Cora. Being careful to support her head, he cradled her against his bare chest. Never in his life had he felt anything as right as this little girl in his arms.

He heard Maddie's rapid steps.

"I'm coming in," she called.

No way would Dylan set Cora down so he could put on his shirt. Blinking, he thought of the Christmas story and how Joseph had loved Mary's little boy. The family had been on the run and he couldn't provide a night at an inn. Silently Dylan thanked God for his run-down cabin and warm fire.

Maddie slipped behind the curtain. Her eyes went first to Cora, then to Dylan's chest. Steam and bay rum tickled his nose. Cora's mouth moved against his skin and he smiled. "I think she's hungry."

"She just ate. Sometimes she just wants to…" Maddie's voice drifted to nothing.

They both understood Cora's need. The baby wanted to suckle. She craved the comfort of being joined with her mother, the peace that came with being loved. Maddie looked into Dylan's eyes. They'd never made love, but he knew it would be good. Judging by the flush of her cheeks, so did Maddie. The old Dylan would have seduced her. The new one wanted more than a passionate night. He wanted forever and intended to fan the flames.

He kissed the top of Cora's head, then smiled at Maddie. "Will she sleep if I put her down?"

"I hope so."

After Maddie smoothed the blanket, Dylan set Cora on the bed. As he reached for his shirt, Maddie looked up. Her eyes landed on his chest and stayed for a good three seconds, long enough to notice the muscles he'd earned with honest work.

As he buttoned the shirt, Maddie's cheeks flamed red. His heart sped up. Brodie had brutalized her body, but he hadn't destroyed her heart. With tenderness and respect, Maddie would soar again.

Still blushing, she slipped through the curtain. "I'll dish up supper."

Maddie paced to the kitchen, where she ladled stew on their plates. Dylan came up behind her, bringing along the scent of bay rum and soap, even a trace of Cora. Maddie refused to look up. She'd see his freshly shaved face and recall the tender way he'd held her baby. Worst of all, she'd see a twinkle in his eyes. She'd noticed his chest and he knew it.

"Need a hand?" he asked.

No, she needed space. She needed air that didn't smell like Dylan. She kept her eyes on the stew. "I can do it."

"It smells good."

"Here." She jammed the plates in his hands. "Take these to the table."

He took the plates but didn't budge. Maddie gave up and looked into his eyes. Instead of teasing, she saw a gentleness that pierced her soul. She could deal with scorn. She'd earned it. What she couldn't endure was kindness. She didn't deserve sympathy, let alone respect.

Dylan's mouth curved. "I want you to know something."
Don't ask.

"This Christmas is the best of my life."
Mine, too.

She didn't say it, but cutting up the red dress had turned into a celebration of sorts. She didn't regret it a bit. She just wished the gray dress didn't make her squirm.

Dylan's eyes stayed on hers. "That dress is almost silver. You look beautiful."

Don't say that!

Warm all over, she pushed past him with the bowl of biscuits. He followed with the plates and set them on the table she'd decorated with candle stubs. When he held out her chair, she sat. He pushed it in, then sat across from her and raised his coffee cup in a toast. "To the best Christmas ever."

Maddie's heart clinked with the cup. "To Christmas."

He took a bite of the stew.

She nibbled a biscuit.

The fire snapped behind her, warming her back and filling the room with a soft glow. Dylan complimented everything about the meal. With each word of praise, she yearned for the future they couldn't have. Dylan needed a wife, not a soiled dove. She hadn't fallen into prostitution, but she could have.

She didn't deserve a man like Dylan. Why on earth had she lit so many candles? The amber glow reflected in his eyes and turned his face to gold. What would it be like to share his life? To feel his strength inside her, protecting her? The thought stole her breath.

Dylan smiled. "This Christmas is special. Do you know what I like best?"

"No."

"Sharing it with you and Cora."

Forcing a smile, she stood and stacked the plates. "We have the cookies for dessert. I baked fresh, but they're too dry."

"Maddie?"

She froze. "What is it?"

"You don't have to apologize for anything. The meal was perfect. In my eyes, *you're* perfect."

How could he say such a thing? She'd ruined her life and tainted Cora's future. With tears welling, she carried the dishes to the wash bucket. As the water sloshed, Dylan clasped her shoulders and spun her around.

She'd never seen such passion in a man's eyes. Brodie had wanted her, but not like this. Dylan's expression went far beyond lust. She saw hope and love, desire on the wings of a promise she couldn't let him make. She bit her lip, but a sob exploded in an ugly hiccup.

He tried to pull her close, but she stiffened. Instead he massaged her shoulders. "Tell me what's wrong."

"Everything."

"Not for me."

She choked on the next words. "I don't belong here."

"You could."

"But I don't… And I don't want to!" Her throat ached with the lie. She loved him. She wanted to bear his children and bake cookies and bread.

Dylan lowered his hands but didn't move. "Do you know what I see right now?"

She shook her head.

"I see a good woman who—"

"Stop!"

She wasn't *good* and never would be. If he kept talking, she'd fall apart. Leaving the dishes in the bucket, she pushed by him and slipped behind the curtain surrounding his bed.

"Maddie?"

"Go away!"

They both knew he had nowhere to go. The snow had stopped, but the cold had grown more intense. Shaking inside, she listened as Dylan walked across the cabin to the kitchen. While he washed the dishes, she slipped into her nightgown, the old one she'd brought from San Francisco. She climbed into bed as gently as she could, but the ropes creaked and Cora stirred against her. Predictably, the baby searched for her mother's breast.

With her eyes closed, Maddie nursed her baby, listening as Dylan moved in a circle around the cabin. One by one, he extinguished the candles until the room was dark except for the fire. She heard the creak of the rocker as he sat. Back and forth, he rocked until the rhythm lulled her to sleep.

Dreams came in a rush, ugly ones of Brodie and her red dress. She ran in the dark but had nowhere to go until she saw Lula and Riley in a silver glow. The light burned even brighter until Dylan's cabin appeared in a meadow of lush grass. Somehow she knew he was inside. If she knocked, he'd open the door.

She felt...good.

But she wasn't.

Maddie startled awake. A log hissed in the dark. Light seeped under the curtain. She heard the creak of the rocker as Dylan sat alone in the dark. Judging by the fading fire, he'd been rocking for hours.

Maddie had Cora to love. Who did Dylan have? No one. Until now, she hadn't thought about his feelings. As always, she'd thought only of herself. Alone in his bed, she felt ashamed...again. She couldn't be the woman Dylan deserved, but for tonight she could meet a need. Barefoot and trembling, she slipped out of bed and went to Dylan with all she had to offer.

Chapter Eight

Three hours had passed since Maddie had slipped behind the curtain and he hadn't slept a wink. He hadn't craved whiskey in months, but he wanted a drink now. Anything to numb the loneliness.

"Dylan?"

He opened his eyes and saw an angel in white cotton. Earlier he'd admired Maddie in the gray dress. What she had on now—a sleeveless nightgown that ended at her knees—turned her into the girl who'd dared him to kiss her. Her hair wisped around her face, hinting at the loose braid falling down her back. He wanted to untangle it with his fingers and watch it fall.

She padded across the floor to the rocker and dropped to her knees. In her eyes he saw a mix of boldness and need. He didn't understand it. He just knew he couldn't stand to see Maddie kneeling at his feet. She had no reason to humble herself before him. Before God, yes. But not before Dylan. He wasn't a lick better than she was. He clasped her hands.

"Stand up," he ordered.

She hung her head. "I have a confession to make."

Whatever she had to say, Dylan didn't care. She'd told him about Brodie. If she'd bedded a dozen men, even a hundred, he had no right to judge her. He loved her. She'd come home with a humble heart. In his eyes, she'd been washed clean. But what about her own eyes? How did Maddie see herself?

He touched her cheek. "I'm listening."

"I lied to you."

"About what?"

"When I said I didn't want to belong here...I do, but I can't."

"Why not?"

"You've worked hard to earn respect. You've changed. I'm not good enough for you. I can't love you, but..." She finished the sentence by lowering her eyes. "Just for tonight, I could—"

Dylan shot to his feet. "Stand up."

She cowered.

"Damn it, Maddie." He pulled on her arms. "I said *stand up*."

She did as he commanded, in part because he refused to let go of her hands. No way would he let her stay on her knees. Did she think she had to repay him for three days of canned stew and a lumpy bed? The thought sickened him, yet he understood it. He knew how it felt to climb out of the gutter. What gave him peace was knowing God loved him anyway. Christmas proved it. Reverend Taylor preached that truth every Sunday. The man lived it, too. He and his wife had invited Dylan to Sunday supper the same way they'd asked the mayor.

Dylan had tried to give that dignity to Maddie.

Give...

The thought settled like snow on a branch. Christmas honored giving. Wives made new shirts for their husbands. Men bought pretty things for the women they loved. Maddie's motives were just as generous. She hadn't come to repay him for his kindness. She'd brought him a gift, the most precious gift a woman could bestow...a gift he desperately wanted but couldn't accept.

A better man would have kept his eyes on Maddie's face,

but Dylan didn't have the strength. Firelight turned her night rail into gossamer. Looking down, he saw the outline of her legs and hips, every curve and shadow. Temptation made his body ornery, but love made him patient. Maddie was offering him something precious and he intended to have it…but not tonight. Not until they took vows.

Intending to speak his mind, he looked into her eyes. Instead of sparks, he saw dying embers and knew he had a problem. If he turned down Maddie's gift, she'd feel rejected. If he hurt her, she might never fly.

He couldn't risk it.

Neither could he take her to bed.

The answer, he realized, was right in front of him.

Maddie tried to pull back, but Dylan wouldn't let go. She'd expected him to welcome her with a sly grin. Instead he'd looked at her with revulsion. She'd been prepared for anything but loathing.

"I'm sorry," she murmured. "I shouldn't have presumed."

With a glint in his eyes, he caressed her fingers. Maddie felt his strength to her shoulders. She tried to take back her hands, but he wouldn't let go.

His voice came out in a growl. "Don't you dare run from me, Maddie. I have something to say."

She didn't want to hear it.

His eyes burned into hers. "Do you know what I see when I look at you?"

"No."

"Then I'll start at the bottom and work my way up."

Her mouth went dry. She knew what *she* saw when she looked in the mirror. She saw the woman who'd wasted her virginity on a shady gambler. Ashamed, she stared at the floor.

So did Dylan. "You have pretty toes."

They curled by themselves.

"Nice legs, too."

He'd spoken in a sexy drawl, the one that made her shiver. Her knees knocked inside the nightgown. Why the scrutiny? Why hadn't he just taken her to bed? She could have handled being kissed and touched. Being admired made her squirm.

Dylan's voice dropped even lower. "Do you know what I like best about your legs?"

She bit her lip. It hurt to hear his voice.

"Those legs carried you home."

She raised her gaze from the floor but got only as far as the open collar of his shirt. His Adam's apple bobbed as he swallowed. She saw brown skin against the blue flannel and thought of earth and sky.

He hummed low in his throat. "I see a lot more than your legs through that nightgown."

She blushed all over.

"I see the womb that carried a beautiful baby girl. I see the breasts that fed her."

Maddie's heart pounded. She'd done those things and felt proud. She wanted to look up, but she feared what Dylan would see when he looked into her eyes. She loved him, but she still felt like trash.

"Maddie?"

She swallowed hard. "I'm listening."

"Look at me, please."

She raised her head but only an inch. Dylan tipped up her chin. His eyes lingered on her lips, then moved to her eyes. "Do you know what I see now?"

She could barely breathe.

"I see a woman who's so caring, so giving, that she came to me tonight with a special gift. I can't make love to you, Maddie. Not tonight. But I want to. I want *everything* you have to give."

Her eyes misted.

"That's right," he said. "I love you and want you for my wife. I want you in my bed and not just for tonight."

Stepping closer, he cupped her face in his hands and kissed her with a mix of tenderness and male demand. The taste of him shot her back to their first kiss. She'd been innocent. He'd been wise. She'd expected a peck. Instead he'd coaxed her lips apart and taken her naivety. He was taking from her now…her pain, her shame.

But what did she have to give?

She didn't know, but she poured her heart into kissing him. The caress stretched from seconds into minutes. He pulled her tight against him. She felt the hard muscles of his chest and the strength in his arms as he kissed her. He slid his fingers into her hair but didn't undo the braid. The restraint honored her.

He brushed his lips against her ear. "I love you, Maddie."

I love you, too.

The words caught in her throat. She smelled the tree and smoke from the fire. Dylan made her feel brand-new, but could she be the woman he needed? Her fingers clutched at his back. Holding him tight, she tucked her head under his chin. "I want to say the words, but I'm afraid."

"I understand." He kissed her temple. "The storm's over and I could take you home tomorrow, but I want something from you."

"What is it?"

"Stay for Christmas."

Maddie liked the idea. By Christmas morning, she'd have sorted her thoughts. She knew how she felt in Dylan's arms, but she had to make this decision with a clear head. Whatever was noble, whatever was unselfish…that's what she had to choose. She heard Dylan's heart beating against her ear.

"I'll stay," she said.

He held her a moment longer, then kissed her forehead and stepped back. "Go to bed, sweetheart. Before I forget my manners."

Maddie gave Dylan an impish grin. "I'd let you kiss me good-night, but…"

His eyes gleamed. "But what?"

"There's no mistletoe."

Dylan liked her spunk. He also liked a challenge. Stepping forward, he brought his lips within an inch of hers. "I don't need mistletoe to kiss you."

Before she could breathe, he matched their lips in a kiss that outdid the first one. Looking proud, he strode out the door, not bothering with his coat. The night air would cool his blood, but nothing could chill Maddie's high spirits. For the first time in forever, she felt cherished.

Someone rapped on the door.

Dylan looked up from his morning coffee, then at Maddie. They'd been sharing a late breakfast. Maddie had just nursed Cora and was holding her against her shoulder, coaxing a burp. Dylan had high hopes for Christmas morning. Maddie still had to see her father, but Dylan had staked a claim and Maddie seemed pleased.

The visitor knocked again. No one ever came to call, especially not after a blizzard. Dylan looked at Maddie and saw her nervously patting Cora's back. They were thinking the same thought. The caller had to be from the Castle. No doubt Sylvia had blabbed all over town and Lord Albert had got word.

"I'll get it." Dylan stood and went to the door.

On the rickety porch stood Wayne Gordon, the man who'd replaced Riley. Dylan knew the foreman and didn't care for his habits. He had iron-gray hair, a moustache and hard features. Behind him stood Howdy Marks. Dylan and Howdy had partnered up when Dylan worked at the Castle. Howdy liked to joke around, but he was serious about cattle. Dylan liked him.

Wayne Gordon didn't like anybody. "Good morning, McCall."

"Good morning."

"I'll get to the point. There's talk that Maddie's back.

Rumor has it she left town with you before the storm. Is she here?"

Dylan fought the urge to lie. He wanted more time with Maddie, but he didn't have the right to keep her if she wanted to go.

"She's here," he said to Gordon. "I was taking her to the Castle when the storm hit. Come on in."

As Gordon stepped into the cabin, Dylan glimpsed a two-seat sleigh. He'd never seen such a fancy rig. The black lacquer boasted gold trim and painted roses that made a double *C* for "Cutler's Castle." Even more impressive were the dappled grays in the harness. The rig put the cutter in Dylan's barn to shame.

Howdy followed Gordon, stopping to slap Dylan on the back in greeting.

Maddie stood. "Hello, Wayne."

"Miss Cutler."

As he removed his hat, his gaze slid from Maddie's face to Cora. Gordon looked disgusted. Dylan wanted to break his jaw. How dare he judge Maddie? Dylan knew for a fact that Gordon kept dirty pictures under his bed. When the man's eyes skipped down Maddie's body, Dylan fought the urge to slug him.

He settled for crossing his arms. "What do you *gentlemen* want?"

Gordon got Dylan's drift and sneered.

Howdy stepped around the foreman. "Hello, Miss Maddie. Is that a baby I see?"

"It sure is." Maddie tried to smile. "Her name's Cora."

Howdy grinned. "She's a beauty."

God bless Howdy.

The foreman glared at Dylan, then focused on Maddie. "I have orders from Lord Albert to bring you home."

No way would Dylan let this man take Maddie to the Castle. Gordon wouldn't harm her, but she'd fuel his fantasies and that made Dylan sick. Maddie belonged in *his* dreams, no one else's. He wanted to order the men to leave, but he didn't have that right. Eventually Maddie had to face her father, but she had the right to say when she did it.

He looked at her standing with Cora. Even in the gray dress, she looked like the frightened bird he'd found in the livery. He'd given food and shelter to that bird. He'd kept it safe while it healed. Dylan wanted to keep Maddie in the cage of his cabin, but birds were born to fly. He'd learned that lesson from the hawk. His belly ached. After setting the bird free, he'd never seen it again.

Maddie had to make a similar flight. Until she faced her father, she wouldn't find peace. She had to go to the Castle, but she didn't have to go alone.

Dylan turned to her. "I'll take you."

She looked upset. "You can't."

"Of course I can." He faced Gordon. "We'll follow in my cutter."

The foreman frowned. "I came for Miss Cutler."

Not you.

Dylan didn't care. "Maddie's coming with me."

Gordon chuffed and left the cabin. Dylan turned to Howdy. "I need a favor."

"Sure."

"Stay and see to things, will you?"

Howdy grinned. "Sounds like you got plans to stay for Christmas dinner."

"Maybe," Dylan replied. If Lord Albert shunned Maddie, they'd be home tonight. If he welcomed her, Dylan didn't know what would happen. Their future lay in Maddie's hands.

She touched his arm. "Maybe I should go alone."

He'd expected gratitude, not resistance. "Is that what you want?"

"No," she said. "But my father might be angry that you helped me. He could ruin you."

"He doesn't scare me."

"He should," Maddie insisted. "He's a powerful man."

In his own way, so was Dylan. When a man had self-respect, he could stand up to anyone. "Get your things," he said to Maddie. "We're going to the Castle."

Chapter Nine

They rode out of the yard in silence, but Maddie's thoughts were far from quiet. Wayne Gordon reminded her of how hard her father could be. Since the moment she'd left San Francisco, she'd imagined facing him alone. Now she had Dylan's future in her hands as well. If he crossed Lord Albert, he could lose everything. Her father had the power to drive him out of business. Maddie refused to let Dylan pay for her mistakes. She couldn't stop him from going with her to the Castle, but she could insist on seeing her father alone.

Sensing her unease, Dylan put his arm around her. "Are you nervous?"

"A little."

"I'll be with you every minute."

"I can't let you do that," she said.

"You can't stop me, either." He stared straight ahead. "I won't leave your side. If your father gets mean, I'll—"

"You'll do nothing."

He scowled. "Why not?"

"I owe him amends. You don't."

She watched the trees as the cutter raced by. Ahead of them she saw the tracks left by Wayne Gordon's sleigh. Cora felt warm in her arms, but Maddie shivered. Everything about the day felt cold and hard.

Without warning, Dylan reined in the horse. He looped the reins, then cupped her face in his hands. "You can push me away if you want, but it won't change how I feel."

She wanted to say that she loved him, but she couldn't speak the words until she knew the cost to Dylan. The future depended on Lord Albert's good graces. If he offered his blessing, she could stay in Crystal River. If he ordered her to leave, she'd consider it penance and leave to protect Dylan. She lowered her eyes to hide her confusion.

Dylan drew her into his arms. "You need to know something, sweetheart."

"What's that?"

"Even if you hated me right now—"

"I don't."

"I know," he said. "But if you did, I'd still go with you. You need to speak to your father. That's certain. But you don't have to do it alone."

But she did.

He gave her a bossy look. "Are you worrying about me?"

"Of course."

"That's sweet, but it's not necessary."

Fear stole her breath. "I know him, Dylan. He could ruin you."

"No, he can't." He sounded sure. "He can make my life hard, but he can't take my self-respect."

Maddie wanted that confidence for herself, which meant facing her father alone. She sat straight and looked Dylan in the eye. "Promise me you won't interfere."

"I can't do that."

"Dylan, please—"

"No dice, Maddie."

He lifted the reins and clicked to the horse. The animal took off through a mix of gray shadows and glistening snow. With

Cora in her arms, Maddie stared across the meadow. She had to stop Dylan from accompanying her and knew of only one way to discourage him.

Sitting straighter, she plastered a haughty look on her face. "I didn't want to say this, Dylan. But there's a reason I want to go alone." She spoke with just a hint of disdain.

"What's that?"

"Frankly, you can't help me."

His eyes narrowed. "What do mean?"

"You're just not…"

He turned and glared. "I'm not what?"

Maddie nearly choked. "My father won't be impressed by you. You'll make it worse for me."

His eyes snapped back to the trail. "I don't believe you."

"You should."

She'd played the part of a snob perfectly, but she didn't feel proud. She risked a glance at Dylan and felt even worse. He looked sucker punched.

"So the truth comes out," he said in a drawl. "I'm not good enough for you."

She lifted her chin. "You've come a long way, but frankly…" She grimaced. "Surely you know what I'm saying."

"No, Maddie. I don't." He clipped each word.

"I'm talking about…table linen."

"I see."

"And clothes," she added. "You're not dressed properly." The gray dress suddenly made her itch. If not for Dylan, she'd have been wearing red.

"So that's how you feel."

"It is," she lied.

"I get the message, Miss Cutler." His jaw hardened. "I'll deliver you to the Castle and head back to my shack of a cabin."

Where she'd decorated the tree with her old dress…. Where he'd given her his bed and honored her by not sharing it. The hill dipped and the cutter sped up. Maddie clutched Cora to her chest and stared at a field of untouched snow. The road leveled, then climbed a hill. When they reached the crest, she saw the Castle. Even from a distance, she could see the balconies and tall windows. The glass looked black and empty. She squinted to make out details but saw none of the Christmas decorations she'd expected. Where were the wreaths? The candelabras in the windows?

Her father always decorated the house for Christmas. He considered it a tribute to Maddie's mother. The absence of decorations confirmed Maddie's decision to push Dylan away. Her father had turned as bitter and cold as the winter. He'd decided to forget her.

Dylan stopped the cutter by the front porch and climbed out. He lifted her satchel, then offered his hand. She took it, felt his strength and fought a wave of indecision. All her life, she'd been selfish. She didn't want Dylan to leave, but staying put his future at risk. No matter the cost, Maddie had to protect him from her father. Being careful of Cora, she climbed out of the cutter and tried to take back her hand. Dylan refused to let her go.

"Did you mean it?" he said a low tone.

Tell the truth.

She couldn't raise her eyes. Was she wrong to protect him? After seeing the Castle with its barren windows, she felt certain her father would send her away to protect the family name.

"Miss Cutler?" Gordon approached from the side. "Your father's waiting."

She dropped Dylan's hand but managed to look him in the eye. "Thank you for helping me."

"You're welcome."

One word and he'd go with her into the house. He'd sacrifice everything for her. Maddie couldn't stand the thought. She didn't deserve that kind of devotion.

The front door swung wide. A manservant came down the steps and took her satchel. With a dismissive nod to Dylan, she walked alone into her father's house. Charles, the butler she'd known since childhood, greeted her with a blank expression. Brigitte, one of four maids, was coming down the stairs with an armload of linen. She gasped. "Miss Maddie!"

"Hello, Brigitte."

"You've come home!"

"Maybe."

Charles cleared his throat. "Your father's in his study, miss."

"Thank you," she answered. "I know the way."

With Cora in her arms, Maddie walked down the hall to the room where Lord Albert conducted business. He hadn't chosen to greet her in the parlor, nor had he met her himself. She prepared herself for a rebuke that would singe her soul. At the end of the hall, she saw the closed door. She took a breath, then rapped on the wood.

"Come in," he called.

Maddie turned the knob and opened the door. Her father was standing at the window with his back to the room and his hands laced. His white hair gleamed in the sun.

"Hello, Father."

Cora mewled.

His back stiffened, but he didn't turn.

Since leaving San Francisco, Maddie had made every decision with one thought in mind. She had to do what was right. Looking at her father's ramrod spine, she felt certain she'd been kind to send Dylan away.

Fear made her tremble, but her voice stayed steady. "I've come to ask your forgiveness."

He said nothing.

"I was wrong to leave the way I did." She cuddled her baby. "This is Cora. Brodie's her father, but we never married."

"Cora…" Her father spoke gently. "After your mother."

"Yes." Her voice cracked. "I'll do anything you ask, Father. If you send me away, I'll go. I'll work as a servant. I'll—" She sobbed. "Please, Daddy. I want to come home."

After the longest ten seconds of her life, Lord Albert faced her with tears streaming down his cheeks. Maddie gasped. She'd never seen her father cry.

His eyes, brown like hers, clung to her face. "Did you doubt that I'd welcome you? Did you feel so unloved that you feared to come home?"

Her throat closed.

"I love you, Maddie. Not a day has passed that I haven't stood at this window, watching for you, praying for you. I hired detectives to search for you. I offered rewards for information, but no one stepped forward."

Tears spilled down her cheeks. "You were looking for me?"

"Of course!"

"I didn't know."

His face darkened. "Brodie did. He wrote me once, asking for money to marry you. I told him no. I wanted you back here, not trapped in a foolish marriage."

"He never told me."

Lord Albert's eyes burned. "He'll pay, Maddie. Now that you're safe, I'll bring the full bearing of the Cutler name against him."

Maddie could barely speak. "I hate him."

"Then it's settled."

Her heart felt free. "So I can stay?"

"Of course."

She hadn't hugged her father in a long time and was afraid to move. Then it happened.... Lord Albert came around his desk, wrapped her in his arms and wept. "My girls have come home."

Cora, feeling squished, kicked her grandfather in the chest. He laughed and stepped back. "May I hold her?"

As Maddie handed Cora to her father, she whispered a prayer of thanks. She also felt a catch in her chest. She'd hurt Dylan for no reason at all. She'd sent him away when she should have told the truth.

"Oh, no," she murmured.

"What's wrong, Madeline?"

"Dylan—" She choked up.

"He's the man who brought you home."

Her voice wobbled. "I sent him away."

Lord Albert eyed her thoughtfully, then offered his handkerchief. "Do you have feelings for this man?"

"I love him," she confessed. "I was afraid you'd be angry with him."

"Nonsense! Where is he?"

"He went home." Maddie looked out the window to confirm what her heart knew. Instead of two sets of tracks, she saw three. Dylan had left.

Lord Albert frowned. "This won't do. I owe Mr. McCall a debt of gratitude. I intend to repay him with the best I have."

"Anything?" Maddie asked.

Her father's eyes twinkled. "Even my daughter's hand in marriage, if she's so inclined."

She blushed.

Lord Albert smiled. "Is that yes?"

"It is."

He gave Cora back to Maddie, then went to the pull rope. Charles came to the door. "Yes, sir?"

"It's Christmas," he said in a crisp voice. "Why isn't the house decorated?"

"But, sir—"

"We need a tree. A big one. And a turkey dinner."

Charles bowed. "Yes, sir."

"And decorations. I want candles in the windows and wreaths on the doors. I want the world to know my daughter's home."

"Yes, sir!"

"And, Charles…tell Wayne to have my sleigh ready first thing in the morning. No driver. I'll be going alone."

Charles left with a small smile. Maddie looked at her father with awe in her eyes. "You're going to see Dylan?"

His eyes twinkled. "Mr. McCall and I need to have a talk if he's going to marry my daughter."

Maddie trembled with worry. "I said terrible things to him."

Sympathy filled Lord Albert's eyes. "We all have regrets, Madeline. Tomorrow is Christmas. I can't think of a better time for a fresh start."

Neither could Maddie. She'd promised Dylan a decision about his marriage proposal on Christmas morning. With her father's help, she'd keep that promise. Her answer was yes…but would he still ask the question? She didn't know, but tonight she'd be on her knees with hope.

Dylan arrived at his ranch in the late afternoon, put up the horse and walked into the cabin. His gaze went to the tree, then to the blanket still hanging around his bed. Two days ago, Maddie had knelt at his feet in humility. This morning she'd stuck her nose in the air. It didn't make sense.

Howdy was sitting in the rocking chair, leafing through a catalog. "I thought you'd be staying for Christmas."

"Me, too."

"What happened?"

"Beats me." Dylan poured coffee and downed it. "Go home, Howdy. If you hurry, you'll make it for supper."

"I'll do that." The ranch hand put on his hat. At the door, he looked over his shoulder at Maddie's tree. "It sure is pretty. So is Miss Maddie."

"Yeah."

As the door shut, Dylan stared at the red ribbons. Maddie had spent hours cutting them. She'd done it for him. Had it all been an act? Or had she been acting when she sent him away? Either way, he had to respect her choice. He walked to the hearth and slung the coffee dregs in the fire. Alone and hurting, he chopped wood, ate beans for supper, then looked at the bed he hadn't slept in for a week.

He wouldn't sleep in it tonight, either. Not while the sheets smelled like Maddie. He spread his bedroll by the fire, stretched on the floor and closed his eyes. Sleep came in fits. He should have heard Cora's mewling and Maddie's breath. Instead he drank in the silence and felt cold. At dawn, he stoked the fire and made coffee. It was Christmas morning, the saddest one of his life.

As he poured the first cup, someone rapped on his door. Dylan nearly dropped the pot. Had Maddie come back? Bleary-eyed, he opened the door and saw Lord Albert Cutler on his rickety porch.

Stunned, he stared at the older man. An expensive wool coat hung past his knees. His hat, a black derby, spoke of idle privilege. A working man needed a broad brim to protect his face from the sun. Between the scent of cigars and fancy soap, the man even smelled like money. Dylan thought of Maddie's fears and wondered if she'd been right about her father's bitterness. Anger churned in his gut. If the man had come to chase him out of Crystal River, he was in for a fight.

Lord Albert removed his hat. "May I come in, Mr. McCall?"

"Sure."

As he entered the cabin, Dylan became aware of his meager existence. He hadn't shaved and looked like hell. His cabin still leaked cold air and he'd left the pot of beans on the stove. Also in view was the blanket walling off his bed. The sight of it filled Dylan with pride and a longing for Maddie. He'd done right by her. He'd respected her and he respected himself for the choices he'd made. Lord Albert couldn't do a thing to change that fact. Who cared if the man was rich? Dylan could stand tall.

He had a guest and would give the man his best. "Can I get you coffee, sir?"

"Yes, thank you."

Dylan indicated the rocker. "Have a seat."

As Lord Albert crossed the cabin, he saw Maddie's tree, stopped and touched one of the bows. "My daughter's handiwork, no doubt."

"She's a fine woman, sir."

"And she's come home."

Dylan tried to read his tone but couldn't. Had he shunned Maddie or welcomed her? And why had he come to the cabin? Dylan didn't know and he didn't care. He loved Maddie and intended to fight for her. He waited for Lord Albert to sit, then handed him the cup and sat across from him.

Lord Albert sipped the coffee, then studied Dylan. "You helped my daughter, Mr. McCall. I'd like to thank you with a gift."

His tone made Dylan wary. Maddie thought her father would do him harm. Was the gift really a bribe to leave his daughter alone? Dylan's brow furrowed. "What kind of gift?"

"Whatever you'd like."

"Are you offering me money, sir?"

"Is that what you want?"

"Hell, no."

Eye to eye, the men took each other's measure. Dylan raised his chin. So did Lord Albert. Maddie's father sipped his coffee. Dylan set his cup on the table. "There's only one thing I want from you, sir."

"Go on."

"I want to marry your daughter."

"Is that so?"

"You bet it is," Dylan declared. "I don't have much to offer, but I love her. I'll be a good husband and I'll claim Cora as my own. I don't want your money. I just want Maddie for my wife."

Lord Albert's eyes twinkled like silver. When his mouth quirked, Dylan realized he'd been tested. Brodie Jones had chased after Maddie for her money. Dylan's feelings were pure and he'd proved it.

Maddie's father smiled. "The decision is hers, Mr. McCall. But you have my permission to ask the question."

His blood raced. "It's Christmas. I'd like to do it today."

"I'll take you to the Castle myself."

Now that was a twist…Lord Albert driving Dylan McCall in his fancy sleigh.

The older man stood and held out his hand. As they shook, Dylan felt the strength of his grip and squeezed back. They were equals. If Maddie agreed, soon they'd be family. He couldn't imagine a better gift.

"Miss Maddie?"

"Yes, Brigitte?"

"Your father thought you'd like to decorate the tree."

"That sounds lovely." Maddie said the words sweetly, but her insides felt like shredded paper. She'd been staring out the library window, looking for Dylan and her father, when Brigitte had found her.

This morning she'd eaten breakfast, then apologized to each of the servants for her past behavior. Belinda, a housekeeper who'd known Maddie's mother, had hugged her and wished her a merry Christmas. Maddie had said it back and then gone looking for her father. She'd learned from Charles that he'd left the Castle and wondered if he'd gone to see Dylan. She considered going to the cabin herself, but she couldn't leave Cora. Her baby girl had endured enough travel this week. Right now, she lay sleeping in a cradle in a warm nursery.

Decorating the tree would pass the time until her father returned. If anyone could persuade Dylan to come, it was Lord Albert.

Brigitte smiled. "I'll fetch the ornaments. The tree's in the front room like always."

After a last look out the window, Maddie went down the hall to the fanciest room in the Castle. A massive blue spruce filled the window. As lovely as it was, the tree didn't match the one she'd shared with Dylan.

Brigitte delivered a chest of ornaments, then went to the

attic for more. Maddie opened the lid and nearly wept. Every bauble reminded her of her mother. She put several on the tree, then selected a silver bell. It pinged as she put it on a branch. Next she added a glass heart.

"Don't drop it," said a familiar voice. "Broken hearts don't always mend."

She whirled and saw Dylan. Instead of dungarees and a flannel shirt, he wore a frock coat, a white shirt and an ascot tie that made him look even more roguish than he looked in leather and denim. He'd shaved and combed back his hair, but his eyes belonged to the man who'd admired her in the firelight.

With the glass heart in her hand, Maddie thought of Dylan's heart and hers, joined and beating in perfect time. At last she could speak the truth. "I love you, Dylan. Yesterday I lied to protect you. Can you forgive me?"

"I already have." He smiled. "I love you, too."

Four strides brought him to her side. He lifted the heart from her fingers, put it high on the tree, then took her hands in his. He kissed her fingertips, then her cheeks and finally her lips. When she thought she'd faint, he broke the kiss and dropped to one knee.

"It's Christmas, Maddie. Do you remember what I asked?"

"I do."

She'd once knelt before Dylan in humility. By kneeling now, he honored *her*. Maddie touched his jaw. "I'd be proud to be your wife."

He stood and pulled her into his arms for a kiss that lasted until they heard a polite cough. Together they turned and saw Maddie's father.

He approached Dylan with an extended hand. "Welcome to the family, Dylan."

"Thank you, sir."

Lord Albert reached inside his coat pocket. He withdrew a red bow from Dylan's tree, fluffed it and placed it front and center on the spruce. For the first time, Maddie understood the depth of her father's love. She'd been completely forgiven.

Lord Albert cleared his throat. "I'd like to give you two a wedding present."

Maddie felt shy. "We have everything we need."

"Don't argue, young lady."

His tone made Maddie smile. Her father could still be difficult.

He turned to her future husband. "You have integrity, Dylan. In my eyes, you're already a wealthy man. Soon you'll add a wife and daughter to your treasures. If you'd be gracious enough to accept, I'd like to build a house for you and my daughter, one that's big enough for more grandchildren."

Maddie worried that Dylan's pride would bristle. Instead he squeezed her hand. "I'd be honored, sir."

"Then it's settled." Lord Albert turned to the tree and put on a gold ball.

Dylan added a snowflake.

Maddie opened a tiny box and found a white dove made of blown glass. She hung it on a high branch, then reached for Dylan's hand. Soon they'd marry and have a nest of their own. Dylan had given her a future full of hope and love. She couldn't think of a more wonderful gift for Christmas.

* * * * *

A BABY BLUE CHRISTMAS

Cheryl St.John

Dear Reader,

I enjoy writing Christmas stories. No matter what time of year, I can always get into the holiday spirit. Christmas is a time of hope, and that's always a timely premise for a love story. It wasn't difficult to come up with a Christmas baby theme, but I did complicate my task when I decided on two babies! Telling twins apart was probably more difficult on paper than in real life. I hope you enjoy Gabby and Turner's story of discovery and commitment.

I wish each and every one of you a Christmas filled with love. May the joy you share with others come back to you many times over, and may the spirit of Christmas live on in your heart all year.

Cheryl

*This Christmas story is lovingly dedicated
to a classy lady and wonderful friend,
Carolyn Davidson, who invited me to participate in
this anthology. Carolyn, I admire and appreciate you.*

Chapter One

There was always at least one rude traveler for the duration of a stage ride, and this time it was an overweight and cloyingly perfumed woman in a bright green traveling suit. She'd slept nearly the entire trip since Salt Lake City, snoring in snorts and whistles that punctuated every tedious, bone-jolting inch of the way.

Gabrielle couldn't complain. She was exceedingly grateful it was Snore Lady beside her and not Whiskey Breath. From his seat directly across from her, the man with the bristly, brown-stained beard gave her sidelong looks that made her skin crawl. The one time she'd accidentally met his gaze, he'd smiled. His teeth were brown and decayed. One of the rules of etiquette required that he offer to share the bottle, and he'd done so begrudgingly. Only one passenger had accepted his invitation. Gabby wouldn't have touched her lips to that bottle if she'd been dying of thirst.

Gabby had taken only short trips with the Wells Fargo Overland in the past. Heat and dust were definitely worse during summer months, so late November was marginally better for a hasty and ill-planned trip. Being packed in like sardines was an advantage this time of year and in this unfamiliar part of the country.

The coach hit another rut and her teeth jarred yet again. Snore Lady gasped in her sleep and then lapsed back into vigorous and prolonged inhaling and exhaling.

The driver struck the side of the coach to gain their attention, and a gentleman in a gray wool suit opened the flap to listen to his message. A flurry of snow filtered in and dusted the buffalo robes.

Gabby stared at the flakes glistening on the dark fur. She was from the Steptoe Valley in eastern Nevada and had only seen snow in stereoscope slides. Having been forewarned about winter, she'd bought a warmer coat at a layover in Utah.

"Last bend before Ruby Creek," the gentleman traveler conveyed.

After being delayed most of the afternoon for wheel repair, they were finally reaching her destination in darkness. Gabby prayed the hotel would check her in at this late hour. To hurry her travel, she'd brought only one small satchel. All she needed was a place to lay her head for the night.

She'd been following her cousin for weeks, traveling by any means available and inquiring from town to town. She had learned that Willow had come to Ruby Creek only a day or two ago. This was the closest Gabby had come to finding her since starting out a month ago. She didn't let herself think about what could happen if she was too late. Willow always landed on her feet, but the baby she was about to give birth to was defenseless.

With a final lurch, the stagecoach slowed, turned in a new direction and came to a halt with a screech of springs. Snore Lady roused. "Where are we?"

"Ruby Creek," Whiskey Breath replied.

The obese woman raised the flap and peered out into darkness. "It's late! Nearly bedtime."

Gabby exchanged a glance with the man in the gray suit.

The coach rocked as the driver and a passenger climbed down from the top seat. The door opened outward, and a bitterly cold draft and more fascinating white flakes swept inside.

"Ruby Creek!" the driver called. "Those goin' on will have to find a room for the night on Wells Fargo's tab. We're half a day behind, but we cain't go no farther in the dark. Too dangerous for the horses."

The reflection of the moon and stars on the snow lit the night with an odd, silent brightness. Gabby stepped down into the freezing, inch-thick blanket of white. Her thin-soled shoes made a squeaking sound with each step. Drat. She'd bought the coat, but hadn't thought of warmer footwear.

Eager to be on the road, Gabby had been the first passenger aboard the coach that morning; her bag was buried between crates and trunks. Waiting impatiently as the driver and a man from the freight line unloaded, she turned to cast a look at the town.

Four gas lamps burning at uneven intervals lit Ruby Creek's Main Street. She made out hanging signs for the hotel, a livery, a mercantile and a pawnshop. Other signs painted on windows were indistinguishable in the dark. Dissipating smoke curled from half a dozen chimneys.

Within minutes, the cold had seeped through her shoes and chilled her toes. Beneath her coat and dress, frigid air encased her legs. Within seconds numbness set into her thighs.

By the time the men uncovered her satchel, she was the only one left standing at the station. She took her bag with a weary thank-you and pointed herself toward the sign that read Friberger Hotel. The frosty layer that had settled on the boardwalk made her final steps treacherous. She slipped and slid and finally grabbed the doorknob as a lifeline. The door opened and she slid into a chilly lobby, relieved to be indoors at last.

"Full up!" a wiry man with hair standing in pewter-colored

tufts around his ears called to her as soon as she closed the door behind her.

Now what would she do? Her whole body ached, and she was so tired she could have fallen asleep standing there.

Carrying a No Vacancy sign, the proprietor limped toward the front door. The crown of his head was bald and pink. "Just let the very last room."

He hung the sign in the front window.

Gabby set down her bag. "I need a place to stay." Refusing to give in to desperation, she thought quickly. "I'll share a room with someone and pay the entire cost."

The man obviously wanted to get back to his bed, but he sighed and obliged her by plodding up the stairs. He was gone a long time, so Gabby looked around for a chair. There was only a long, narrow bench beside the door. She remained standing.

At last he returned. "Won't nobody share. The new arrivals ain't payin' their own way, so they don't care."

With her hopes in shreds, she closed her eyes against the discouragement crushing in. "What am I supposed to do?"

"Sometimes Miz Sims takes a boarder overnight. How long ya stayin'?"

She only wished she knew when she'd find Willow and be able to head home. When she'd made up her mind to do whatever she could to get to her in time, Gabby'd had no choice but to come on this trip alone. There was no other family besides her parents. Besides the fact that they'd given up on Willow, they had a business to run. "I'm not sure."

"Other'n that, maybe the reverend. No, come t' think of it, he's a widow man and don't take in no females on account of propriety. Sometimes Turner over at the livery lets a fella stay the night with his horse. 'Specially in poor weather. Ya might ask 'im."

Tired, hungry and supremely frustrated, Gabby picked up her bag and tugged her collar around her neck. She forced herself to thank the man politely. In the morning half the travelers would move on and, if she hadn't found Willow, she'd still be in need of a room by tomorrow night.

Long about three o'clock, Ruby Creek and the day closed in on Turner Price. He tended the horses as usual, did chores and ate simple meals, but come nightfall and the locked silence of the businesses along Main Street, he saddled his gelding and rode out, staying away from the hills and the creeks and finding clear, moonlit trails.

Often, no matter the weather, he dismounted and walked, his Mexican spurs jangling and silencing night creatures as he passed.

This snowy November night made for a bitterly cold ride and a colder walk, but he was accustomed to the elements and had dressed warm. With the stars spread overhead and the frigid air biting his lungs, it was easier to keep his thinking focused on the present.

Snow glistened in the moonlight and brightened the landscape. His horse didn't care what Turner said or didn't say, didn't have an opinion or feel pity. Comanche just plodded along at his side, offering an occasional snort or soft whinny. Comanche didn't demand Turner talk or feel or change, and Turner liked their relationship just fine.

Judging by the stars, it was time to head home. He mounted and urged the Appaloosa toward the livery. He reached the door, dismounted and rolled the wood sideways to lead the gelding inside.

One of the other horses nickered from its stall, and Comanche responded with a soft snort and a shake of his head.

Turner hung his coat and hat, unsaddled Comanche and picked up a blanket to dry him. "Hold on. I'll get you dry and warm and you can settle in for the night."

He was brushing the animal's withers when a sound arrested his attention. His hand fell still. A cat? A pair of cats?

Not impossible that felines had sought lodging in the warmth and safety of the building for the night. But why in tarnation were they making so much racket?

The sound registering more clearly, Turner rolled around additional possibilities. He was either losing his mind or…

Laying down the brush, he gave his horse a pat on the shoulder and grabbed a lantern that hung from a nail on a beam. His spurs jangled a beat as he strode down the long row of stalls.

The horses were agitated, stamping and moving restlessly. A bay he was boarding for a traveler pinned his ears back and rolled his eyes, a distinct reaction to a disturbing smell. More than Turner's late return was exciting these horses. Something—or someone—had disturbed them.

The high-pitched sound had grown louder and was definitely coming from the back of the barn. These end stalls were always the last ones rented.

Turner's gut clenched at the sound he now recognized as a baby's cry. And not just one slender, reedy trill—two.

The stall gate was unlatched, and he swung it outward to enter. Two impossibly tiny infants wrapped in brightly colored cloth lay on a mound of hay, their tiny fists flailing in the chill air.

For a full minute, he couldn't make sense of what his eyes told him. He stopped breathing to simply stare and absorb.

Just looking at them hurt.

He'd been gone only a couple of hours at the longest. How could this be? Hesitant, but unerringly drawn, he stepped forward and knelt. Their eyes were squinched shut, their faces red with agitation. Turner touched one finger to the nearest infant's matted, damp hair. Like newborn colts, these babies still bore evidence of their recent birth. They were mere minutes old, barely over an hour at the most.

An unsettling sense of trouble clawed at his nerves. Where was their mother? Unwilling to leave them alone, he glanced around as if their parent would appear or he'd find the answer in the wooden enclosure.

Both infants' stiffly held arms trembled as they screamed. They kicked at the cloth covering their legs until the material was pushed aside. Boys, both of them. Hungry, frightened, tiny boys.

Stricken by the unexpected sight and the tormenting effect on his mind and heart, Turner acted instinctively.

Shrugging out of his heavy flannel shirt, he knelt and—one at a time—gingerly placed the babies against the warm fabric and tucked the bulky garment around them. He folded back the excess, careful not to bury their faces.

He lifted the bundle gently and held it against his chest, his mind racing. Turning on his heel, he inspected the stall, the space leading to it and each of the surrounding pens. Twelve contained restless horses. Eight were empty.

None hid a woman.

He checked the tack room and even walked back to his quarters. The room held everything he needed for his sparse existence: a bed, a small coal burner, a table and one chair.

Warmth and motion soothed the babies. Nestled against each other in the soft bundle of his shirt and against his heart, they grew silent.

He studied their miniature features, and a torturous ache weighted his chest. He didn't want to look at them, didn't want to add to his misery, but he couldn't keep his gaze away. The child with the most hair had a hand splayed against his cheek, and his fingers were unbelievably tiny with perfect little nails. The other opened his heart-shaped mouth and turned his seeking face against the flannel. Turner couldn't catch his breath for seconds. His head swam.

Tiny and helpless and alone. The fact that someone had abandoned them chafed Turner's temper. The act was inconceivable.

And now what in blazes was he to do with them? They

wouldn't survive a day without milk and proper care. He stirred the ashes in the coal burner and added fuel to get the room warm.

The bell outside the entrance clanged once, then silenced abruptly as though someone had placed a hand on it. It was rare that anyone came for his mount or to leave a horse this late. He'd heard the stage earlier, though, and occasionally, if the small stable behind the freight station was full, the drivers boarded animals here overnight.

He placed the babies on his bed, making sure they were bundled snugly before he strode through the building. He hadn't tethered Comanche. His horse had wandered to the other side of the open area, and stood with his head lowered. "I'll get you bedded down in a shake, boy."

Two lanterns still burned on either side of the entrance. Turner opened the door and peered out.

A feminine form in a dark coat and fur-lined hat moved into the glow of the lantern. "Pardon me for disturbing you so late."

So here she was. He looked her over, suspicion sending a warning signal to his senses. Her hat was pulled low so that it almost hid her eyes, and her nose was red. "Who are you?"

"My name's Gabrielle Rawlins. I need a place to stay. The hotel's full, you see. The man there told me—"

"What were you tryin' to pull?"

"Pardon me?"

"Takin' off like that?"

She glanced over her shoulder and repeated, "Pardon me?"

"Looks like a mighty warm coat you're wearin' there."

"It's sufficient. What I need is—"

At that moment, a thin wail rose from the back of the building and echoed through to the front. It was immediately joined by a second.

The young woman's eyes widened and she stared at Turner.

"Had somewhere important to go?" he asked, narrowing his gaze.

"I told you, I—"

"Tell me anything you like, but what kind of woman leaves two spankin'-new babies alone in a horse stall?"

The squall was unmistakable. Her shocked gaze traveled past his shoulder. Eyes a rich tawny color like dark honey widened.

"Yeah, I found 'em. What did you think would happen?"

So quickly that he didn't have time to stop her, she slipped past him and ran toward the source of the pathetic cries.

Taking note of her bag sitting in the snow, he moved it inside before he bolted the door and followed.

Chapter Two

Gabby stepped into the room with her heart in her throat. She had eyes for nothing except the bundle on the bed. Holding her breath, she approached.

Two delicate, red-faced babies cried and flailed tiny fists. Gabby peeled away the flannel shirt in which they'd been carefully wrapped and stared. Her attention fell to the paisley scarf wrapped around their legs. Her heart stopped.

Willow's scarf.

Her cousin had given birth to not only one baby, but two. For weeks, her concern had been that she wouldn't get to Willow in time, that Willow's obsession with that outlaw would lead her to do something terrible to the baby.

Grief, panic and relief warred for prominence. Relief won, and gratitude made Gabby's throat tight. Two babies right here. Safe. Her greatest fear had been calmed. This was without a doubt her cousin's scarf. Her favorite. Gabby peeled it away.

These were her cousin's baby boys. Hot tears streaked Gabby's frozen cheeks.

"You aren't what I expected."

She didn't move her gaze, but dashed away the tears with her sleeve. "What?"

"I was wonderin' what kind of woman abandons her babies."

"I'm not... I mean..." She bit her lip. Heaven only knew where Willow was now. For weeks her cousin had been single-mindedly chasing her outlaw lover across the country without a care for her health or that of her baby. *Babies,* Gabby corrected herself. As if the fate of one hadn't been enough to fear, now there were two.

Obviously Willow hadn't grown up or thought of anyone other than herself. Knowing her, she was glad to be rid of the burden and well on her way to the next county.

They were incredibly tiny. Helpless.

Gabby's heart melted. Her pleading and entreaties had had no effect on their mother. She thought she'd done everything possible to convince Willow to stay where she'd be safe and looked after, but Willow had always run her race her own way. This had been no different.

Gabby hadn't been able to do anything about Willow, but she could do something about these two boys, boys with her blood running through their veins.

Finally, she turned to look at the stern-faced man. Suspicion and anger were evident in his scowl. If he believed the babies had been deserted, would he have her locked up? What would happen to them then? She couldn't let that happen. "I had something to do," she quickly improvised. "I only left for a few minutes and I came right back."

His black eyes held more than passing concern. She'd been around men all her life, and she knew what anger could make them capable of. A little quiver of anxiety shot up her spine, but she fought it down.

He speared her with that dark glare. "What in the hell could be more important than taking care of those babies? They were cold! Where's your family? Where's their father?"

She looked away, lest he see the lie in her eyes. She'd never been a good liar. She'd never had cause to lie. "He got killed on our way here."

"What were you doin' stumbling around in the dark? And what were you doin' in my livery?"

"I tried to explain that. There was no room at the hotel. The boardinghouse wouldn't even answer their door, and the proprietor at the hotel said you let travelers stay here sometimes."

He grunted. "Isn't that story a little overdone? I suppose next you'll be tellin' me you're a virgin."

Warmth edged up Gabby's neck to her cheeks. "There's no call to get insulting, Mr....Mr.... What's your name?"

"Turner. This is my livery you chose as your place to birth children."

"I can assure you it wasn't voluntary, Mr. Turner. I had no other choice. As I said, the—"

"Yeah, yeah, the hotel was full. Lucky for you I always leave the sliding door unbarred when I'm away in case there's an emergency."

Lucky indeed.

The babies were still squalling. Turner studied them and then eyed her. "Where'd you go that was so all-fired important?" His thoughts snagged on the stall where he'd found the babies. There had been no evidence of their birth. "The afterbirth could've been cleaned away later."

"I went for help, but I don't know the town or any of the businesses, so I came right back. I was only outside a few minutes."

She'd run back here without any indication of infirmity. He'd heard stories of Indian women giving birth along the trail without stopping, but experience told him Eastern women were frailer. Thinking now about the logistics, it was a miracle that this woman had given birth all alone. Even more amazing that she and the babies seemed perfectly fine.

An arrow of guilt pierced his conscience. She needed to lie down. She'd already done too much runnin' around. Maybe she was touched in the head, or the ordeal had made her a little crazy.

And now he was stuck with two babies and a deranged woman.

He reached up and tugged the hat from her head, and the sight he uncovered surprised him. Her wildly curling hair was an unusual shade of dark gold, with deeper tones running through the coils. It was gathered against her neck with a clasp of some sort, mussed but not damp with sweat. She didn't look like she'd been through much of an ordeal.

Her coat was clean, and she appeared to be wearing a deep-blue traveling suit underneath. He caught himself giving thought to her clothes. Could be events happened just the way she said, and he was making her stand here and defend herself. No denying when she looked at those babies, her heart was in her eyes.

"Give me your coat."

"What?"

"Give me your coat."

"Why?"

"So I can hang it and you can tend to those screamin' babies and get off your feet."

"Oh." She glanced down, managed to unbutton her winter garment and give it to him. "I'm fine."

"I don't know much about carin' for 'em, so tell me what's needed. I expect they should be cleaned up. Even mares do that."

Gabby searched his eyes for a moment. There was something dark and troublesome in their depths, something that touched her when she should be thinking only of her task. She looked away. "Well. Maybe warm water to clean them off first? I suppose I'll need something for nappies."

"I brought your bag inside," he said, suggesting she had come prepared.

"There's nothing useful in my bag. I traveled light."

He cast another suspicious glance over her. "Travelin' in your condition and you didn't have anything ready?"

"I thought I'd have more time."

Without hiding his disapproval, he went into motion, adjusting the vents on the coal heater to further warm the room. He set an enamel basin on top of the scarred table and went for water, which he poured into a kettle and placed on the heater.

"I can go get the doc for you," he said.

"What for?"

"Well…" He looked at her and then away. "Don't womenfolk need a doctor when they have a baby?"

"I don't want a doctor, thank you."

"He could look at the babies."

Concern etched her brow and she leaned over them. "What's wrong with them?"

"From the sound of them, nothing."

"Maybe in a few days," she suggested. "Not right now."

He held up a palm. "Okay." Taking a stack of flannel shirts from a bureau drawer, he produced a folding knife from his trouser pocket and sliced the shirts into pieces. "Use one of these for a washrag," he said, handing her a sleeve.

She took it.

When she reached tentatively and picked up the first baby, he wrapped the other in the scarf and nestled it in the crook of his arm. It stopped crying immediately.

The young woman held the other as though terrified to drop or drown him. He continued his bleating wail the whole time she poured water over his head, dried his hair, then immersed his body in the water and rinsed him clean.

She placed the infant on a blanket on the bed and haphazardly tied a folded piece of flannel shirt around his bottom.

"I'll take the clean one," he offered, and they made an exchange. His hand brushed hers in that brief trade, and the contact brought her surprised gaze to his face. She quickly looked away and continued her task.

The freshly washed baby quieted in his arms, but the other

began a tremulous caterwaul as she sponged water over his scalp.

"What're you gonna name 'em?"

She looked over at him.

"What names are you givin' these boys?"

"I—I don't know," she stuttered. "I hadn't thought about it."

His questions were unrelenting, but the situation had him off balance and he liked stability. "You had three-quarters of a year to think about it, and you didn't come up with any names?"

She continued her chore. "That wasn't very smart, was it?"

He shook his head and perched on a wooden chair. "What's their pa's name?"

"They won't be named after him," she said too quickly.

He cocked a brow. "Somethin' like Percy or Carol?"

"Yes, that's it. His name is unsuitable."

"What's your pa's name?"

She barely paused in rinsing the tiny body. "Howard."

"Don't seem quite fittin' for a mite, does it?"

She carried the baby to the bed, dried and then awkwardly dressed him in the same manner as the first. "No, it doesn't."

"Samson is a good, strong name. So is Elijah."

With her next glance, her tawny eyes filled with skepticism.

"Jack, too. Jack's kind of plain, but it's a strong name."

"Jack's a good name," she agreed. "My grandfather's name was Marcus."

"Solid," he said with a nod.

"This is Marcus." She wrapped the infant in an extra shirt.

"I'll bunk down in a clean stall tonight." He laid down the baby and gathered a few things. He looked from one infant to the other, wondering why he should be so concerned, but unable to hold back. "A mare feeds two foals at once. What're you gonna do?"

Her cheeks turned bright pink. None of his damn business— except she was here in his place with nowhere else to go.

"I'll need extra milk for them." She was silent for a moment and finally said, "I'm supposed to drink milk, too. Do you have any?"

He started to ask another question, but caught himself. "Miz Friberger has a couple o' cows in a shed just back of the hotel. I'll slip over and fill a pail."

"I don't need a whole pail," she clarified. "Half. And a couple of jars to store it in if you can find any."

"I'll bring your bag." He stopped and his suspicions caught up with him. "Where did you leave it when you came inside the first time?"

She looked away. "I hid it under a wagon in the alley next door and came looking for a dry place."

The bell out front clanged a dozen times in succession. Wells Fargo needed to put up their horses. His barn would be full tonight. He donned his coat and settled his hat on his head before leaving her alone with the now-sleeping babies.

Another hour had passed by the time he'd warmed more water, stuffed his things into a saddlebag and shown her how he'd seen motherless pups fed. She'd fed the babies using a clean cloth soaked in milk. He obviously thought she was the most inept and stupid woman he'd ever met. She couldn't really deny it. Chasing after Willow had been a crazy plan— even her father had urged her not to go—but knowing her fanatical cousin was about to bring a baby into the world without a care for its well-being, she'd had no choice.

Mr. Turner was big and blustery, his expressions fierce, but his actions had been gentle. His concern for the newborns was evident, an anxiety they shared, and she couldn't help warming toward a man who'd acted so responsibly…kindly, even. His resentment toward her was blatant, but he'd helped her anyway, providing shelter and food she so desperately needed.

And she'd lied. Every word of explanation that had come

out of her mouth had been a lie. Every time she thought of the story she'd told, a sick regret washed over her.

She'd had no choice. He'd been so angry thinking the babies had been deserted. If he'd believed the twins had been abandoned, he'd have taken action, she was sure of it. At least now he only thought she was an idiot.

Icy snow blew against the glass panes of the single window in the room where she lay, but their rescuer had tacked yet another of his seemingly endless supply of flannel shirts around the frame so that not a single draft reached past the glow of the coal burner to where she and Jack and Marcus lay snug and sound. The sturdy building and the man who owned it were their fortress against the world and its elements.

Looking at the tiny, sleeping boys, fear lodged in her heart and set it to thumping erratically. She didn't know the first thing about taking care of babies. Mr. Turner had suggested she bathe them: he'd provided sheets and blankets, shown her how to feed them, and all she'd done was stumble along feeling foolish and inadequate. Not to mention terrified.

They were so tiny and helpless. Caring for them wasn't instinctive, as he seemed to expect. She was alone with two brand-new human beings whose lives depended solely on her. What was going to become of them? Anger at her cousin welled up and spilled over in hot tears.

Willow had come to live with Gabby and her parents when Gabby had been eight. Willow had been ten that year, and her father had been killed in a mine cave-in and her mother had taken up with a man who didn't want a kid underfoot.

Looking back, Willow had always been self-centered and focused on things that benefited her above anyone else. And because of her situation, Gabby had always given in to her. When it came to a decision of who got which color of fabric for their school dress or who handled the most unpleasant chores, Gabby had acquiesced. By having both of her parents alive and having grown up in the same town where she'd been born, she felt more fortunate than Willow.

At some point over the years, Willow's selfish behavior had gotten out of hand. When it came to something she wanted to do, Willow never considered anyone else, or the price tag. She tossed caution off a cliff and went to any measure to get her way.

They'd been twelve and fourteen the first time Willow had set her sights on a boy and barreled ahead, consequences be damned. Even Howard's shotgun hadn't resolved anything. After the initial threat, the boy and his parents had moved out of town, never to be heard from again.

Afterward Willow was slightly more discreet. Gabby's father had threatened to cut her off from the things she valued most: her clothing allowance and spending money. The warning had worked.

Until Drum Jennings rode into town.

Though she wasn't cold, Gabby shivered. Just his name was enough to make her skin crawl. Willow thought the sun and the moon rose and set on the outlaw's shoulders. From the first time he'd eaten in Howard's saloon and she'd waited on him, Willow had closed out common sense, tossed away restraint and ignored the rest of the rational world.

Gabby had known all along that Willow was secretly seeing him. The cousins shared a room. Every time Drum and his robber gang passed through, Willow left by way of the window and the porch roof.

She'd disappeared with him once, returning three weeks later in need of a bath and a delousing. Howard had drawn a line and told her she was on her own if she was taking up with the likes of that outlaw.

Willow's packing took less than an hour. She rented a room at the hotel, and when Gabby questioned how she was paying for it, Willow assured Gabby it was none of her business.

Willow was gone longer the next time. Nearly six months.

Gabby had worried, of course, but without the constant chaos, she and her parents had settled into an easy routine.

Eventually Willow had shown up at their door begging for a place to stay. Howard let her back in. That night, while preparing for bed, Gabby had recognized Willow's condition. Drum Jennings had dumped her when her pregnancy inconvenienced his life on the run.

Willow wasn't repentant or ashamed. She was despondent. Obsessed. Gabby could barely get her to eat. Finally, after weeks of coaxing, she was able to draw her out of bed and encourage her to eat three meals a day. Soon after she'd been doing a little light work in the kitchen.

Resuming work at the saloon had been a mistake. Only a few weeks later one of Drum's hooligans had shown up. When Willow had spotted him, she planned to follow him back to find the man she wanted.

Gabby figured out her cousin's plan too late. By the time she'd realized what had happened, Willow was gone.

The baby's birth had been only weeks away, and Gabby had been driven to do whatever she could to save a helpless child endangered by the web of its mother's selfishness. Gabby had never doubted for a moment that Willow would do whatever it took to get in Drum's good graces again. Even if it meant abandoning—or harming—the baby neither of them wanted. Not knowing where and when that would happen had been Gabby's greatest fear.

She was tired of coming to Willow's rescue, but now there was more at stake. More than just her self-indulgent cousin.

Safe in the warm room and enjoying the softness of the stranger's bed, she closed her eyes. It smelled like a man's room, like a man's bed. Not unpleasant by any means, but like leather and wood and hay. If safety had a scent, this was it.

The fact that Willow had given birth and left the babies here, in a place where they could be found and rescued, brought a rush of gratitude. Gabby was indebted to the man who'd taken her in out of the cold. A man with something deep and tormenting behind his dark eyes.

A man she knew only as Mr. Turner.

Chapter Three

Turner opened the rolling door at the rear of the livery and set half a dozen horses loose in the corral. They would have the snow trampled by noon. He turned back for Chick Spurling's barn-sour mare and led her out with a little more coaxing. She didn't like to leave the barn no matter the weather. "Look there, Debbie, the sun's full in the sky and nary a cloud in sight. It's a fine mornin' to greet the world."

With a final slap on her rump, he watched the bay plod away, her breath billowing white gusts into the morning air.

Closing the door, he set to work shoveling the stalls and spreading fresh hay.

Sounds from his quarters told him his uninvited guests were awake. He cleaned his boots on a pile of hay and tapped on the door.

"Need anything in there?"

The door opened.

Dressed in a plain, dark blue skirt and white, pinstriped shirtwaist, the woman from the night before stepped back for him to enter. A crease had formed between her brows, and she looked tired. "I've been trying to figure out what I'll do."

Turner couldn't help noticing her surprisingly slim shape in her plain clothing. He'd only known a few women who'd had babies, and they'd worn loose clothing for months afterward. But then she'd only brought one bag.

She had gathered her hair into a cascade of ringlets on the back of her head. The woman had the prettiest hair he'd ever seen. "What do you want to do?"

"Well…" She paused as though she didn't want to say more. "I need to get them some clothing." She cast him a curious glance. "Do they sell ready-made clothing for babies?"

Again he couldn't help wondering how she'd been so unprepared, how she wouldn't know the answer to her own question. "Catalog orders take a couple weeks. Don't think the mercantile has anything like that made up. Most women make their own, I suppose."

Thank God she didn't ask how *he* knew.

"And I can't keep them here. Not in your barn." She glanced around, then back at him. "Not that it isn't a very nice barn, because it is. We were quite warm and comfortable last night, thank you. I've thought about taking a room at the hotel."

"What're you gonna do, wrap them in a shirt and carry them out in the cold to see if there's a room? There hasn't been a stage out this morning, so I'm guessin' there aren't any empty rooms, either."

"How do you know the stage hasn't gone on?"

He jerked a thumb over his shoulder. "Horses are all still here. Eatin' my hay, earnin' me another six dollars."

Her face crumpled in disappointment, and she caught the edge of her lip with her teeth. The sight made him uncomfortable. "They were awake every hour all night, one crying while I fed the other. I don't suppose the hotel guests would appreciate having their sleep interrupted anyway."

"You plannin' on taking a stage somewhere?" he asked.

She only looked at him and blinked.

"Where's home?" he asked.

She shook her head. "Nevada. They're too small. The trip is

difficult enough for a woman, let alone a woman with two infants."

"What're you gonna do?"

She put her hands on her hips, and the motion outlined her breasts under her clothing. Disturbed that he'd noticed, he looked away. She was a widow. A new mother—even if she didn't look like one.

"Even if they didn't cry all night—and most likely they will—can you afford to stay at the hotel?"

"Not indefinitely," she replied. "I'll think of something."

"Where were you and your husband headed?"

A pained look came over her face. She closed her eyes and drew a breath before opening them again. She said nothing.

"You said he was killed, is that right?"

"I said that, yes."

"How were you traveling? You didn't bring horses."

"I appreciate your help, Mr. Turner, but I'm uncomfortable with all your questions."

He looked her over, from her bright, tawny eyes and wild curls to the fancy stitching on her collar. She wore a pearl-encrusted brooch at her throat. She was tired. She'd just been through harrowing experiences one on top of the other. "Sit tight. I'll go get breakfast."

She lifted a brow in surprise, but her posture relaxed. "Thank you."

He switched the horses that he'd let into the corral and led others out before saddling his, putting on his coat and hat and riding into the morning cold. She was right. It wasn't fittin' to keep those tiny babies naked and in the back of a stable, and now he had to do something about it. Much as he didn't like it, they had become his problem.

Minutes later he sat atop Comanche, staring at a two-story house painted pale green, with white porch banisters and gingerbread trim. Unlike all the others nearby, the walkway had not been shoveled and the curtains were still closed. No smoke curled from the brick chimney. It was a house filled with haunting memories. A house that stirred deeply buried feelings that stabbed him with helplessness, so he quickly accomplished what he'd come to do.

Tying Comanche at the gate, Turner plodded through the snow and let himself in with a key. He removed his wet boots, then, looking straight ahead, climbed the stairs and entered a room.

He found a cloth bag and opened a bureau drawer. The scent of sachet powder drifted to his unaccustomed nose, evoking painful images he didn't want to remember. He set his mind on finishing his tasks and hurried from the house.

At the Wells Fargo station he learned that snow was still falling to the north. The stage had been delayed yet again. He ran a couple more quick errands before returning to the livery with his arms full.

He knocked on his own door.

Gabrielle Rawlins opened it.

"No rooms anyhow," he told her.

Her expression showed her disappointment. "What am I going to do?"

He set a crate holding food and milk on the table. Mustering words and fortitude, he looked at her. "I have a place you can stay."

Her wary gaze touched the bed, the table and the row of brass hooks by the door.

"Not here," he clarified. "I mean I have a house."

Her eyes widened. "Oh?" Then, as though she'd thought of the possibilities, she asked, "A home you share with a wife? Or parents?"

"Just a house. Empty."

"But you stay here."

He set out two plates of eggs and sausage he'd bought at the café. "We'll eat, then I'll take you there. You can stay as long as you want. At least till you figure out what you're gonna do."

One of the babies fussed. Brow creasing, she turned to where the flannel-wrapped twins lay on the bed.

Turner opened a cloth bag he'd set aside and showed her the contents. "Things to put on 'em. Nappies'n such."

Gabrielle took out the tiny garments, a look of wonder crossing her face. Then curiosity. "Where'd you get these?"

"Someone didn't need 'em anymore." He found two forks and upended the crate to use for another seat at the table. Leaving the chair for her, he sat. "Mind if I eat? I need to move you and get to work."

"Go ahead. I'll join you in a minute."

Gabby had removed his shirt from the window that morning, and now bright sun reflecting off snow lit the little room. Today she had a good view of the man.

He was big, but not clumsy, appearing at home though the room was too small for him. Seeing him perched on the crate would have been comical had she dared let herself dwell on the sight. She would guess his nose had been broken a couple of times, but the imperfection didn't take away from the clean lines and rugged symmetry of his face. He had a stubborn jaw that had seen a razor recently, and his eyes weren't really black or even dark brown now that she saw them with the sun streaming through the windowpanes. They were a deep, troubled blue, and his brows and lashes were black as a raven's wing.

She made herself look away, and pinned one of the clean, folded squares of cloth on Marcus, then wrapped him in a tiny white gown with delicate stitching and embroidery. She could have sworn it had never been worn or laundered. Carrying him in the crook of her arm, she took the chair.

Turner uncovered a plate of bacon and eggs and pushed the aromatic food toward her.

Gabby picked up the fork and ate her breakfast. She hadn't eaten since noon the day before, but she forced herself to take small bites and chew well. "I can repay you," she said once she'd finished. "For the food and milk and even for letting me use your house."

"No need," he answered. "It's not of any use empty."

He didn't seem inclined to talk anymore and that was fine with her. She didn't need him asking more questions she had to lie to answer. He didn't deserve deception in return for kindness.

Finding Willow before she had the baby and perhaps abandoned it—or worse—had been Gabby's goal all along. She hadn't planned on this development. She'd been so focused on reaching Willow that she hadn't thought out what she'd do or say if she caught up. Had she imagined her cousin would suddenly listen to her pleas, turn over a new leaf and return to Nevada a loving mother?

She'd always known Willow was too selfish, had always suspected she herself might be the only one willing to take care of Willow's baby. *Why couldn't you have once thought about someone besides yourself?* she thought. *I can't just abandon these babies like you did, and I can't take care of them alone.*

Sadly, she realized that chasing Willow had been impulsive, but instinctive. Her plan seemed idealistic now that she was faced with the harsh facts. What a fool she'd been. Even now she fought a nagging determination to go after the selfish woman and convince her to go home even though it was impossible. Gabby couldn't take two newborns on a stagecoach, nor go traipsing around the country without guarantee of ever finding their mother.

At this point she couldn't even get them back to Nevada, and if she could, what would be the point? There was no one there with any ties to them except Gabby's parents, and they wouldn't be able to take them. Besides, everyone in Steptoe Valley knew about Willow and Drum Jennings. What kind of life would that make for two young boys?

This dilemma had grown to greater proportions. What was she going to do now?

* * *

A black buggy sat at the ready in front of the livery, and Turner carried the babies toward it while she minced her way along the shoveled path and climbed up to the seat. He raised the wrapped bundle for her to take before perching beside her, lifting the reins and clucking to the horse.

The back had been packed with crates and burlap bags, in which, she assumed, were food and provisions she'd need at the house.

It was a brief ride along brick streets sparsely lined with houses. Some had carriage houses; most were constructed with wide porches. Some had pillars, others iron gates. Turner's home was two handsome stories with a wrapping porch and a thin stream of smoke curling from the brick chimney.

He helped her down and steadied her as she made her way to the steps. The entrance was stark now, but Gabby pictured the porch in the summer, with bushes in bloom at either end and cushioned chairs situated in the shade. She really was a dreamer. Turner opened the door and ushered her inside.

"I'll show you to your room," he said, automatically removing his boots on the wooden jack without bending down. Noticing the smooth, waxed wood floors, Gabby gestured for him to take the babies.

"Keep your shoes on. Your feet will get cold. Here." He knelt and used his neck scarf to dry her shoes. Straightening, he took the babies in one arm and held her elbow with his other hand. "Up the stairs."

She figured he was deferring to the physical state he believed she was in having just delivered two babies, so she took her time.

"This one." He stopped outside a doorway and waited.

Gabby entered the average-size room. A coal heater emitted enough warmth to take the chill away. So he had planned on her agreeing to come here? She walked to a double window and moved a lace curtain aside to observe the side yard and the distance to the nearest neighbors down the way.

He moved behind her and she turned as he laid the babies in a white iron cradle with elaborate scrolled legs that raised the bed three feet from the floor. He had lined it with a blue-and-white embroidered quilt.

"You just happened to have a cradle, too?"

"In the attic."

He made a few more trips, carrying the supplies for the baby. "The rest of the things go in the kitchen," he told her. "Want to see the stove? I'll bring in more firewood before I leave."

She followed him down the stairs and to the back of the house into a long kitchen. Two upholstered chairs draped with cloths sat by a brick fireplace at one end.

"Take the covers off any of the furniture you want to use," he told her. "The dishes in the cupboards are probably dusty."

"I can wash them."

"Make a list." He glanced around. "Anything else you need. I'll get it this evening."

Gabby was still absorbing the knowledge that he owned a perfectly good house he didn't use and the fact that he had opened it up to her. "Why are you doing this?"

He didn't meet her eyes. She admired the line of his jaw and the way his hair curled over his collar. "Like you said, you couldn't keep the babies in the livery."

"But why let us use your home? Why go out of your way at all? Why trust me here with all your things? I could steal you blind and disappear."

He turned his head, drilling her with a vivid blue gaze. The look sent a surprised quiver to her belly. "You plannin' to steal from me?" he asked.

Warmth flooded her cheeks. "I don't know why, but I have the feeling you'd give me anything I wanted if I asked."

His expression turned to a frown. He strode in his stocking

feet to the fireplace, where he turned the brass handle to open the flue. He knelt on the hearth and stuck his head into the opening, twisting to gaze upward.

By the time he'd finished his inspection and sat up again, Gabby had moved in front of him. He looked at her in surprise.

"What's your first name?" she asked, wondering now. Here she was, staying in his home and accepting his help, while she didn't know anything about him.

"Turner," he replied.

"I thought that was your last name."

"Last name's Price."

She blinked, feeling silly for calling him Mr. Turner until now. "Well…thank you. You don't have to worry about me stealing from you."

He stood and moved away, brushing his hands together without speaking. Within minutes, she heard the front door open and close. She hurried to the entrance and turned the lock.

In the dining room, she moved the drape aside and watched the buggy disappear down the street. The fabric smelled like dust. She released it and glanced around the room. The table was covered with a white drape, as were what she assumed were a sideboard and a china cabinet. A framed painting of a homestead with a house and barn and various outbuildings hung by a wire from the crown molding.

Gabby returned to the babies, who were now waking, and unpacked the crates Turner had placed inside the door.

He had miraculously supplied a few small, narrow-necked bottles with maroon-colored rubber nipples, and she nearly wept when she saw them. Feeding two babies by soaking fabric had been frustrating for all of them.

She padded an empty crate with a blanket and carried it to the kitchen, where she kindled the stove, washed the bottles and heated the milk. By the time it was ready, Marcus was hollering wholeheartedly and Jack was just joining the chorus.

She uncovered both upholstered chairs and found a comfortable position to hold Jack on her lap and Marcus in her arm, and feed them at the same time. She would have to get them on a schedule so that they ate separately.

What was she thinking? A sick feeling washed over her, ebbing from the pit of her belly. She couldn't stay here indefinitely. She didn't even know Turner Price. What little she did know stabbed her with guilt. He had taken her and the babies in and was generously providing for them on the basis of her lies. Being afloat on the whim of his generosity and her deceit was a sickening feeling.

She had to make a decision, and make it soon.

Chapter Four

～～～

Two days later Gabby had realized there were no good choices, only realistic and heartbreaking ones. She hadn't actually had a spare moment to think clearly when she wasn't exhausted. At night she slept in fitful breaks spanning only one or two hours between feedings. No matter the hour, she no more than got one baby to sleep before the other was screaming for milk and a dry nappy. She'd barely taken time to bathe and eat. Her clothing was rumpled, and she smelled like curdled milk.

Turner came morning and evening to bring fresh milk, fill the wood bin and pump water. That day he caught her by surprise at noon. He carried a covered basket into the kitchen and ducked under the line of drying nappies she'd strung between the stovepipe and the pantry door.

"I brought dinner," he told her, his gaze taking in her appearance.

Gabby reached up and tucked stray tendrils of hair into the chignon, which had fallen loose hours ago. She couldn't remember if she'd looked in the mirror that morning. "Don't you have to work?"

"It's Sunday. I have a hired man who takes care of the horses after church."

"Oh. For other people returning horses after church, or after you go to church?"

He removed his coat, revealing dark trousers, a white shirt that made his shoulders look broader than ever and a string tie. After rolling back his sleeves, he filled the coffeepot with water and measured grounds. "Both."

Self-consciously, Gabby studied him in his Sunday clothes, imagining him in his church, worshipping with all the respectable citizens. Her deception pressed in harder. Her family might not be churchgoers, but she'd been raised to know the difference between right and wrong.

He gestured to a chair. She smoothed her wrinkled skirt under her and sat. He poured them each a glass of milk and placed silverware beside their plates, then took the seat across from her.

He'd selected a pot roast with potatoes and carrots, and when he uncovered the plates and the savory aroma of beef wafted upward, her stomach growled. Gabby picked up her fork. She had just raised the first bite to her mouth when one of the babies fretted in their crate near the stove. Her heart sank, and she prepared to get up.

"Stay put," he told her.

She watched as he towered over the makeshift cradle, observing the babies for a moment. He plucked up Jack, tucked his blanket tightly around his legs and carried him back to the table.

He sat with the baby against his chest, his enormous hand and hair-dusted wrist supporting the baby from bottom to head. Jack's fair head was a contrast to Turner's dark jaw and the ebony hair that reached his collar.

Gabby had become increasingly curious as to why he had a fully furnished home and yet slept in that narrow room behind the livery. There was evidence that a family had lived here in the past, and everything she noticed led her to believe a woman had been one of the occupants. The house's furnishings reflected a woman's taste. Gabby often looked at objects and wondered about their owner. "Why don't you live here?"

He rested his fork on the edge of his plate, but didn't raise his gaze from the utensil.

Seconds ticked by. She'd crossed a line.

"Too big for just one," he said finally.

"Was it your parents' home?"

"I barely remember my folks."

"I'm sorry. Did your grandparents raise you?"

"No." He picked up his fork and finished eating. When his plate was empty, he leaned to uncover a pie tin holding two enormous slices of apple pie.

"I'll have to save mine for later," she told him. "I couldn't eat another bite. That was delicious."

She stood and carried the plates to the enamel dishpan, then set about preparing a bottle of milk.

"I haven't told anyone that you're here," he said, adjusting Jack in the crook of his arm. He touched a finger to the baby's delicate ear as he spoke. "But neighbors can see the lights and the smoke from the chimney. One of 'em asked if I was stayin' in the house."

She simply looked at him.

"I told 'em I had a guest."

She nodded, uncomfortable with the secrecy.

"Are you ready for the doctor to call on the babies…or on you?"

She took Jack from him and sat in one of the upholstered chairs to feed him. "Do you think there's a need?"

"Don't know." He poured hot water into the dishpan. "Thought it might give you comfort."

"I suppose he could check on Marcus and Jack. To make sure they're eating enough and healthy. Who will you say I am?"

"A widow who was passin' through and needed a place to stay. What else would I say?"

She shook her head again. She was exhausted and probably wasn't thinking clearly. "I don't know."

He washed and dried the plates so he could return them to the café. "Heard the trail for the stage is clear."

Jack had satisfied his initial hunger, slowed his nursing and was now making little sounds of contentment while his eyes drifted shut.

She could leave.

She couldn't go after Willow *and* take care of the boys, too. That was plain. After days and nights of bone-weary thinking, she'd realized she didn't want to go after her cousin. Willow didn't care about these babies, and even if Gabby did find her, Willow would never take care of them like they deserved. Gabby swallowed hard.

She had narrowed her choices down to reality.

Turner moved to the fireplace, where he coaxed the flames with a poker and added a log. "I s'pose you'll be movin' on."

It wasn't really a question. Her heart thumped erratically.

Gabby rested Jack on her shoulder and patted his back until he burped, then she wiped his chin and placed him in the crate beside his twin, who was still sleeping peacefully.

She rinsed the bottle, dried her hands and turned toward Turner. Her stomach lurched at the thought of exposing her lies, but she couldn't continue to mislead him. She still needed his help to find the best life possible for those two boys, and she wanted to ask for it with dignity. "I haven't been truthful with you, Mr. Price."

He turned to face her.

She took several steps toward him. "I've lied since the very first night I got here. I was scared and desperate. It's no excuse, I know. I just had nowhere to turn, and you were kind."

"Never were married, were you?"

That question stopped her. "No. I've never been married."

"Did the babies' father run off on you?"

She couldn't think of anything to say. Their father was long gone, that was for sure.

After a lengthy silence, he said, "I got no respect for a man like that." His expression darkened. "So you were fishin' for a pa for your baby?"

"No. Nothing like that. Please. Just let me tell you."

He eased onto the upholstered chair, resting a hand on each arm. "Go ahead."

She couldn't sit. Or catch her breath. She clasped her hands together and walked to the window and back, inhaling deeply and placing a hand on her midriff. "Those aren't my babies."

His eyebrows climbed his forehead, but he held his tongue.

"I was chasing after my cousin, afraid she would give birth and abandon them—which she did. I followed her all the way from Nevada, never quite catching up, because she'd taken up with Drum Jennings. He's wanted for stage robberies, but—"

"I know who Drum Jennings is."

"But his life of crime makes no difference to her." The whole story came rushing out now. "She found herself in the family way and just kept chasing after him.

"My pa told me to let her go, but I couldn't. I couldn't stand not knowing what would happen when she had the baby on the run, whether she'd leave it… Or maybe Drum… Maybe he would have…" She shook her head to dispel nightmarish thoughts. "I don't know, I just knew the baby wasn't safe.

"So when I came here the other night and you'd found two of them and they were safe, I was so grateful. I thought you'd turn them over to the law if you knew what had really happened, and I was afraid."

She finally stopped talking and looked at him. He was absorbing the information with a line between his black brows. She already knew he wouldn't hurt her, but she hated disappointing him. She prepared for his anger and the results.

"I'm sorry I lied to you," she said pleadingly. "Please forgive me."

His jaw worked for a moment.

Gabby's heart raced. Would he call the law on her? What would they do?

"I reckon you did what you thought you had to in order to keep 'em safe," he said at last.

The fire crackled in the grate while she took in his words. Just like that? she thought. He could dismiss her betrayal so easily? She looked at him as if he were a stick of dynamite in which the fuse had fizzled out, but which still wasn't safe to approach. "You're not angry?"

"I'm a trifle aggravated about bein' lied to. But you didn't know me from Adam, so I reckon you thought you had to. You've come clean now."

She sat down across from him in a rush of relief.

"Makes sense, o' course. You bein' so slight and not filled out. All that milk you were supposedly drinkin'."

She gave him a sheepish smile.

"Some mares don't have milk for their foals, so I thought there was a problem like that."

She felt herself blush. "I'm sorry."

He truly was the kindest man she'd ever met. But then she'd only met the sort who ate and drank in saloons and not the type who went to church on Sunday mornings.

Her conscience won out. "Here's the whole truth about me. My father owns a saloon. My mother was a dance-hall girl before they got married. Willow and I work in the kitchen, cooking, washing dishes and glasses and serving meals. Well, we did until she ran off. Then it was just me. Now…I suppose my father has hired help to replace me."

"No shame in honest work," he told her. Then after a moment he added, "You talk like you're educated."

"We always went to school," she answered with a shrug. "We suffered ridicule and disapproval from teachers and students alike. Willow hated every minute of it and used every excuse to quit. Me, I wanted to be as good or better than those who held themselves in such high regard, so I endured their contempt and continued studying after grammar school. Read everything I could get my hands on."

He simply nodded, as though digesting her words.

"I worked hard to be accepted and respected," she added. "But I never was. Not in Steptoe Valley. Not as the daughter of the saloon keeper." She hadn't meant for her story to be so revealing, but emotion had crept into her words. She sighed before saying, "I'll be going back."

He met her eyes.

"But…" She had rocked the babies for hours while making this decision, knowing it was best, and hating that there was no other way. She hadn't known a person could fall in love with tiny little human beings so quickly. The growing attachment was making everything more difficult now. "I need you to help me do one last thing before I do."

"What's that?"

"I—" Her throat tightened and she fought the sting of tears. "I can't take care of two babies. Even here in your lovely home with all I need, I-I'm inadequate. They deserve better than me, better than what I can do for them and give them. The trip to Nevada would be too difficult, and even there…well, they'd grow up to work in the saloon."

"Would that be so bad?"

"Everyone in town knows about Willow and Drum. Jack and Marcus would grow up with people knowing they were an outlaw's sons." As difficult as it was to say the next words, she stopped and pushed them past the lump in her throat. "I need to find an agency that will find them homes." Bitter tears burned her eyes. "They'll be better off with parents who want them, respectable people to—"

"No." The syllable he bit out was harsh and unrelenting.

She dashed away tears with an open palm. "What do you mean, no?"

"I will not help you sentence two innocent babies to a life like that."

"I'm only thinking of what's best for them."

He got up and thrust his fingers into his coal-black hair, a muscle in his jaw jumping. "No." Turner slashed the air with a palm. "That's final."

His body was tense with anger now. Nothing had enraged him until her plan, and this reaction was confusing her. She experienced a trickle of fear that doused her confidence. She'd already asked enough of him. "Of course. I can go talk to the sheriff. I'm sure he'll be able to put me in touch with—"

"No," he said again, this time louder. He turned back and pinned her with a steely blue glare. "I won't let you send those babies off to a life of neglect and work and unfair punishment. They wouldn't get to be together. Do you care about that? They'd probably be kept in a foundling home until they're old enough to be of use to someone. Then they'd be worked sunup to sundown without proper food or clothes."

"You don't have to paint such a bleak picture."

"It's the facts, lady. I barely remember my folks. But I remember every foster home I ever lived in. I remember the spoiled kids that never lifted a finger while I hayed and milked and plowed and picked corn. I remember bein' punished by goin' without food, and I remember bein' too small to defend myself when an angry farmer swung a fist or used his boot-strap."

Gabby flinched.

"All I knew was work and hate. Bein' hungry. Plannin' the day I could run away." He speared her with that fiercely determined stare. "I won't let you do that to those boys."

The images he'd created were too much to bear. It was no wonder he objected to her plan. Tears choked Gabby's next words. "I'm sure it's not always like that. There must be good people who truly want children."

"Probably are," he told her. "And your boys have about as much chance of findin' 'em as they do strikin' gold in my dooryard." He walked to a cabinet and took out a revolver.

Gabby's heart lurched. What was he going to do? She jumped to her feet.

He took four bullets from a wooden box and loaded them into the chambers, spun the cylinder, walked toward her and extended the butt.

"There are two empty chambers in there. A chance the gun won't fire when you pull the trigger. Go ahead. Aim it at me. Fire and hope for the best."

Gabby stepped back and shoved her hands behind her back. "You're crazy!"

"I'm not crazy. You're talkin' about taking a chance on those children's lives, a chance that they'll get placed in decent homes. I know better. I know the way it really is."

"Please. Put the gun away."

He tipped the cylinder and let the bullets fall into his palm. "I was makin' a point."

"I got your point." Angrily, she brushed a tear from her cheek.

"Didn't mean t' scare ya."

"I'm already scared!" She hadn't meant to say it so vehemently. She couldn't bear to think about anyone being treated the way he had described, especially not the children she was now responsible for. "What am I going to do? I'm not married. I have a little money." She fingered the brooch at her throat. "A few things I can sell, but that money wouldn't last us long." She dared a look at him. "I thought giving them a good home was the best choice."

His expression softened. "Giving them a good home is still the best choice." His voice had lost its edge as well. "The state agency just isn't the way to go about it."

"What then? Do you know anyone who'd want them?"

He closed the cupboard. "I might."

She studied him as he padded in stocking feet to set the clean plates in the basket. "Who?"

He shrugged.

A thin wail rose from the babies' crate. It was Marcus's turn to eat. Gabby moved to unpin a clean, dry nappy from the makeshift clothesline. Folding it into a square, she shot a look at Turner.

He picked up the basket and glanced over his shoulder without looking directly at her. "I have to go after a couple buggies and put up my horses. Anything else you need?"

"Thank you, no."

With that, he headed for the front door. Was that all he was going to say? Gabby stared after him, her insides trembling with uncertainty. The future was terrifying.

Thank goodness he'd been adamant about not letting Marcus and Jack go to a foundling home. The miserable picture he'd painted forced her to agree. It was a good thing she hadn't taken off on her own to turn them over to authorities. She'd almost made a terrible mistake. But he hadn't let her. One more debt she owed him.

She picked up Marcus and held him close. At least they were secure for another day. Turner said he might know of a family, so she had to believe he was going to come up with someone he trusted…. Gabby was out of options.

Chapter Five

On Wednesday, the babies were a week old. Turner thought about the recent troubling events as he saddled the deputy's horse and led the chestnut out of the barn. Turner hadn't asked around about a family. He hadn't told anyone that the babies didn't belong to the woman staying in his house. He'd been pondering the situation day and night.

Freezing drizzle pebbled his duster as he met young Lester Faraday and handed over the reins. "Miserable day for a ride."

The deputy peered from under the low-settled brim of his hat. "Marshal got news of a standoff up this side o' Medicine Pass. Seems Emory French and his men cornered the Jennings gang on their way back from a train heist." Emory French was a Texas Ranger turned bounty hunter, and he'd been on Drum Jennings's tail for the better part of a year. "Marshal wants me to scout the area, just to be on the safe side and make sure none of 'em are comin' this way. We've dealt with that Jennings bunch before, and we ain't fixin' to let 'em anywhere near Ruby Creek."

"Want me to ride with you?" Turner offered.

"No call you freezin' your parts off, too. Unless o' course you got a hankerin' to ride out in this miserable weather."

Turner made up his mind. "I'm comin' with you."

Riding in the cold, he questioned why he had involved himself when it wasn't in his best interests. His attachment to those boys had been instant. But Gabrielle? Well, a woman who went to such lengths to see to their welfare was to be admired. And he admired her.

An hour and a half later, they located Emory French and his men at a campsite outfitted with tents and a makeshift corral.

"They're in a line cabin up yonder," Emory said, pointing to a ridge overgrown with trees and weeds. A faint trail of smoke hung low in the dense sky. "They know we're out here. They're not hidin' their smoke. They're trying to keep warm and not use much ammunition. Every once in a while we exchange fire. Don't think anyone's been hit yet. We'll starve 'em out if need be."

"Anybody seen a woman with 'em?" Turner asked.

"Can't say," Emory replied.

"You sure nobody's been able to sneak away?" Lester asked.

"One o' my men found tracks and blood. They could've shot a rabbit or some other small game. I got men posted around the perimeter. Nobody's gettin' past."

Les and Turner had a cup of coffee at the campfire and traded news with Emory before heading back. No matter what he did, Turner's thoughts swung like a compass needle, unerringly shooting back to the woman staying in his house. He didn't like his notion that she felt obliged to him. Nobody worked harder than she did, spending every spare minute when not caring for the babies cleaning his house, cooking and baking. She wasn't afraid of hard work, but he was growing concerned.

The drizzle had turned to slippery snow by the time they got to Ruby Creek. Les unsaddled and curried his own horse while Turner put up Comanche.

"Wanna come to our place for Thanksgivin' this year?" Les

asked. One of the local families usually asked Turner to join them, and sometimes he accepted.

Turner didn't want to leave Gabrielle alone on the holiday.

"Your houseguest can join us," Les added as though he knew what Turner was thinking. "Marcia told me to say so."

"Thanks." Turner had guessed that the news of someone staying in the house would get around town. People were probably curious. Letting them know the situation should quell the tongues of the gossipers. And Gabrielle deserved a day out. "I'll let you know."

Les finished his task and Turner led both horses to their stalls.

He was on edge the rest of the day, looking over his shoulder, gazing out at the street and up at the gray foothills that lined the horizon. Emory had a dozen lawmen up by Medicine Pass. They could handle the situation.

All the same, he packed a saddlebag with his shaving gear and clothing and carried it into his house that evening. He cared what people thought, but not enough to overshadow his protective nature.

An unrelenting high-pitched cry was the first thing he heard as he hit the porch. Once inside, the scents of lye soap and starch that he associated with happier times assailed his senses. He paused for a moment to gather his wits and to think only of today and what had to be done.

In the foyer he called out, so as not to catch Gabrielle off guard. She appeared at the top of the stairs, one of the babies over her shoulder. "Turner?" she called over the persistent wail. "Is something wrong?"

"Nothin'." He removed his boots and climbed the stairs. "Who's that?"

"Marcus. He's been doing this for two hours straight." Her hair was tied at her neck haphazardly, her skirt and shirtwaist were wrinkled and her eyes showed bone-deep weariness. She looked aside, pursing her lips in a stubborn gesture of control.

Turner dropped his bag and removed his coat before reaching for the baby. "Marcus," he said, peering at the boy's reddened face. "What's the matter?"

"He's eaten," she said, "but it's Jack's turn, so now he's working up to a howl, too."

"Go tend to Jack." He followed her into her room.

She had a bottle already prepared, so she picked up the other baby and settled herself in the rocker. Jack took the nipple eagerly.

Turner looked the child over, even removed his nappy, which was barely damp, and replaced it with a dry one. He wrapped him snugly in his flannel blanket and tucked him into the crook of his arm.

Marcus had not been appeased throughout the process, but when Turner strode out into the hall and walked back and forth, bouncing the baby with little rocking motions, he finally quieted. "You're not the only one who needs attention, you know," he said to the baby. "You're gonna have to learn a little patience. All that squawkin' is unbecomin' of a man."

Marcus squinted up at him, his tiny brow furrowed as though he was listening.

"That's much more respectable," Turner told him.

Marcus closed his eyes.

Turner carried him back to the bedroom and propped a few pillows against the oak headboard before settling on top of the coverlet. "Did you eat supper?" he asked Gabrielle.

Her attention drifted to one side as though she was trying to remember that long ago. "I'm not sure."

"Are you hungry?"

"I think I might be."

Once Jack was finished eating, they tucked the babies into the cradle together and went down to the kitchen. Turner sliced cheese and bread and set out a jar of blackberry jam. Gabrielle ate a couple slices of each and drank a glass of milk.

"I found out today," Turner said, "that Emory French has

the Jennings gang cornered. Jennings and his men are holding them off, but Emory is prepared to starve them out."

The color drained from her face. "Is Willow with them? Did you ask?"

"I asked. Emory didn't know."

She steepled her fingers over the lower half of her face in a gesture of concern, and closed her eyes. "Oh, Willow, what have you done?"

"I brought my things. I'm stayin' here," he said.

Her eyes flew open. "Why?"

"Been uneasy ever since I heard. The law has it under control," he said to assure her, "but…I'm staying."

She nodded distractedly. "Do you think those outlaws will actually starve?"

"The need to eat is mighty powerful. They'll give themselves up. At least there's food in jail."

"She's not a bad person. She's just *foolish!*" She smacked one hand on the table to emphasize that word. The sugar bowl rattled. "A foolish, *selfish* girl!"

Turner got up to pump water into the kettle and put it on to boil. He found the tin of tea he'd purchased and placed the china pot and ingredients on the table in front of Gabrielle. She set the tea to steeping without conscious effort while he cleared their dishes and poured water into the dishpan, then scraped soap shavings and made suds. By the time he had the plates, nursing bottles and nipples washed, her tea was ready and she was sipping it thoughtfully.

Was she regretting her choice to follow her cousin? It wasn't Gabrielle's own foolishness that had landed her here and given her the tedious care of two babies. She'd done what she'd believed was right, and she was still trying to make the best choices at the sacrifice of her own life—and her rest. "Maybe you should get some sleep while the twins are quiet."

She looked up at him. Something in his chest shifted, exposing an aching cavity. Her heart was in her eyes, love and concern and loneliness shining as clear as day. He admired everything about her, from her stubborn determination to her compassionate nature. The trust in her dark honey eyes created an unexpected tug in his chest.

"Next week is Thanksgivin'," he said. "Deputy and his missus invited you—us—to their place. Wanna go?"

She furrowed her brow with a quizzical frown. "Will I still be here next week?"

Confident and capable were attributes he'd hang on her, but he'd caught her at a completely vulnerable moment. She needed to feel safe. He'd brought her here. He was responsible for setting her mind at ease. "Let's say you'll be here and make a plan."

She raised her eyebrows in concern. "They don't know what I am or who Willow is, do they, Turner?"

What she was? She was a caring, unselfish person trying to do the best she knew how for two helpless children. "You're a widow who was passin' through and needed a place to stay."

She searched his face as though hoping to find assurance. "And the truth is our secret?"

She made it sound clandestine, intimate…and he reacted to her words and trusting expression in a physical way that caught him off guard and delivered a sucker punch to his lungs.

Her gaze fell to his mouth.

Turner had to concentrate just to breathe again. When he did, her clean, soap-and-talc scent washed over him.

"Our secret," he agreed and the words made his body tingle. She'd raised her chin, and her lips were so near that he could… Had he leaned over that far without intending to?

Turner lowered his mouth the last few inches and rested his lips against hers. Her surprised sigh fluttered against his mouth, sending sensory signals to his brain. He added slightly more pressure and tasted the sweetness of her sugary tea and the essence that was uniquely hers. For an endless moment there were no other distractions, no past, no future, and he was free to experience the softness of her lips and the pleasure of unhindered discovery.

It had been a long time since he'd felt anything so soft, since he'd experienced a sensation so pure and without a dark edge of pain. There was unexpected honesty in these fleeting moments.

The gentle touch of her fingertips against his cheek startled him. Embarrassed him. Brought reality into acute focus. He opened his eyes and drew away.

Her eyelids fluttered open. "Oh," she said on a sigh and touched her fingers to her lips.

He hadn't done anything that reckless for a long time. Maybe not ever. He'd guarded his heart so carefully. Turner backed away. "You won't be of any use to those babies if you don't take care of yourself. Go get some sleep."

She watched him retreat, uncertainty in her eyes now. She nodded, set her cup aside and stood. "Yes."

Without another word, she hurried from the room, the swish of her skirts loud in the silence.

He kept his gaze on the chair where she'd been.

No arguing, he had tender feelings for the woman. For her plight and that of the babies. He'd felt protective toward her from the first. Gabrielle and her tiny wards were ripping open wounds that had never properly healed. Being back in this house, being near her, *smelling her,* holding those babies…his defenses had been relentlessly bombarded. Now what was he to do?

The thought of anything happening to any of them was unbearable. Her obvious unhappiness and fearful uncertainty tore at his conscience.

Turner picked up her cup and looked at the dark liquid in the bottom. He had the power to do something about her situation. He'd been powerless over the things that had happened in his past, but he could do something about this.

Fierce determination rose inside him.

He *would* do something about this.

* * *

Gabby couldn't get that kiss out of her head. She'd been kissed a few times, usually by a drunk whom her father promptly tossed into the street, but once or twice by a young man attracted to her. Those times had been all right, but she hadn't understood Willow's fascination with men and flirting and kissing. She'd watched her cousin do it enough for both of them, and maybe that's what had soured her on the prospect.

But kissing Turner had given her a whole new perspective. *Aha!* her awareness had shouted mere seconds after his lips had touched hers. *So that was what all the hullabaloo was about.*

It hadn't lasted near long enough. She'd only experienced the first, startling realizations of pleasure when the kiss had ended.

Would he kiss her again?

What did it mean, that kiss? Nothing, probably. She was setting too much store on an impulsive act that he had maybe immediately regretted.

But the possibility was in her head. And in her heart, which thumped erratically every time he came near. She was thinking of him as a man. Not a rescuer. Not a concerned citizen. Turner Price was a strong, competent man, and she wanted to kiss him again.

He came home at noon each day that week, and sometimes she warmed up stew or made potato soup. Once or twice he sliced ham and cheese and they ate it between crusty slices of her bread. He let her know at lunch if he'd be bringing home supper, and if not, she cooked a meal for the two of them. A comfortable routine developed.

It almost felt like they were a family.

Whenever Gabby questioned him about his ideas for the boys, he told her he was working on it. On Saturday, he invited her to attend church with him the following day.

"I don't go to church," she replied automatically.

"Why not?"

She rested the broom she'd been using against the door frame of the pantry. "I don't have any boots."

"I'll bring you a pair of boots. That's not the reason, is it?"

She shook her head. "Saloon workers don't sit beside town officials and respectable people."

"You're talkin' about life in Nevada."

"Well, yes."

"Nobody in Ruby Creek even knows you're a saloon-owner's daughter. Nobody will look down on you."

The thought of church made Gabby uncomfortable. "What do you do there exactly?"

"Sing hymns. Listen to Reverend Thomas's sermon. See neighbors. Sometimes there's food."

"I don't know any hymns."

"There are books with the songs in 'em."

He had an answer for everything. The whole idea made her uncomfortable.

"You can read."

"Of course I can read. I just don't know about the God parts." She turned to pick up a stack of nappies she'd taken from the line and folded. "I don't want anyone telling me how bad I am. I've heard enough of it my whole life."

Turner didn't say anything for a minute, and she thought he was going to forget the idea, but then he suggested, "How about you try comin' this once? If you don't like it, I won't ask you again."

How reasonable was that? Drat, the man *was* reasonable. She couldn't argue, especially since he'd been so kind and generous and had only asked this one little thing of her. "All right."

"I'll help get the babies ready in the morning."

He had been helpful every evening when he got here after his day at the livery. No task was too big or too small for him to tackle efficiently—in fact she often felt incompetent beside him. She nodded and resumed her task. Turner left and returned with suitable boots.

The following day, true to his word after bringing home a buggy, he dressed and bundled the boys while she prepared bottles. Together they carried them outdoors to the vehicle and Turner directed the horses through town.

Gabby's stomach fluttered at the notion of showing up at church with these babies. What if someone recognized her from Steptoe Valley? Not likely, but not impossible, either. What if her ineptitude and deception was so glaring that the preacher could see right through her? Did he have special, Godly powers?

The first person Turner introduced her to was Marcia Faraday, the deputy's wife. The petite, dark-haired woman smiled warmly and made appreciative comments about the handsome babies.

"I'm so sorry about your loss," she said to Gabby, her blue eyes swimming with concern. "What an awful thing to have happen, and now you're a new mother. I'll be praying that you're taken care of."

Gabby couldn't think of a thing to say. Apparently news of her fabricated widowhood had spread. She smiled her appreciation while feeling like a fraud.

"I'm pleased you'll be comin' to dinner on Thursday. Don't worry about bringing anything. You just come and enjoy a day with no cookin' or dishes."

"You're very kind, thank you," Gabby managed.

"I know how tirin' it is to have one new baby, let alone two." With that, she moved away and a bevy of women homed in on Gabby and Turner, admiring the babies, smiling and offering their condolences on the loss of her husband.

The service commenced, and Gabby took it all in: Turner's voice raised with the others standing around them, the reverent atmosphere and the preaching. Reverend Thomas spoke about the goodness of God's love and didn't single her out as a heathen. The service ended without a single embarrassing incident.

Relieved, Gabby accompanied Turner through the crowd

toward the door. As they reached the back of the church, an older woman with silver-gray hair tucked under a little feathered hat glanced from Marcus in Turner's arm up to his face, and smiled perceptively. "That big house has been empty long enough, hasn't it? It's a joy to see it filled with life again."

"This is Mrs. Halverson," Turner said to Gabby. "She lives across the street and down a couple houses from mine."

"You call me Viv, dear," the woman said. "Don't be a stranger. You're welcome to knock on my door any day. Tuesdays I'm sewing with the mission circle, but the rest of these long winter days I'm home."

"Thank you, ma'am. I'll remember that."

Gabby hadn't been around many women save her mother and Willow and the girls who worked in the saloon, and she'd never had respectable ladies address her in such friendly fashion. Of course, it was because of Turner and his standing in the town that she'd been greeted with such surprising warmth.

There was a commotion at the door just then, and one of the men pushed through the crowd to reach Turner.

"French and his men just brought in half a dozen bodies in the back of a buckboard. They're bein' identified for the reward money now."

Fear leaped in Gabby's chest. "Is Drum Jennings among the dead?" she asked.

"Not sure, ma'am," he answered. "Marshal's got the papers on 'em."

"Papers?" she asked.

"Wanted posters," Turner explained.

The man moved into the thinning crowd. Most of the men had already left, but he found a few to tell his news to.

"I want to go see," Gabby whispered.

Without hesitation, as though he understood she was determined and wouldn't be dissuaded, Turner helped her with her coat. "I'll take you."

Chapter Six

A crowd had gathered around the front of the marshal's office. The bodies were displayed on old, warped doors and slabs of wood in the frozen, rutted street. Men and women alike crowded around to get a look at the dead outlaws.

Turner gave Marcus to Vivian Halverson, then took Jack from Gabby and handed him to another lady who didn't appear inclined to go forward. With a firm hold on Gabby's elbow, Turner led her closer. They were forced to wait their turn while onlookers gaped and pointed before moving on.

One of the bodies, though dressed in black trousers and a Hudson's Bay coat, was smaller than the rest, slender and delicate like what most would probably assume was a young boy. Gabby recognized the ivory-skinned cheek and a barely visible wisp of golden hair the moment she saw it. She made herself look at the face. Her breath caught painfully. She half turned away, grasping Turner's arm and biting back emotion. She was afraid she was going to be sick, but she couldn't stop staring.

"That one's her," she whispered. "It's Willow."

Turner steadied her. "Stay right here."

He pushed through the crowd to reach one of the unshaven strangers. He spoke quietly to the man, whose gaze shot to

Willow's lifeless body. They exchanged words and Turner strode back to Gabby.

"There's no reward for her. The marshal will turn her body over to us privately. We can have her buried proper."

Gabby felt numb. She took several deep breaths to keep the nausea at bay. Finally nodding her understanding, she scanned the other bodies. "I don't see him. Didn't they catch Drum?"

"Emory said a couple of the outlaws were shot during the siege and he thinks their men buried 'em somewhere on that ridge. Others are lookin' for graves now, but they might never know for sure."

Gabby took a last, sorrowful look. For her pretty young cousin to end up laid out dead in the company of outlaw thieves was a travesty. What a waste of her life. And for what? Tears blurred Gabby's vision, and she turned away before anyone could notice. "I want to go home now."

After gathering the babies, Turner guided her to the buggy. The ride to the house barely registered. She stood in the foyer, numb with shock and regret. Turner helped her out of her coat and led her up the stairs to her room. He turned back the covers and sat her on the edge of the bed before placing the sleeping babies in their cradle. Only then did he unbutton and shrug out of his coat.

Coming back to Gabby, he knelt to remove her boots. "Do you want to get out of your clothing?"

She nodded.

This was no time for the lustful thoughts that barraged him when he reached for the buttons down the front of her shirtwaist. He focused on taking care of her the way she deserved. He drew the shirt away, revealing white shoulders, heartstopping curves beneath a prim white camisole and pale, slender arms.

She helped him with the skirt, and he hoped she couldn't tell his hands were trembling by that point. A gentleman would avert his eyes from the lacy pantalettes that showed off her rounded hips, but he wasn't claiming to be a gentleman right then. He looked his fill, even as his palms tingled with the urge to touch her.

Instead he urged her under the covers. "Rest, Gabby," he told her, his voice gruff with what he hoped sounded like concern rather than lust.

She turned onto her side and curled up. "Don't go just yet," she pleaded softly.

Turner understood grief. He studied her, helpless to control the situation, helpless to comfort her. All he knew to do was give her time and offer his silent support. He built a corral in his head and herded all the carnal thoughts in and closed the gate so he could concentrate on helping her.

Following instinct, he knelt on the bed's edge, then stretched out behind her, atop the covers, but so that his body touched the outline of hers from shoulder to feet. Her clean, feminine scent made his throat constrict. It had been a long time since he'd let himself experience closeness like this.

He liked the feeling, but it scared him. He wasn't ready to let down his defenses. Eventually Gabrielle slept.

When the first baby woke, Turner got up silently and carried both to the kitchen where he prepared bottles. One at a time he changed and fed the boys. Their mother was dead, most likely their father, too. At least they had someone who cared about them enough to have traveled the country alone to find them before harm could befall them. It was plain that Gabby wanted only the best for these boys. He'd successfully discouraged her from her foundling-home idea. A life of poverty and struggle wasn't what she wanted, but she wasn't left with any good choices.

Should she get the notion to take off, there was nothing he could do. He had no right to keep her here without offering stability. He was angry with himself for the vulnerability he'd felt ever since the three of them had come into his life, but he couldn't shake his need to make sure they were safe. He had to protect old wounds by not letting himself care too much, but he also needed to do what was right.

It was dark out, but still early evening when Gabby came downstairs in a dark green wrapper with a sash tied around her waist. She entered the warm, cozy study where Turner was reading. He sat with one ankle over the opposite knee, and both babies on a pillow in the crook of his leg. As Gabby approached, she saw that Jack was asleep and Marcus was frowning at the flickering shadows on the ceiling.

"You've taken care of them all afternoon," she said, feeling guilty.

He laid down his book. "They were fine."

She settled in the upholstered chair across from him.

"Are you hungry?" he asked.

"I'll get something in a little while." She stood. "I should take over now."

"They're fine, Gabby." He stopped her with a raised palm. "Sit."

She eased down onto her seat, liking the way he said her name. Her thoughts drifted to the safe and peaceful feeling of having him lying behind her as she fell asleep earlier. What would it be like to know that kind of contentment for a lifetime?

Turner got up and placed Jack and Marcus on a quilt she hadn't noticed on the floor, a safe distance from the fireplace. He covered them with their blankets.

"I have a hankerin' for coffee. Want some? Or maybe tea? Hot cocoa?"

"I'll drink a cup of coffee with you."

He returned a few minutes later with two mugs of dark, sweetened liquid. "I reckon we need to talk now," he said.

She nodded.

"I've come up with an answer."

He had her interest. "What is it?"

"You love those boys."

She blinked back tears and nodded. "Yes."

"You want the best for them."

"Of course."

"I already told you foster homes are not the best, and you agreed."

Her gaze moved to the babies sleeping nearby. "I wouldn't want that for them. Not after what you told me."

"The best thing is a good home. A woman to care for 'em, a man to protect and provide."

"It sounds so simple when you say it," she said. "But you might as well say I should catch them a falling star."

"We could get married."

His words pierced her fuzzy thoughts and arrested her attention. The suggestion took shape and full comprehension dawned. Her gaze shot to his in astonishment. "What?"

"I have my own business. I'm on the town council and people respect me. I have a house. I'm hardworkin'. I don't drink."

She suspected where he was going with this, but she couldn't be right. Maybe she was still asleep. He couldn't have just suggested they get married.

"I'm probably not what you dreamed of as a girl when you thought of a husband, but I'd take care of you. All of you."

Marriage *was* what he was talking about. He'd said *husband*. She didn't need a list of his attributes to know he was a good man. Her character paled in comparison to his qualities. Why he would offer himself was her concern. He was sometimes overbearing and gruff, but he'd shown his level head in every situation. It was no secret that the attachment he felt to the twins went beyond a stranger's kindness. He had more to offer than she could ever hope to give them.

For a brief second she allowed herself to wonder if he would ever have given her a second thought had it not been for the boys. If she'd shown up at his livery or attended his church alone one Sunday, would he have paid her any attention? Right now security won out over pride and vanity. She let herself think on the idea he'd planted in her head.

"You're talking about a lifetime," she said finally. "About forsaking your independence, and even the possibility of meeting a suitable young woman, by taking on the burden of ready-made children."

His expression showed she'd touched on something delicate.

"Maybe you want a wife of your choice and children of your own," she pressed.

Turner got up then. He walked to the window and pulled back the drape to gaze out at the night.

The fire crackled and Gabby waited for him to reply.

Without turning to face her, he spoke. "I had a wife and a child once," he said, his tone flat.

Well, that explained a lot. Except why that fact should cause a peculiar sinking feeling in her stomach. She had suspected just that. She noticed things every day that made her wonder who had lived here and what had happened to them.

"I'm not lookin' to replace them. I can't do that." He shook his head. "I'm sayin' this all wrong."

He dropped the curtain but still didn't face her. "My life has to mean somethin' more than work and sleep. If you stay, if you let me, I'll do everything in my power to give those boys a good life."

What about *us?* Gabby wanted to ask. What about you and I? But she knew better than to expect more than he could give. He'd had a great love and lost her. He was looking to fill his days and find worth in his work. And she understood. She'd never met a man like him, a good, upstanding man. Staying in Steptoe Valley, working in the saloon, she never would have. He was offering her security and respectability. For the first time she would be able to hold her head up and not be judged by her parents' occupations or their status in life.

"And the townspeople will believe I'm a widow?" Her

question revealed the merit she'd already placed on his idea. "They'll think the boys' father was a good man who took sick and died? No one could ever know or look down their noses at them."

"Never," he promised, turning at last to look at her. "They'll grow up here and attend school like all the other children. I'll be…" He paused. "I'll be the best father to them that I can be. You have my word."

And *husband?* she wondered. Will you give that much effort to being a husband? But she had no right to question, or to demand more when he'd already offered so much. Offered enough. Enough to assure her she was making the right decision.

"Then I agree," she told him. "I'll telegraph my parents to tell them about Willow. I'll let them know I'm marrying and staying here. My father will send the rest of my belongings."

"You can buy whatever you need. I'll arrange accounts for you in town."

For the hundredth time, she thought about that kiss they'd shared in the kitchen and wished he would make a move to seal this moment with a similar gesture. Then she once again cautioned herself not to expect more than the man was able to give. She'd just accepted an arrangement that held no room for romantic notions.

"You have to let me help," Gabby told the deputy's wife. "Your children are pacifying the babies and I need to feel I've contributed something."

"Go ahead and mash those potatoes." With a smile, Marcia gestured to a bowl. "Less than two weeks, and you and Turner will be married. I still can't get over the surprise."

"Me, neither," Gabby admitted. "I never dreamed I was coming to Ruby Creek to get married."

Marcia stacked slices of turkey on a platter. "This is a harsh land. Women have to take care of themselves and their young'uns. You couldn't have done any better than Turner," she added.

"Did you know his wife?"

Marcia shook her head. "That was before I came to Ruby Creek with my folks. I was only here three months before I married Lester."

Gabby turned her attention to smashing the boiled potatoes.

"Lester knew his missus, though," Marcia added. "He said Turner didn't come out of that house for weeks after she and their baby died. Then one day he closed it up and never went back. Stayed at the livery after that."

Gabby could picture that very scenario. "It's sad that he lost them."

"Just as sad as you losin' your man. People do what they have to do to keep goin'. You and Turner are going to do just fine."

As they finished dinner preparations, Gabby's thoughts flitted around the questions she'd entertained ever since accepting Turner's proposal. She was doing the right thing for Jack and Marcus, but what about for her? How difficult would it be to marry a man she barely knew?

She always managed to reason with her doubts and convince herself of the benefits. If she'd stayed in Steptoe Valley, her chances of ever meeting a good man and marrying would have been slim. Eventually she may have settled anyway—settled for someone older or with less means—and still have never known a grand passion. At least this way she was getting a husband in his prime, a kind man with a business and an upstanding position in the town.

Grand passion wasn't for people like her. She would do well to focus on that fact and to remember she was going to be living a far different, and better, life.

Gabby's father had always kept the saloon open on Thanksgiving. They ran one of the two establishments in town that served a meal, so she had always helped her mother cook and serve the men. Gabby had spent holidays clearing tables and washing mountains of dishes. Today, sitting down at the table with the Faradays and their children, with Turner beside her and the babies sleeping peacefully nearby, she experienced a true taste of what it would be like to enjoy life with family and friends.

The Faraday home wasn't as large or as well furnished as Turner's, but love and kindness were evident in all they did and said. They treated Gabby as though she was one of them, and Gabby's heart could barely contain her pleasure.

While Lester said a brief prayer to bless their food, Gabby studied Turner, who had his head bowed and his eyes closed. Pleasure and trepidation overwhelmed her. She was out of her element, but there was no turning back now.

Chapter Seven

Turner made arrangements for the wedding, had a small stack of announcements printed and gave Gabby a list of townspeople to invite. He set up accounts at the mercantile and the dressmaker's and told her to ask Marcia to keep the babies whenever she needed time to shop or try on her dresses. The next two weeks passed rapidly.

She stood on a stool in Effie Carter's little shop while the petite redhead pinned finishing touches to the skirt of the wedding dress and measured the hem. "I only have a chance to make a wedding dress once a year or so. This is so much fun that I almost feel guilty taking your money." She giggled. "But I will, of course. What do you suppose Turner will present you with as your bride's gift? Have you dropped sufficient hints?"

Gabby had been gazing at her image in the full-length mirror, stroking the skirt, still disbelieving that she would be wearing such a lovely gown. Though Turner had given her complete choice over the dress, even assuring her the gown didn't need to be practical, she'd chosen a design she could wear again on Sundays and special occasions. She was too sensible to have done otherwise.

Mrs. Carter's chatter caught her attention. "A bride's gift?" Gabby asked.

"You know, it's tradition for the bride and groom to exchange gifts." She gave Gabby an odd look. "You do have something planned for him, don't you?"

"Well, I—I guess it slipped my mind."

"You still have time unless you want something that has to be ordered."

Gabby had one more thing to preoccupy her thinking for the rest of the day. When she went to pick up the boys from Marcia's, she dared ask, "What is a proper gift for the bride to give the groom?"

"Customarily, it's something like a stickpin or a watch chain, but we're practical people in these parts, so anything meaningful will do."

"What did you give Lester?"

"I monogrammed handkerchiefs with his initials and gave them to him in a cedar box." She smiled. "He keeps the box on the bureau and he takes one of those handkerchiefs to church every Sunday."

Gabby had no idea how to monogram letters, and she certainly didn't have time to learn. A stickpin or a watch chain were definite possibilities, however. She glanced at the boys, who slept contentedly in a cradle Marcia had brought from her attic and set in a corner of the kitchen. "Would you mind if I ran another errand?"

It took her ten minutes to hurry home, dash up the stairs and locate the flannel bag in the drawer of the chest she used. Finding it quickly, she hurried downtown.

She'd spotted the sign on a tiny brick building when she'd first come to Ruby Creek, and she'd kept McCann's Pawnbroker and Jewelry in mind. A bell clanged, startling her as she pushed open the door. A man in a canvas apron came from the back to stand behind the counter. "How do, ma'am. What can I do fer ye t'day?"

"I'd like to sell this necklace." She reached to lay a strand of pearls on the polished mahogany counter, but the man stopped her and tucked a square of black velvet under the necklace first.

He bent over, then appeared to remember his glasses were on top of his head, and settled them on his nose to peer at the pearls. "Oh, my. I don't keep enough on hand to buy these on the spot. If you give me a day or two, we can make an arrangement."

Gabby just wanted to be certain she had a gift for Turner. "I need a watch chain or a watch by next Saturday."

"Take any watch and chain you like." He gestured to the display case to the right of where she stood.

She stepped over and looked at the prices. "Any of them?"

"I've only seen quality pearls such as these in jewelry shops in the East. I won't cheat you, ma'am. I just need to take some cash from the bank to pay you the rest. I want this necklace."

His interest was understandable. It was a lovely piece of jewelry. It had been a tip from a customer. Gabby had tried it on a few times and admired it. She'd never had anywhere to wear it, but had always known it would come in handy when she needed cash. "I can have any watch I want, plus cash?"

"Tell you what. I'll lock the shop and walk to the bank with you right now."

"You have a deal, Mr. McCann. May I see that gold pocket watch with the horses engraved on the cover?"

"You picked the best 'un, you did." He unlocked the flat case and wrapped the watch in another square of velvet before handing it to her.

Gabby opened the watch and gazed at the face with a sense of satisfaction. The second hand ticked in precise movement as she studied it. She was going to be able to give Turner a useful and beautiful gift. "It's perfect."

"It's new," he told her. "The retail side of the business is my cash flow, so I keep a few quality pieces. Didn't expect to see that one gone so soon. Just picked it up in Denver a month ago."

"And a nice chain," she told him. "Do you have a box?"

"The missus makes these little bags for me," he answered, taking a small, black velvet bag from under the counter.

She accompanied him to the bank, where she promptly stared in astonishment at her cashier's check, then turned right around and asked the teller to split the money into two accounts for Jack and Marcus.

And to think she might have kept those pearls tucked away without ever knowing how much they were worth! She bought a tart and a tin of tea for Marcia at the bakery and offered them to her new friend when she picked up her babies. "I'm indebted to you," she said, wrapping the boys in their blankets.

With her youngest grasping her apron, Marcia waved Gabby on with a shake of her head.

Gabby was overjoyed that she'd been able to buy such a nice gift for Turner. He'd been nothing but generous, and now she had something that she'd paid for herself to give in return.

A month of Sundays wouldn't have been enough time to prepare Gabby for the church filled with people dressed in their best clothing and wearing expectant smiles. Especially disconcerting was the fact that their attention was focused entirely on *her.*

Gabby's face burned in discomfort. Her knees trembled. Her hand shook, but she determinedly extended it toward Turner and he slid a wide gold band on her finger. She stared at the ring, and then up to catch his introspective gaze on their hands. He'd never held her hand—had only kissed her once—and here they were making vows that bound them to one another forever.

Married.

"By the power vested in me by the state of Colorado, I pronounce you Mr. and Mrs. Turner Price. Turner, give your bride a kiss."

A spattering of applause and murmurs surprised Gabby.

She'd been to two weddings in her entire life, both nuptials for saloon girls who'd been married right there on the premises by a justice of the peace. The events had gone nothing like this.

Turner leaned forward to give her a perfunctory peck on the lips, and that was that. A traitorous sliver of disappointment revealed that her girlish hopes had been raised, regardless of her every effort to convince herself this was nothing more than a practical union.

She accepted good wishes and stood beside her new husband as church members moved the pews to line the walls and make a larger area for the gathering.

Tables had been set up and were laden with sandwiches and cake, coffee and punch. Reverend Thomas's wife, Urlene, cut the cake and served frothy slices on white china plates. The bride and groom received the first pieces of white cake with red berry filling, and Turner led her to one of the pews.

Gabby tasted the sweet confection. "Oh, my."

"Vivian Halverson made it," he told her.

She discovered his gaze on her as she raised the fork to her lips again, and heat infused her cheeks. Why was she suddenly feeling giddy and expectant? That mister and missus declaration had thrown her off kilter.

"She offered," he added, and she searched her thoughts before remembering he was talking about the cake.

Gabby spotted the silver-haired woman watching them from across the room and gave Viv an appreciative smile.

After refreshments had been enjoyed, Urlene suggested they open their gifts. "I didn't know there'd be gifts, too," Gabby whispered to Turner.

He urged her to open the bundles, and, feeling awkward yet delighted, she discovered tea towels, embroidered linens, tins of spices and useful kitchen items. Nothing extravagant, but all thoughtful and practical, like the people who had so generously accepted her into their community.

By the time they'd gathered up the babies and headed home,

Gabby was exhausted. She fed the boys and put them to bed. Turner had ordered two iron baby cribs and they'd arrived a few days earlier. He'd set up the beds in the room next to Gabby's and told her she could begin using them whenever she chose.

She decided tonight was a good time. This was the day that started the rest of their lives on a new path.

She laid Jack and Marcus in the beds that seemed so large for such tiny little fellows, then stood gazing at them, and touched each of their down-soft heads and grazed their cheeks with the backs of her fingers. She had never imagined her heart could be so full, that it was possible to love so completely and selflessly. In a few short weeks, her tiny, demanding charges had become so precious that she couldn't imagine life without them.

The floor creaked behind her.

She turned. Turner's wide form was silhouetted in the light from the gas lamp in the hall.

"They seem so small," she said softly.

He entered the room and gazed from one to the other. "They're used to having each other," he thought aloud. "They might miss that."

"Then again they might not wake each other up as much."

"Join me downstairs?" he invited, and ushered her ahead of him. He'd made coffee and now he poured them each a cup. She took a seat at the kitchen table.

"I have something for you," he told her.

Gabby's heart fluttered expectantly. She'd been waiting for Turner to let her know when the time was right. "I have something for you, too." She hurried upstairs, returning with the black velvet bag.

Turner's raised eyebrows showed his surprise. He studied the bag she set on the table, then took a similar bag from his jacket pocket. He didn't meet her eyes.

"We didn't have a regular courtship," he said to her. "Or *any* courtship. I already made all my promises, and I aim to keep my word. I know this whole thing isn't what you would've chosen for yourself, and…I'm sorry we're not takin' a honeymoon. As soon as the boys are old enough, I'll take you somewhere nice."

"I don't need a trip, Turner. Fancy weddings and trips like that are for…well, for people different from us. From me, I mean."

He frowned, but nodded and extended the black velvet bag.

Gabby reached for it. It wasn't nearly as heavy as the one she had for him. She loosened the drawstring and hesitantly tipped the bag so the contents fell into her palm…and draped over her wrist.

A pearl necklace. *The* pearl necklace. She stared at the strand, realization dawning.

"Was the nicest thing in all of Ruby Creek," Turner told her, his voice conveying his concern over her reaction. "I wanted somethin' special for you. Do you like it?"

There was no question the necklace was lovely. But it hadn't held any particular sentimental value for her. Until now. Gabby's throat closed and an overwhelming sensation threatened her composure, though she didn't know why. She managed a nod. "I do like it."

"Here." He took the strand and worked the delicate gold clasp with calloused fingers until he had it open. Gabby turned away so he could fasten the pearls around her neck. His fingers brushed her skin, and a delicious shiver ran all the way to her toes. He gestured toward the grainy mirror over the washstand just inside the back door.

With a swish of satin skirts, Gabby approached the mirror. Her pearl necklace complimented the ivory-and-lace dress he'd bought her. Knowing how much she'd gotten for the pearls, she could only imagine how much Mr. McCann had marked them up to make a profit by selling the necklace to Turner. They were an extravagance.

He had wanted something nice for her, and it was true there was nothing nicer in Mr. McCann's store. The irony of him buying the necklace she'd sold wasn't lost on her. She would never let on. "It is a lovely gift, Turner. Thank you."

"You'll wear 'em?"

She never had, but now she would wear the gift her husband had given her. She nodded. "Often."

He returned to discover the watch and chain she'd purchased for him. His eyebrows rose in surprise. He looked as though he was going to ask something, but then thought better of it. Was he wondering how she'd been able to buy such an expensive watch? "Mighty generous present" was all he said.

"I wanted the best for you, too."

His mouth tightened and he dropped his gaze. Was he thinking of his wife? Of the woman he'd loved and lost? Was he having second thoughts? "Thank you," he said finally.

Gabby couldn't help wondering in that moment how different things would have been between them this day—all along—if she had been his first wife. If she'd been the woman Turner had loved and desired.

They drank their coffee and Turner carried warm water to Gabby's room. They hadn't spoken of their sleeping arrangements, and he hadn't moved his belongings or asked her to move hers, so she had no idea what to expect.

Effie Carter had come that morning to help her dress, and Gabby couldn't unbutton or remove the dress on her own. Turner poured the water and was turning toward the door when she stopped him with a quiet request. "I need help removing my dress."

Chapter Eight

Clearly uncomfortable, Turner set down the pail. He brushed his hands together as though stalling, then stepped behind her. He slowly, painstakingly unfastened the buttons from neckline to waist. Cool air touched her skin and sent a tingle all the way through her. She didn't want to seem forward or demand affection he didn't feel, so she bit her lip and closed her eyes.

He'd held his breath, and he released it now in a gust of warm air that brushed her neck. "That's all of 'em."

"Thank you, Turner."

He picked up the pail and hurried from the room.

Gabby removed the dress and hung it. Heart racing in anticipation, she washed up quickly before donning her cotton night rail. After blowing out the light, she opened her door, telling herself it was so she'd hear the babies when they woke, but knowing it was her unspoken signal that she was waiting…and willing.

Would Turner return? She didn't know how to act or what to do or say, but she shamelessly wanted him as her husband in all ways. From beneath the covers, she listened to the creak of the wind under the eaves, the whoosh of air in the coal heater pipe.

Eventually, her heart slowed its frantic beat. A lonely ache yawned in her chest. He wasn't coming. The sense of expectancy and hope she'd tried to deny withered. She wasn't his first choice. He'd married her for the sake of the babies, nothing more.

The house was dark and still…and she slept alone.

December had arrived with a foot of new snow, and brought a cheerful atmosphere to Ruby Creek. Store windows displayed feather trees and wooden toys, and many of the shop owners draped evergreen garlands above their doorways and windows.

Gabby had nearly set the house in order. She'd uncovered the remaining furniture, aired rooms, dusted and polished until everything gleamed. She'd never lived anywhere so nice, had never before had the freedom or time to make a home the way she liked it. The privilege was almost too good to be true. Cooking, serving and cleaning up after meals for two was a big change from feeding streams of cowhands, drifters and gamblers, most of them dusty and unshaven, many of them drunk.

Turner had assured her he'd been taking his laundry into town for several years and he didn't mind adding hers and the babies' to the tab, but she found she didn't mind laundering her items with the boys'. Turner kept a path shoveled to the clotheslines, and many times she brought in stiffly frozen nappies and ironed them dry.

She had telegraphed her parents and heard back from them, and now she sent a letter once a week. She missed them, and she grieved for what had happened to Willow, but she didn't regret the corner she'd turned in her life. She could be happy here. She wasn't fooling herself that Turner desired her or would ever love her, but she had a husband and children and a lovely home. Her story didn't have to have a fairy-tale ending. As long as Turner always respected her and lavished his attention on the boys, she would be content.

Now that the babies were no longer newborns and had

fallen into a mostly shared sleep-and-wake schedule, she agreed to help whenever volunteers were needed at church. Staying busy helped take her mind away from what was missing in her marriage. She helped Effie sew a dozen white angel costumes and hosted the quilting ladies when Viv's parlor was being repainted. She was the first to answer a call for pastries needed after the children's Christmas program.

Several of her new friends were surprised that making half a dozen pies at once was no hardship, and her ability to contribute reassured her. She wasn't failing at everything. She was making friends and contributing to the community. Even church wasn't as awkward as she'd feared it would be.

"There is a church service on a Wednesday morning?" she asked Turner at supper one night the second week of December. "Christmas morning, I mean."

"Christmas Day service," he answered with a nod. "The young'uns do a skit and Reverend Thomas reads the nativity story from the Bible. There's refreshments and then we go home to our families."

He'd been without a family for enough years, Turner thought after he said the words. Having Gabby and the boys here gave him new perspective. Made him look at his life and what he'd been doing with it in a new light. On one hand a sense of guilt tortured him. No one could replace his wife. He'd loved her. No one could replace his own little-girl baby, who'd never drawn a breath on her own. But he had a reason to get up every day. A reason to come home.

He looked across the table at Gabby, really thinking for the first time of all that she'd given up to do right by her cousin's children. She'd left her family behind to come to an unfamiliar part of the country. She'd married Turner because he'd promised to help her take care of Jack and Marcus. She'd buried her dream of being married to the man of her choice, someone who spoke fancy words of devotion and made her heart flutter.

He'd been watching her do her best to fit in and give this arrangement her all. Whatever Gabby did, she put forth her best effort. He recognized that fact and he admired her for it. He'd been going about life halfheartedly for a long time, and still he held back. But not Gabby. Gabby didn't hold back.

He wondered what it would be like if she threw herself into loving him the way she applied herself in everything else. What would it be like to be on the receiving end of all that devotion? He couldn't open himself up to finding out, of course. He could appreciate her compassion and quiet strength, but he couldn't become soft. That kind of weakness was too big of a risk.

From time to time he recognized her loneliness in her expressive face, and it disturbed him. He didn't want her unhappy, but what they had together was based on their agreement to make a home for twin boys. Their bargain hadn't included feelings, but he felt responsible for her contentment.

She gave him one of those smiles that had an electrical effect on him. "Won't be long before we'll be watching Jack and Marcus in that church play."

He would like to stop the years from passing and hold on to this time right here and now, but she was right—the boys would be grown up before long. "I reckon it won't."

"Church isn't what I expected," she admitted in a voice that revealed her awe. "Of course, they don't really know me, and they might treat me differently if they did. I'm careful what I say around them. On Monday I was humming a tune without thinking, and Viv asked me what it was. I was so embarrassed."

"What was it?"

"A song about red garters. Saloon music is all I ever heard till I came here."

Turner grinned. "No, Gabby. They wouldn't treat you differently. I treat you respectfully, don't I? I know all about you."

She nodded.

"They're good people. It was different where you came from. People aren't like that here."

She didn't look convinced, but she finished her supper without contradicting him.

He raised a questioning brow. "Will you sing that song for me? The one about the red garters?"

She had finished her meal, so she stood and picked up her plate. "I will not."

He chuckled.

She turned back to look at him. She'd never before heard him laugh, and the sound gave her pleasure. She poured water she'd kept hot on the stove into the dishpan and set to scrubbing pans and bowls.

Turner finished eating and brought his plate.

Gabby reached for it with soapy fingers, and it slipped. They both grabbed for it, but it teetered on the edge of the pan before sliding harmlessly into the water. Turner had somehow enveloped her hand, however, and they stood that way, with her slippery hand in his grasp. Gabby's heart thrummed so loudly she was sure he could hear it.

She studied his expression, wondering about his thoughts, hoping he would stop resisting what was happening between them, but terrified of being disappointed. She made a loose fist, and his hand wrapped around it, the warm, slick contact riveting. He met her gaze, his deep blue eyes filled with uncertainty.

What is it? she wanted to ask. *What keeps you from loving me?*

One of the babies howled from the cradle he'd moved down to the kitchen. Turner let his gaze fall away and released her hand. "I'll get 'im."

He moved away, and she closed her eyes against the sense of loss. Was this how it would always be? Less than she hoped for?

She collected herself and finished the dishes.

Changing and feeding Marcus gave Turner something to do while he struggled with the confusion of his attraction to

Gabby. She deserved more than he could give her. His inability to be more open with her, to let himself care about her, was his flaw, but he didn't know how to change it.

Turner was tucking Marcus into the cradle when a blood-curdling scream and a metallic thunk scared the bejeebers out of him, and he was glad he'd already laid the baby down.

The back door flew open and Gabby raced inside, her apron and skirts drenched, her face white with fright. "Out—out there!" she gasped, unable to speak past her fear.

Turner grabbed his rifle from atop the pie safe and flung open the back door. A small black bear sat on its haunches and looked over at him. It appeared the animal had been scratching at the door of the storm cellar, probably smelling the food-stuffs stored down there.

Turner fired the rifle into the air and the beast turned and loped off toward the aspen-covered hillside beyond the neighborhood. Turner picked up the dishpan from where it had landed outside the door.

"Did you kill it?"

He turned to find a terrified Gabby clutching her wet skirts. "I didn't try. He ran off."

"You didn't try? What if it comes back?"

He gestured for her to move inside ahead of him, and hung the pan on a nail. "He's fat and ready to hibernate for the winter. They don't usually come down this far."

Both babies were fretting now, probably startled by Gabby's scream and the gunfire. "Go change. I'll get a bottle for Jack," Turner said.

"How can you be so calm?"

She was mighty peeved with him, but he'd just wanted to calm her. He didn't respond.

"I was nearly eaten by a grizzly bear!"

"It wasn't a grizzly, Gabby, just a young black bear. He was lost and smelled the storm cellar. He'll find a nice cave now and settle in for the winter."

"What about in the spring?"

"In the spring we'll keep a watch out."

She stood for a moment, then removed her apron. With an uncertain glance at him, then another at the back door, she spun and headed for the hallway. He heard her tread on the stairs, and heated milk for Jack's bottle.

Gabby couldn't believe Turner was so cavalier about the whole incident. She was on edge the rest of the evening, starting at every little sound. She wasn't the fearful sort, but she'd never come face-to-face with a bear before. Not even a little one like this one was, as Turner had so maddeningly pointed out.

"Can bears climb fences?" That evening they sat in the study where she was sewing a pocket on a new apron. She never had enough aprons, and Effie had given her a bag of leftover-fabric scraps.

"They climb trees. I reckon a fence wouldn't stop 'em." He was sitting on the braided rug in front of the fire, polishing his Sunday boots.

"We'll need a fence when the boys are bigger anyway."

"Fence'd be good, Gabby. I'll make one come spring."

"Thank you."

He glanced at her over his shoulder, then stood by bracing his hands on his knees, elbows out, and straightening. He stretched, arching backward. Watching him gave Gabby an unexpected fluttery sensation in her belly.

"Gonna heat up that leftover coffee. Want a cup?"

She looked away. "Thanks, but I don't think it would sit well."

"Feelin' poorly?" Concern creased his forehead.

"No, just a little jumpy."

He returned several minutes later, smelling of soap, and seated himself in the comfortable chair across from her. Resting one ankle atop the other knee, he studied her as he sipped from his mug.

After looking up several times and finding him studying her, she laid down her sewing. "What are you looking at me like that for?"

He shrugged.

"Go ahead and say whatever's on your mind," she encouraged.

He set his cup down. "Don't be scared about the bear. It's rare one comes into town. Probably only happened a dozen times that I know of."

"A dozen times is a lot! Maybe I should have a gun."

"I can teach you to use a rifle, but you would've had to run in to get it anyhow, and by then you'd be safe inside."

He was always so logical. She was irritated and on edge, but it probably had less to do with bears than with her uncertainty about where she stood with him. "Did you love your wife very much, Turner?"

Obviously startled, he glanced aside, then right back. "'Course I did."

"How did she die?"

His jaw tightened, and she knew he didn't want to talk about it, but he said, "She died givin' birth."

Gabby had suspected as much. The unused baby clothing that he'd produced on a moment's notice had been pretty conclusive. "And your baby died at the same time?"

He nodded with grim affirmation. "Doctor couldn't do anything to save them. Baby was too small. A girl, it was. And my wife…well, she didn't suffer any, just went real peaceful like."

"I'm sorry."

He nodded, but didn't say anything.

"How long ago was it?"

"Six years come May."

"I know you loved her, Turner. I'm sorry you lost her. But you know, caring for someone else doesn't take anything away from your love for her."

"I know that."

She poked the needle into the fabric she'd been sewing and set it aside. "I just wanted you to know that I understand your love for her, and I don't want to take away from that."

"You couldn't. My wife doesn't have anything to do with you."

Those words pierced her heart and her already-lacking confidence. "*I'm* your wife now, Turner. And I believe she has a lot to do with us. I believe she's the reason you can't care about me."

"I care about you."

"I don't mean concern or compassion, I mean *love*. Loving your dead wife is keeping you from loving me."

"That's not so."

She gathered her thoughts…her words. "Then you just don't love me because of me. It's Gabby you can't love."

He stared at her, his throat working, but no words coming out.

"I understand," she said quickly. "At least I know where I stand." She tucked her sewing into a cloth bag and stood to stow it behind her chair. "It's better having things out in the open. I can live with our arrangement as long as I know."

"Guess you expected more."

"Everybody hopes for more."

"It didn't come out the way I meant it."

"It came out fine, Turner. Thank you for being honest."

She gathered her skirts and her last shred of dignity and headed for the stairs, trying not to run. She wasn't escaping. She was hurt and humiliated and wanted to nurse her wounds in private.

He watched her leave, her name on his tongue, but he couldn't push it out. He didn't want her hurt, but he didn't know what to say. It wasn't that he was heartless.

It was that he wanted to be.

Chapter Nine

The days leading up to Christmas were full. Gabby baked and they attended Sunday church, then he brought her home while he found a tree to cut. Friends and neighbors dropped by with packages of baked goods and jars of pie filling and preserves, and Gabby was proud to have her own baked goods to share in return. If no one looked closer than the surface, everything was just fine.

Her belongings had arrived, along with a check for her pay and a surprising amount her parents had included as a wedding gift. It was a cold but clear day, so Gabby bundled the babies and tucked them into a sturdy basket with a handle. She put on her coat and boots and walked downtown to the bank.

Effie waved to her from inside the dressmaker's shop, so her first stop was a quick cup of tea. "I have a gift for you," the woman told her, and produced a stunning beaded collar.

"I can't thank you enough," Gabby said. "It must have taken hours."

"I don't have my own family and I like to make things, so it gives me pleasure."

"I'm afraid all I have for you is a pie."

"I love pie."

After thanking her again, Gabby tucked the babies into

their basket and worked her way toward the bank. She reached the boardwalk, and had just waved to the proprietor of the mercantile when a man in a hat and long coat backed out of the bank with a long-barreled weapon drawn.

The sight of the gun registered immediately, and she stopped in her tracks.

From inside the bank came a ruckus and loud shouts, and then a shot was fired.

Gabby screeched her surprise.

Grimacing, the man dropped to one knee. He staggered to his feet and cast her a glance.

Her heart dropped to her feet.

Drum Jennings. She took note of the saddlebag over his shoulder as realization dawned. He was alive. He'd robbed the bank.

His sharp gaze shot from Gabby to the basket and back again.

Gabby went numb with panic. Would he figure out about the babies? What would he do? How was he alive and why was he here?

The moment he made a decision, she recognized it in his stance. If she was fast enough, she could get them into the mercantile and to relative safety. Turning, she shielded the basket with her body and ran.

He was faster, motivated by the gunfire that would have alerted the nearby shop owners and the marshal. He lunged toward her.

She didn't make it to the door. With a desperate grasp at the back of her coat, he caught her up short. It took all her strength to bend forward enough so that, with the collar of her coat choking her, she could set down the basket. There wasn't time to push it away, because the next thing she knew, Drum's arm went across her throat from behind and he dragged her backward.

Grasping his sleeve, she strained to free her neck so she

could breathe, at the same time recognizing that the commotion had drawn people out along Main Street. The bank teller peered out with a rifle. Drum's other arm came up beside her head and he fired a deafening shot. Gabby's ear rang. The man ducked, and wood splintered.

Two more men appeared in the doorways to their businesses with gun barrels aimed. Her terror was real. If they fired at him, they would shoot her. She might be killed in the next minute and leave Marcus and Jack orphaned. Someone watching the incident would take them in out of the cold. Turner wouldn't let any harm come to them.

Turner. Her eyes smarted, but she didn't have time for more panic. Drum reached his horse and tossed the saddlebag over its hindquarters. Still holding her by the neck, he mounted clumsily, grunting in pain.

Gabby's vision blurred and everything became red. She was aware of being lifted and jostled, but nausea and lack of air stole her senses.

When she drew a painful breath again and the cold air seared her lungs, they were galloping away from Ruby Creek. Every pounding of the horse's hooves on the frozen ground jarred her teeth. But Drum had released her throat and lashed her to him with a length of rope.

They rode like that for an unbearably long time. Gabby attempted reaching back to strike the man, but he hit her on the head so hard she saw stars.

"Where are you taking me?" she yelled into the wind. "Why don't you let me go now?"

He cuffed her again, this time striking her cheek with his gloved fist, so she kept silent.

He stopped once to relieve himself, cursing as he got down and put weight on his wounded leg. He had tied her to him with a length of rope so she had to turn away or watch. "If you gotta go, this is the time."

"Not tied like this."

"Suit yourself. Get yourself up," he told her. "If you jump off, you'll get dragged under the horse, so don't bother."

"Why don't you let me go? You're out of Ruby Creek."

"But I ain't outta Colorado, so shut your mouth or I'll shut it for ya."

After a couple more hours, Gabby faced the humiliation of relieving herself while tied to the outlaw. Night fell quickly. He stopped, tied her to a tree and set up a crude camp. He limped from tree to tree, gathering sticks and a fallen limb to make a fire. She observed silently as he packed snow around the wound on his leg and tied a rag around it.

While coffee boiled he pried open a can of beans with a wicked-looking knife, and ate them cold. "Shoulda grabbed your damn basket, too. Coulda used a solid meal."

He thought she was carrying food in the basket? It had never occurred to him that it held Willow's babies? But then, why would he jump to that conclusion? she reasoned. People usually carried food in baskets, and it was the holiday season.

He didn't offer her any of the beans, but she wouldn't have eaten anyway. She felt like throwing up. Her head throbbed and her throat hurt. She hunkered down at the base of the slim, white-barked tree, keeping her coat between her and the snow. She was thankful for the boots Turner had bought her.

"Maybe if you let me go, they'll find me and stop chasing you."

"Maybe if you shut the hell up, I won't have to kill you."

He tossed the empty can into the brush and pulled out a bottle of whiskey. After a long draw at the bottle, he poured a measure over the gunshot wound. Gabby wondered how long it took to die of lead poisoning. She didn't want to be tied to this tree if he died. But she hadn't actually seen his leg. Maybe the bullet had passed through or only grazed the flesh.

"I'll take a cup of that coffee," she said finally. Her teeth were chattering, and she couldn't imagine how cold the night ahead would get. She could freeze to death so far from the fire and without a blanket.

He ignored her request.

"I'll never know what Willow saw in you," she said with disgust.

He jerked his head around and narrowed his gaze on her. "What'd you say?"

"I don't know what Willow saw in you. She ruined her life chasing after you. She died because of you."

He tossed his tin cup aside and came toward her. He got close enough that she could see the stubble along his jaw and the glint in his pale blue eyes. "How do you know about her?"

"How do I know?" she asked. "How do I know?"

Drum leaned over her.

The truth dawned on her then. "You don't know who I am."

He straightened. "You're a loudmouth pain in the ass."

Incredulous, she looked away. "You don't know who I am."

"Make it a habit of sayin' ever'thing twice, do ya? I ain't deaf, lady. Who are you, the Queen of England? Should I be fearin' the redcoats are on my trail?" He snorted, obviously pleased with his sarcasm. "Had tea in that basket, did ya?"

She didn't want to tell him. She didn't want him to know she'd followed Willow and found her babies. If she died at his hands or froze to death, she didn't want him causing any trouble for them, now or ever. One thought kept her from despair: Turner would take care of them.

Drum went back to his fire and made himself a bed on the ground with his saddle under his head.

"I'll freeze without a blanket!" she called.

"Good. Then you'll stop yappin'."

Blackness descended and eerie silence enveloped the night. In the distance a wolf howled. Gabby thought of the bear. They were all hibernating now, Turner had assured her. But there were wolves and coyotes. Mountain lions, too. She hoped she was frozen before any predators found her tied helplessly to this tree.

She'd never been so miserable in her life. Her teeth chattered and her body shook with tremors. Some time later, sounds caught her attention. Someone or something was approaching. "Something's out there!"

Drum grunted.

Two horses with riders appeared in the dim circle of light from the fire. Were they men from Ruby Creek? Had they come to rescue her? The men dismounted.

"Why'd ya start a fire with the law on our tail?" one of them called.

Drum sat up, but didn't grab his rifle. "Freezin' to death don't sit too well with me, neither," he replied.

Gabby's last hope faded to nothing. He knew these men.

Turner didn't feel the cold. It was too dark to keep following the outlaw who had taken Gabby hostage. He'd considered the risk of going on, but if his horse got injured, he'd be useless to help her and wouldn't even be able to get back to town. So he hunkered beside his fire, waiting for first light.

Once they'd lost Jennings's trail, Turner, the marshal, Les Faraday and two others had split up in order to cover more ground. His head was filled with images of Gabby at the hands of cutthroat outlaws. Gabby afraid. Gabby cold. Gabby beaten or bleeding or… He couldn't cope with the remaining possibilities.

He worked to think of her as he wanted to remember her: rocking a baby; turning from the stove, a tendril of that amazing gold-shot hair falling over her shoulder, a smile on her face; sewing by the light of the gas lamps and the fire; looking at him with that wistful expression he often noticed.

He pulled the blanket around his body more tightly, chastising himself for thinking of her as though she were dead. He was using the same old behavior he used when he didn't want to think of his wife dying, and thought of the good times. But Gabby wasn't dead.

Please, don't let Gabby be dead.

But it felt as though she were. Why was that? The same fear gnawed at his belly. The same sick ache consumed his wits until he wanted to scream.

He'd told himself a thousand times he would never feel that way again. So why did it feel the same? He'd held her at arm's length to make sure there would be no risk.

Turner sat up again and felt something on his face freeze in the frigid air. He used his wool scarf to scrub it off.

He hadn't wanted regrets, but here he was regretting every fool thing he'd done to push Gabby away. He felt remorse for every blessed night that had passed without going to her bed, without lying beside her and making her his. The most foolish thing he'd ever done was to pretend he didn't care.

He loved her.

It had been weeks since he'd felt the need to take Comanche out at night and ride until his thoughts were purged. It had been longer than that since he'd visited the graves at the little cemetery north of town. Circumstances had changed—he had changed and he'd been too stubborn to realize it until now.

He loved her, but she didn't know. He loved her, and she might die without hearing him say it.

Holding back affection so he wouldn't get hurt hadn't stopped him from falling in love. Now it might be too late. Fate couldn't be that cruel, could it? Turner used every shred of faith he still possessed to pray that Gabby would be spared. And then he added a prayer that she would forgive him.

Gabby had been wary when the youngest of the new arrivals had carried a blanket and bedroll toward her. She'd watched him approach with suspicion. When he'd gotten close enough, she'd recognized he was no more than a boy, maybe fifteen or sixteen.

"I ain't fixin' t' hurt ya, ma'am," he said. "It's mighty cold, and we might just as well keep each other warm."

She hadn't spoken, but hadn't opposed him, either. By then she couldn't feel her fingers, and her ears were on fire. He brought kindling and wood and lit it, spread out his gear where she sat and gestured for her to lie down. After she obeyed, he covered her with two blankets and stretched out in front of her, facing away, sharing the wool covering.

"Is she purdy?" the other man who'd ridden in with him called across the clearing.

"Don't make no never mind to you 'cause she's with me," the boy returned.

He was protecting her. She didn't question it: she was simply grateful. Sometime later, her fingers tingled as warmth prickled back into them. Her ears still burned, but she stopped shaking.

Everyone on Main Street had seen Drum take her today. The lawmen were on their trail, and she didn't have to wonder if Turner had ridden out as soon as he'd heard. He'd probably made sure Jack and Marcus would be looked after and immediately taken off.

The boy snored evenly. Eventually, she succumbed to exhaustion.

When morning arrived, she was the last one awake.

The boy brought her coffee and jerky.

She ate the tough meat and drank the bitter brew, grateful for its warmth and the satisfying feeling of food in her belly.

The third man, whom she hadn't seen up close, moved off into the brush, while Drum crouched before his fire.

"Why are you with Drum?" she asked the boy who'd been kind to her.

"Ain't none o' your concern." His voice had that awkward pitch of a not-quite-man.

"He'll get you killed."

He looked aside and then at his cup. "Reckon I'll take my chances. Ain't never had it no better in a town."

"Living by the law has to be better than on the run," she said.

"Shut her up!" Drum called across the clearing. "It's nearly daylight. We're headin' out. You're so all-fired cozy, you ride with her and her yappy mouth tied to you."

The boy gave her a look to quell her talk.

"I have two babies," she told him quietly. "Little boys. My husband will have to raise them alone if anything happens to me. He's a fine man."

He didn't look at her, and she kept her voice low. "Their names are Jack and Marcus. I'm Gabby."

The boy half chuckled, then hid his amusement behind his cup. "Gabby. Fits, don't it?"

She ignored his barb. "What's your name?"

His gaze skittered across the way. "Jim. Now don't talk no more."

"All right, Jim."

He set aside his cup, got up and bent to pick up the blankets he'd curled into a tight roll. A shot exploded and he fell backward, his hat bouncing across the ground toward the fire.

Gabby jumped back. Had Drum shot him?

Drum had lunged to his feet and picked up his rifle. He swung the barrel in an arc, searching the surrounding woods for the shooter. "Tram!" he shouted. "Where the hell are ya?"

Another shot rang out, and Drum grabbed his arm with a howl.

Confused, Gabby tried to comprehend what was happening.

Drum swung an accusing, hate-filled glare on her. She pulled at her restraints, but couldn't budge from the tree. As sure as she knew anything, she knew he'd try to grab her as cover from whoever was out there unloading their gun on them.

Crouching low, he limped toward her.

She flattened herself out on the ground, so he couldn't pick her up easily. "Get up or I'll shoot you!" he hissed.

She covered her head with her arms and shook it. He had

two bullets in him now. She could resist. He grabbed her by one arm and tried to lift her deadweight.

She fought with all her strength, landing a sturdy kick on his knee. He gasped and raised the handle of his gun to strike her.

A gunshot rang out.

Gabby could hear her own breath, see it puff in the crisp dawn air.

Drum fell to his knees. His pale blue eyes held a vacant look before they rolled back, and he toppled forward over her.

Gabby sobbed with relief.

"Gabrielle!"

Turner's voice. She looked up. He was running toward her, a rifle in his hand.

Chapter Ten

"Turner, there's another one out there!" Gabby shouted in warning. That third outlaw would have heard the commotion by now, and she cringed at the thought of a bullet aimed at Turner.

Turner reached them, riveting the gun barrel on the man lying still across her lower body. With one booted foot, Turner rolled him over and off of her.

"Is he dead?" Gabby asked.

Turner placed a hand against Drum's chest, inside his coat, and waited a moment before straightening. "He's dead. Are you all right?"

"There's another man out there. Untie me."

"I took care of the other one." He knelt and fumbled with the rope, finally grabbing a knife from a sheath at Drum's waist and slicing the binding away from her wrists and middle. "Are you all right?"

Tears blurring her vision, she nodded.

Turner hauled her to her feet and grasped her against him so tightly she could scarcely breathe. "Did they hurt you?"

"No," she murmured against his wool coat. He smelled so good. He smelled like leather and wind and home.

He hauled her away, holding her face between his palms. "Your eye."

"I'm fine. Really. The boys?"

"They're with Marcia."

A moan alerted them, and Turner released her, shoved her behind him and grabbed his rifle.

The kid, Jim, was sitting up, holding his shoulder. Blood had seeped through to the outside of his coat. He wore a look of shock. "I'm shot."

Turner pointed the rifle at him.

Gabby stepped in front of Turner, then knelt beside Jim. "We'll take him to the doctor. He looked out for me last night. He kept me warm. Look at him. He's just a boy."

Turner lowered his gun. "Let's get moving. I'll load 'em. The other fella's tied up in the woods. Found 'im in the bushes."

She searched through Drum's bags. The first one was full of money, the other clothing, shaving gear and food. She made a bandage out of a shirt and stuffed it inside Jim's coat. "We'll get help for you," she told him.

Turner loaded the dead man onto his horse, secured Tram and Jim to their saddles and then tied the horses in a string. He helped Gabby onto Comanche's back and mounted behind her. She leaned back against him, never having felt so relieved or so safe.

They soon met up with the marshal and Lester, and together the group took Drum and the prisoners the rest of the way back to Ruby Creek.

"There's a mighty purdy reward for Jennings," Lester said. "Wait'll we tell French you got 'im. He'll be mad enough to swallow a horned toad backward. He had his mind fixed on that reward."

"Guess we can find a good use for the reward," Turner answered. A mile later, he said to Gabby, "We could help out some other young'uns that need a home, maybe. Boys like Jim here, so they don't end up on the wrong side o' the law."

The last thing Gabby wanted to think about right now was reward money, but the seed of Turner's suggestion had been planted. She wanted to see their boys. She closed her eyes and endured the wait.

"We're home, Gabby," Turner said finally.

She raised her head and took in the same buildings along Main Street that she'd seen that first, snowy night of her arrival. Turner directed Comanche west along the street where their house as well as the Faradays' was located. She was indeed home.

He reined in and helped her down. "Will you be all right at Marcia's while I help the marshal and take care of the horses?" Turner asked.

She nodded. "I'll be fine."

As he left her in Marcia's kitchen, his expression was one she didn't recognize. It seemed that he didn't want to leave her, or even release her hand, but he finally let go and backed toward the door. "I won't be long."

"She'll be just fine." Marcia wrapped her arm around Gabby's shoulder. "She wants to see her babies—don't you, Gabby?"

Turner gave Gabby a final nod and was gone. Gabby turned and swept past her friend, approaching the cradle. The babies were both wide-eyed and alert. Jack blinked up at her and kicked excitedly. Marcus studied her with a frown while chewing his fist.

She plucked up Jack first, kissing his cheek and rubbing her face against his downy head. His familiar smell melted her heart. She turned her attention to Marcus next, kissing and hugging him until he squirmed. "I missed you," she whispered.

Marcia fried eggs and bacon and warmed rolls, and they sat together in the toasty kitchen. Marcia's toddler ate the eggs she'd given him with his fingers, getting as much in his hair as in his mouth. She cleaned him up and set him to play with a stack of wooden blocks and horses.

Gabby didn't want to lay the boys down, so she held one or the other the rest of the morning until Turner came for them.

He ushered them home, stoked the stove, heated water and filled the bathing tub. The kitchen was warm by the time he left her alone, and she stripped out of her clothing to sink down into the steaming water.

She luxuriated in being so warm and feeling safe, then

finally began washing and dressing. Turner had a fire blazing in the other room. The twins lay contentedly on a coverlet near the fireplace.

Turner unfolded a soft blanket. "Get comfortable on the divan."

"I'm not sick," she objected. "I'm fine, really."

"I'll sit with you," he encouraged.

It was a workday, shortly before noon. "Don't you have to be at the livery?"

"My hired man took over for the day."

Settling, she pulled her feet up. "What about yesterday?"

Turner sat on the other end of the divan, facing her with one leg curled on the cushion and one foot on the floor. He reached for her feet, pulling them into his lap. After tugging off her soft leather slippers and tucking the blanket snugly over her feet, he caressed them beneath the covering. "I left the livery open yesterday. People took care of their own horses. Chick Spurling locked it up last night and opened it this morning."

The sensation of his strong hands massaging her feet gave her shivers all the way through her body. She wished she wasn't wearing her stockings. "It feels so good…to be warm," she clarified.

"If you're up to it, let's decorate the tree tonight," he suggested.

Her eyelids grew heavy with exhaustion. "That sounds wonderful."

"I didn't sleep last night, either," he said.

She looked at him. "Where were you?"

"In the woods. Waiting for light, so I could find you." He didn't look away. His tender gaze took in her face and hair.

"I kept thinking how you would take care of the boys," she told him. "I knew if anything happened to me that they'd be all right."

"I couldn't have borne it if anything had happened to you." His voice was thick with an emotion she didn't recognize.

A quiver of expectation darted through her.

"I lay awake thinkin' 'bout all the time I wasted lyin' to myself and thinkin' if I didn't feel anything I could never get hurt. I did my best to hold it all back."

"I guess it's just natural," she told him. "Not wanting anyone to take your wife's place."

His hands stilled on her feet. He swallowed hard. Looked away for a moment and then right at her. "I was wrong."

"No."

"It was mean what I said the other day. Hurtful."

"It's okay."

"No, it's not. When I said how I felt about you didn't have anything to do with my wife, I was trying to keep the two feelings separate, trying not to love you. I didn't want to love you because I was a coward."

"You're anything but a coward. You followed Drum Jennings into the wilderness and risked your life to save me."

He drew a hand from under the blanket and held it toward her to stop her objections. "Just let me say this. Ever since you got here, I've had a reason to get up in the morning. A reason to eat and sleep and shave and work. It probably sounds mighty silly, but I was just goin' through the motions before you came. Now I have somethin' to look forward to."

"The boys—"

"Not the boys, Gabby. Not entirely the boys. They have my heart, you know that, but it's you. When I'm standin' over the forge, hot and dirty, I think about comin' home to you. When I go to bed at night I think about seein' you at breakfast. I remember how you look in your dresses and the way you smell and your smile." His mouth inched up at the corners. "Your smile could light up the blackest night, Gabby."

She could barely see him through the haze of joyful tears. He did care for her. She was amazed that he had those kinds of thoughts and even more amazed that he had expressed them. If she didn't know better...

"I could stand outside and announce it's summer every day

of December, but that wouldn't make it so. Just like tellin' myself I couldn't love you didn't make it so."

He had her attention now. "It didn't?"

"No, ma'am. I guess I loved you right off. Problem was I didn't want to. But it was too late. And I figured it out when I thought somethin' might happen to you. I don't want to live without you. And I don't want to live without lovin' you."

Gabby rose up on her knees and slid in front of him. He pulled her onto his lap. She laid her hand along the side of his face. "So just say it."

"I love you, Gabrielle."

"And I love you," she answered.

Their second kiss was better than their first because it held all the emotion they'd reserved. He kissed her long and hard, and she loved every moment of it. He caressed her hair, circled her ear with a fingertip and whispered against it, "I have everything a man could want."

Delight shimmied along her nerve endings and kiss after kiss stole her breath.

A whimper that turned into a squall let them know the babies wouldn't be content to lie across the room forever. Turner laid his forehead against hers. "Which one is that?"

She caught her breath. "Marcus. He's usually the first to complain."

"Let's each feed one, then they can watch us decorate the tree."

She nodded, and he gave her a tender kiss before releasing her and heading into the kitchen. "I'll warm the milk."

That evening she popped popcorn, and they strung it, then artfully draped it on the tree alongside glittery pinecones and glass ornaments Turner had retrieved from the attic.

Stretching out before the fire, they sipped hot cocoa and appreciated their handiwork. "We're gonna share many, many Christmases just like this one," he assured her.

She admired her husband in the flickering light. His size, which at one time had been intimidating, now portrayed strength and security. He wanted to share his life, and share responsibility for Jack and Marcus, and she trusted him to make good on his promises. She had finally found the place where she belonged, where she fit in and where she was accepted for who she was.

This man loved her. She couldn't see the future, but she had his promise that they would discover it together.

That night, after changing into her night rail, she left her door open, so she could hear the babies when they woke. After turning down the wick on the oil lamp, she climbed under the covers, content to be home and warm.

Gabby listened to the creak of the wind under the eaves and the whoosh of air in the coal heater pipe. The house still smelled of the cinnamon that had been in their hot cocoa. Her heart beat with a peaceful rhythm. He loved her. Whatever the future held, he loved her. The house was dark and still…save for the unmistakable creak of wood in the hallway.

A broad silhouette appeared in the doorway. The rhythm of her heartbeat increased. She rose on an elbow and turned back the coverlet in invitation.

Turner padded to the side of the bed. "From now on, Gabby, this marriage is for you and me. Not just for the sake of the babies."

"Hurry," she said. "I'm getting cold."

"I can't believe this has happened," he said, taking her in his arms. "That I've found you."

"Actually, I found you," she teased.

"Actually, Jack and Marcus found me first."

"Well then, I'm indebted to them for life," she said with a laugh before his lips came down over hers.

Outside a fresh blanket of snow fell on Ruby Creek, bringing with it all the hope and promise of the true spirit of Christmas.

* * * * *

Here's a sneak peek at
THE CEO'S CHRISTMAS PROPOSITION,
the first in USA TODAY *bestselling author*
Merline Lovelace's HOLIDAYS ABROAD *trilogy*
coming in November 2008.

American Devon McShay is about to get the Christmas surprise of a lifetime when she meets her new client, sexy billionaire Caleb Logan, for the very first time.

Silhouette®

Desire

Available November 2008

Her breath whistled out in a sigh of relief when he exited Customs. Devon recognized him right away from the newspaper and magazine articles her friend and partner Sabrina had looked up during her frantic prep work.

Caleb John Logan, Jr. Thirty-one. Six-two. With jet-black hair, laser-blue eyes and a linebacker's shoulders under his charcoal-gray cashmere overcoat. His jaw-dropping good looks didn't score him any points with Devon. She'd learned the hard way not to trust handsome heartbreakers like Cal Logan.

But he was a client. An important one. And she was willing to give someone who'd served a hitch in the marines before earning a B.S. from the University of Oregon, an MBA from Stanford and his first million at the ripe old age of twenty-six the benefit of the doubt.

Right up until he spotted the hot-pink pashmina, that is.

Devon knew the flash of color was more visible than the sign she held up with his name on it. So she wasn't surprised when Logan picked her out of the crowd and cut in her direction. She'd just plastered on her best businesswoman smile when he whipped an arm around her waist. The next moment she was sprawled against his cashmere-covered chest.

"Hello, brown eyes."

Swooping down, he covered her mouth with his.

Sheer astonishment kept Devon rooted to the spot for a few seconds while her mind whirled chaotically. Her first thought was that her client had downed a few too many drinks during the long flight. Her second, that he'd mistaken the kind of escort and consulting services her company provided. Her third shoved everything else out of her head.

The man could kiss!

His mouth moved over hers with a skill that ignited sparks at a half dozen flash points throughout her body. Devon hadn't experienced that kind of spontaneous combustion in a while. A *long* while.

The sparks were still popping when she pushed off his chest, only now they fueled a flush of anger.

"Do you always greet women you don't know with a lip-lock, Mr. Logan?"

A smile crinkled the skin at the corners of his eyes. "As a matter of fact, I don't. That was from Don."

"Huh?"

"He said he owed you one from New Year's Eve two years ago and made me promise to deliver it."

She stared up at him in total incomprehension. Logan hooked a brow and attempted to prompt a nonexistent memory.

"He abandoned you at the Waldorf. Five minutes before midnight. To deliver twins."

"I don't have a clue who or what you're..."

Understanding burst like a water balloon.

"Wait a sec. Are you talking about Sabrina's old boyfriend? Your buddy, who's now an ob-gyn doc?"

It was Logan's turn to look startled. He recovered faster than Devon had, though. His smile widened into a rueful grin.

"I take it you're not Sabrina Russo."

"No, Mr. Logan, I am *not*."

* * * * *

Be sure to look for
THE CEO'S CHRISTMAS PROPOSITION
by Merline Lovelace.
Available in November 2008 wherever books are sold,
including most bookstores, supermarkets,
drugstores and discount stores.

Silhouette®

Romantic
SUSPENSE

**Sparked by Danger,
Fueled by Passion.**

Lindsay McKenna
Susan Grant

Mission: Christmas

Celebrate the holidays with a pair
of military heroines and their daring men
in two romantic, adventurous stories
from these bestselling authors.

Featuring:

"The Christmas Wild Bunch"
by *USA TODAY* bestselling author
Lindsay McKenna

and

"Snowbound with a Prince"
by *New York Times* bestselling author
Susan Grant

Available November wherever books are sold.

REQUEST YOUR FREE BOOKS!

Harlequin® Historical
Historical Romantic Adventure!

2 FREE NOVELS PLUS 2 FREE GIFTS!

YES! Please send me 2 FREE Harlequin® Historical novels and my 2 FREE gifts (gifts are worth about $10). After receiving them, if I don't wish to receive any more books, I can return the shipping statement marked "cancel". If I don't cancel, I will receive 6 brand-new novels every month and be billed just $4.94 per book in the U.S. or $5.49 per book in Canada, plus 25¢ shipping and handling per book and applicable taxes, if any*. That's a savings of 20% off the cover price! I understand that accepting the 2 free books and gifts places me under no obligation to buy anything. I can always return a shipment and cancel at any time. Even if I never buy another book, the two free books and gifts are mine to keep forever.

246 HDN ERUM   349 HDN ERUA

Name	(PLEASE PRINT)	
Address		Apt. #
City	State/Prov.	Zip/Postal Code

Signature (if under 18, a parent or guardian must sign)

Mail to the Harlequin Reader Service:
IN U.S.A.: P.O. Box 1867, Buffalo, NY 14240-1867
IN CANADA: P.O. Box 609, Fort Erie, Ontario L2A 5X3

Not valid to current subscribers of Harlequin Historical books.

Want to try two free books from another line?
Call 1-800-873-8635 or visit www.morefreebooks.com.

* Terms and prices subject to change without notice. N.Y. residents add applicable sales tax. Canadian residents will be charged applicable provincial taxes and GST. Offer not valid in Quebec. This offer is limited to one order per household. All orders subject to approval. Credit or debit balances in a customer's account(s) may be offset by any other outstanding balance owed by or to the customer. Please allow 4 to 6 weeks for delivery. Offer available while quantities last.

Your Privacy: Harlequin Books is committed to protecting your privacy. Our Privacy Policy is available online at www.eHarlequin.com or upon request from the Reader Service. From time to time we make our lists of customers available to reputable third parties who may have a product or service of interest to you. If you would prefer we not share your name and address, please check here. ☐

HH08R

MARRIED BY CHRISTMAS

Playboy billionaire Elijah Vanaldi has discovered
he is guardian to his small orphaned nephew.
But his reputation makes some people question
his ability to be a father. He knows he must
fight to protect the child, and he'll do anything
it takes. Ainslie Farrell is jobless, homeless and
desperate—and when Elijah offers her a position
in his household she simply can't refuse....

Available in November

HIRED: THE ITALIAN'S CONVENIENT MISTRESS
by
CAROL MARINELLI
Book #29

COMING NEXT MONTH FROM

HARLEQUIN®
HISTORICAL

- **ONE CANDLELIT CHRISTMAS**
  by **Julia Justiss, Annie Burrows and Terri Brisbin**
  (Regency)
  Have yourself a Regency Christmas! Celebrate the season with three heartwarming stories of reconciliation, surprises and secret wishes fulfilled....

- **THE BORROWED BRIDE**
  by **Elizabeth Lane**
  (Western)
  Fully expecting to marry her childhood sweetheart, Hannah Gustavson is torn by his sudden disappearance. With Hannah desperately needing the protection of a man, Judd Seavers cannot stand by and watch his brother's woman struggle alone.... So begins their marriage of convenience....

- **UNTOUCHED MISTRESS**
  by **Margaret McPhee**
  (Regency)
  Guy Tregellas, Viscount Varington, has a rakish reputation, and when he discovers a beautiful woman washed up on the beach he is more than intrigued. Helena McGregor must escape Scotland to anonymity in London—for the past five years she has lived a shameful life, not of her choosing. But she needs the help of her disturbingly handsome rescuer....

- **HER WARRIOR SLAVE**
  by **Michelle Willingham**
  (Medieval)
  Kieran Ó Brannon sold himself into slavery for his family, but despite steadfast loyalty, he cannot deny the intensity of his feelings for his master's betrothed—Iseult. She, too, must decide if succumbing to her fierce desire for the captured warrior is worth losing what she prizes most....